"Hey!" she yelled.

Up ahead, the car came to a sudden stop right next to a group of preteen girls. The door opened. A gun emerged first. Then a man got out and pointed the gun at the tallest girl.

"What's going on, Harper?" Ridge asked through her phone's earpiece.

No sound would come out of her mouth other than another strangled "Hey!"

The girls responded to the sudden threat by pulling their arms in tight, getting small, but staying locked in place. Harper ran closer.

She had no idea what she was going to do against a muscle-bound man with a sneer and a gun. But her body did. She ran to the open car and leaped into the seat. Harper jammed the idling engine into gear and stomped on the gas.

"Ridge, help them!" Her shocked brain grabbed at words.

"We're coming, Harper. Tell me what's happening."

"Gun! Girls! I…I…I stole the car."

Horror washed over her as she realized what she'd done. This might be the knee-jerk reaction that would end up getting her killed.

Fiona Quinn is a six-time *USA TODAY* bestselling author, a Kindle Scout winner and an Amazon All-Star.

Quinn writes suspense in her Iniquus world of books, including the Lynx, Strike Force, Uncommon Enemies, Kate Hamilton Mysteries, FBI Joint Task Force, Cerberus Tactical K-9 Team Alpha and Delta Force Echo series, with more to come.

She writes urban fantasy as Fiona Angelica Quinn for her Elemental Witches series.

And, just for fun, she writes the Badge Bunny Booze Mystery Collection of raucous, bawdy humor with her dear friend Tina Glasneck as Quinn Glasneck.

Quinn is rooted in the Old Dominion, where she lives with her husband. There, she pops chocolates, devours books and taps continuously on her laptop.

Facebook, Twitter, Pinterest: Fiona Quinn Books.

PROTECTIVE INSTINCT

FIONA QUINN

HARLEQUIN

This book is dedicated in memoriam
to my friend Laura Demchuck.

Recycling programs
for this product may
not exist in your area.

ISBN-13: 978-1-335-47326-4

Protective Instinct

First published in 2020 by Fiona Quinn.
This edition published in 2022.

For questions and comments about the quality of this book, please contact us at CustomerService@Harlequin.com.

Harlequin Enterprises ULC
22 Adelaide St. West, 41st Floor
Toronto, Ontario M5H 4E3, Canada
www.Harlequin.com

Printed in U.S.A.

PROTECTIVE INSTINCT

Acknowledgments

The main character Ridge Hansen was named by one of my Street Force members, M. Strilka, to honor her father.

Her dad, Carroll Vincent Yeatts Jr., goes by the name Vincent. He's been married to his childhood sweetheart for fifty years. Vincent proudly served for over twenty years in the US Air Force.

Vincent got his call sign, Ridgerunner, when he worked on the F-117 Stealth Bomber. Vincent lives by the motto: laugh and learn something every day.

Isn't that advice worth following?

A huge thank-you to Vincent Yeatts Jr. for inspiring the Ridge Hansen character.

My great appreciation:

To my editor, Kathleen Payne.

To my publicist, Margaret Daly.

To my Beta Force, who are always honest and kind at the same time: E. Hordon, M. Carlon.

To my Street Force, who support me and my writing with such enthusiasm.

To the real-world K-9 professionals who serve and protect us.

To all the wonderful professionals whom I called on to get the details right:

Dr. K. Connor for her consistent K-9 inspiration both through her stories and her amazing photographs.

Virginia K-9 search and rescue teams for their work in our community, their dedication and professionalism. Every time I search and train with you, I'm inspired.

Please note: This is a work of fiction, and while I always try my best to get all the details correct, there are times when it serves the story to go slightly to the left or right of perfection. Please understand that any mistakes or discrepancies are my authorial decision-making alone and sit squarely on my shoulders.

Thank you to my family.

I send my love to my husband along with my great appreciation. T, you are my encouragement and my adventure. Thank you for giving me a solid foundation on which to rest.

And of course, thank YOU for reading my stories. I'm smiling joyfully as I type this. I so appreciate you!

Chapter 1

Harper

With her earbuds blasting a hip-hop beat, Harper Katz hit her stride.

This was the point in her run where she could zen out, letting her body do its thing.

As she powered past the neighborhood gardens, their riotous colors fed her creative mind.

Compositions swirled through her imagination. If one of these ideas sparked her curiosity, she'd go back to her hotel room and explore it in watercolors or ink until her boss woke up.

Berlin Tracy—Hollywood rising star and Instagram phenom—rarely climbed out of bed before lunch.

Harper relished these early morning solitary runs. This was the time she set aside to let her creative juices flow, reminding herself that her present choices didn't erase who she was. She was merely in hibernation. Taking a time-out. Soon, things would be normal again. Normal-ish.

A gawker car slowed as it drove past, and Harper averted her eyes. She had no desire to see the occupants ducking low, staring wide-eyed out the window at her.

It was inevitable. It happened *repeatedly* every run.

Harper was a curvy girl, pounding down the pavement.

She had decided long ago to just let them look.

"Bring it," Harper would love to call out. People liked to judge her while forgetting they didn't rise to her capabilities.

Harper could outpace and outlast a high percentage of the folks who slowed, stared, and judged.

It was cognitive dissonance—the point where the reality the person was seeing didn't match with their preconceived understanding of how things worked.

Fast-paced runners were lean, mean fighting machines.

And she was only the mean and the fighting machine part of that equation.

All right, she wasn't mean.

Nor was she anything like a fighting machine.

Harper simply wasn't what the looky-loos expected from someone built like she was. They expected red-faced and struggling.

Once upon a time, Harper had been both red-faced *and* struggling.

She'd come a long way, diligently working herself up to marathon-length runs.

Harper couldn't complain about her curvy-girl size. She was here in her present form because her ancestors evolved a genetic storehouse to endure crop failures, condemning lesser gene pools to death by famine. Her forefathers and foremothers had outlasted frigid Polish nights of centuries past by maintaining a warm blanket of insulation around their vital organs.

She, Harper Katz, was a *winner* in the Darwinian survival race.

Remembering that had taken the sting out of those looks of incredulity and censure that accompanied her runs a long time ago.

Now that the car had passed by, picked up its speed, and powered out of sight, Harper called out, "Not bad for a curvy girl, huh?"

Girl?

That was a stretch.

Today was her birthday.

Thirty-two.

No one knew, and no one cared.

By design, Harper reminded herself.

Tonight, she'd put on a classic movie, order a nice meal brought to her hotel room, and eat it without those public eyes saying, "Girl! Look what you're eating. No wonder you've got that caboose." She'd heard it all her life, no matter that she ate healthfully three-hundred and sixty-two days of the year. Harper allowed herself to eat whatever she wanted, no limits *whatsoever*, on three specific days—Thanksgiving, Christmas, and her birthday.

Tonight, she was going for it—a celebratory cocktail with *hors d'oeuvres*, a glass of wine, mmmm, the macaroni and cheese with truffle oil she'd seen on the hotel's five-star menu, and a decadent dessert.

Alone in her room.

All by herself.

Away from Berlin and her neediness and the rest of the "crew."

Yup. Harper could eat naked and cross-legged on her bed if she wanted. She could dress in a cocktail dress. It didn't matter. It was a no-judgment zone. Whatever felt right at that moment was what she was going to do.

Harper filled her lungs with a deep breath, pulled through flared nostrils, then exhaled her distressing thoughts through pursed lips. Robin Williams had said, "I used to think that the worst thing in life was to end up alone. It's not. The worst thing in life is to end up with people who make you feel alone."

You're in this place by design. It's a survival strategy. By January, things will be different.

Checking her body mechanics, lifting her chin, pulling her shoulders back, Harper kept her pace steady as the melody slowed and faded.

With the first phrase of the next song on her playlist, Harper tugged her phone from the thigh pocket on her don't-run-me-over, blaze-orange-and-black jogging tights and tapped the button to skip to the next in the queue.

Harper was in a lonely mood and didn't need anyone extolling the joys of finding the love of their life, heading toward their much-awaited blissful ever after.

As the next song on her playlist queued up, Harper's ringtone jingled through the earbuds.

Ha!

Harper knew, without even looking, who was calling.

It was uncanny.

Almost without fail, when the notion of a love connection crossed into Harper's awareness, Ridge was on the phone. An etheric joke by some snickering helper-guide with a sick sense of humor.

"Hello?"

"Hey, we're here," came the warm baritone rumble.

Yup. Ridge. Like clockwork. Harper looked at the sky and stuck her tongue out at the imaginary trickster-fiend before she asked, "Where's here?"

She glanced around the suburban D.C. street, empty except for a klatch of preteens shuffling their feet, waiting for the school bus to come. It was the end of May. Freedom was a few dismissal bells away. Then the long lazy stretch of summer.

Harper remembered those days. Everything still felt hopeful way back then.

She raised her hand in a salute as she passed them by.

"We just pulled into your hotel's parking lot," Ridge said.

Harper slapped a hand to her forehead. "It's Wednesday. I said I'd help you and Tripwire with the K9s' scent work Wednesday morning. *This* morning." She sucked in a deeper breath so she could speak despite her seven-mile-an-hour pace. "Working for Berlin, I keep exquisite track of her every moment. I don't normally have things on my own schedule. I'm sorry. I'm not at the hotel." She was able to get all that out without sounding breathless in Ridge's ear. Kudos to her.

Harper had no reasonable explanation for knowing the date but not the day of the week.

Sure she did. Harper was confused because she'd had very little sleep for the last forty-eight hours researching Berlin's speech and powering through Berlin's unending to-do list with a cross-country flight—California to Washington, D.C.—in the middle.

While Harper knew the date, she honestly hadn't realized today was Wednesday, which was how she'd pinned this event in her mind.

Berlin and her ambitions are going to be the death of me.

She heard Ridge say off to the side, "Harper got her schedule confused."

Ridge Hansen was the lead operator on Iniquus's Cerberus Tactical K9 Search and Rescue Team. Tripwire was his number two. Their team had saved Berlin and her camera crew from the bomb cyclone that hit Wild Mountain, Virginia, at the beginning of March.

"Ah, okay. Tell Harper we'll probably see her at Iniquus." Tripwire's voice was off to the side. "Berlin has her security intake this afternoon."

Now that Berlin was back on the East Coast for a few days—doing what she did best, garnering attention—Berlin wanted to hire Iniquus to do her close protection for her D.C. appearances.

There wasn't *any* reason for Berlin to need security.

Berlin was simply dressing for the job she wanted. She wanted to be a Hollywood A-lister. That role required hunky security in her pictures. The operatives working for Iniquus—in their uniform dark gray compression shirts, showing off their broad shoulders and hard bodies—looked like they came through central casting.

Add in their gorgeous K9s, and you had Instagram gold.

Ridge was ex-Delta Force. Tripwire Williams was an ex-SEAL. They were both powerful athletes who worked with tactical K9s.

Did Harper mind helping them out with a training exercise for their K9s?

Nope. She didn't mind.

Glad to. Anytime.

No, really. Anytime at all…if Harper could remember what day of the week it was.

"Did you hear Tripwire?" Ridge asked, jarring Harper back from the memory of Ridge squatting down near his K9 Zeus, muscular thighs flexing against the constraints of his tactical pants. She reached up and swiped the sweat from her lips with the back of her wrist. Could have been drool. She wasn't going to judge herself right now.

"Yeah. Hi there, Trip. Look, I'm not that far away. I took a stroll to clear my head. I can turn myself around." She purposefully didn't say "exercise" or "run." She didn't need incredulity from Trip and Ridge.

"Where are you right now?" Ridge asked.

She looked at the signage. "Corner of Maxwell and Hathaway, heading toward the sunrise, so eastbound." Harper had kept her pace despite the phone call. She frequently had to make coordination calls for Berlin while out on her daily run, and her legs could function on autopilot.

By the volume of Tripwire's voice, Ridge must have tapped on the speakerphone. She could easily hear Trip say, "Two and a half miles."

"What do you think?" Ridge was obviously conferring. That question wasn't directed toward her.

"Doable if she wants to keep going," Tripwire said. "I've got a scent source for Harper in the back with the dogs. If we know what door she came out to cut down on time, we could catch up to her."

Ridge was back on the phone. "Hey, Harper, did you catch that?"

"Yeah. Does that mean Zeus and Valor are going to trail me from the hotel?"

"It shouldn't take too long," Ridge said.

"I'm not worried about the time. I'm not scheduled for work until we head over to Iniquus after lunch. So I'm all yours." She rolled her eyes as she heard that pop out of her mouth.

I'm all yours? She was a moron. This day sucked.

Harper moved farther into the street away from the gravel that could make her slip. "I came out the lobby door, through the parking lot to the left, and took that street. It doglegs to the right. I'm straight ahead. Eventually, it hooks around and comes back at the hotel."

"That's a six-mile circuit back," Tripwire told Ridge.

"Are you comfortable continuing on for a bit?" Ridge asked her.

"That's fine." She stopped her mouth from injecting that her fat rear end wasn't going to keel over in the street.

Harper was a little surprised at the way her thoughts had strung together during this run. She wasn't usually the kind of gal that beat herself up like this. These thoughts were probably a rancid combo of the last day of monthly hormones, exhaustion, jet lag, and it being Harper's birthday with a bleak future on her near horizon. Tonight's planned cake-icing coma would fix this.

"We're good then. We've got a plan. A perfect exercise, thanks, Harper," Ridge said, then Harper heard Ridge tell Trip he was getting the dogs unloaded while Trip found Harper's scent.

The scent source was one of her pillowcases that they stuffed into a PVC pipe, capped on either end.

Harper had given them the pillowcase when she helped them train the week they were snowed in on Wild Mountain. The handlers would open the tube and let their K9 tracking dogs, Zeus and Valor, take a big whiff, then send them off to see if they could find her.

It had been fun. Kind of like grownup hide and go seek with fur-joy and lots of slobbery kisses when they made the find.

Harper knew that no matter how long and fast she ran down this road, those dogs would be on her in no time if Ridge and Trip were working them off-lead. Since they were in a suburban neighborhood with cars, she knew the handlers would be jogging with their dogs on long leads as they tracked her.

She was fast; the handlers were faster. Longer legs. Bigger feet…

She shouldn't envision the size of Ridge's feet. *Shouldn't.*

Huge!

Stop.

Ridge had left the line open as he went about his prep. It wasn't unusual for them. Since their time at Wild Mountain Lodge, they often opened a line and companionably went about their tasks, throwing out bits of conversation as if they were inhabiting the same shared space, like roommates.

There was a pop of a hatch. The dogs whined to get on task.

"Zeus, loveykins," she cooed.

Zeus gave a sentence-long series of barks and whines.

"That riled him up. You're not allowed to do that," Ridge said.

"Sorry." *Not sorry.* She had a thing for Zeus. He was a magnificent Belgian Malinois–long-haired German shepherd mixed breed. Regal. Intelligent. He just gave her such a sense of safety. And she craved that feeling.

A car headed toward Harper and slowed.

Her skin prickled with anger at the driver. Then, she watched him do a three-point turn before she could make a stink face. Okay, not a looky-loo. That was a relief.

Man, she was in a bad mood.

And on top of her birthday blues, here she was running down the road in her sweaty neon orange T-shirt with Ridge heading her way.

As if it mattered.

Harper needed to be careful there. There was no good outcome in letting her chemical reactions brew. They were pals. It was dangerous to her well-being to let any Ridge-feelings take root. Luckily, she would just have these three days here in D.C., then the Berlin Tracy crew would be on the plane, heading back to California. No need to get her panties in a—

"Hey!" she yelled.

Up ahead, the man who had done the three-point turn had come to a sudden stop in the middle of the street right next to a group of preteen girls. The door opened. A gun emerged first. The man who got out of the car had it pointed at the tallest girl.

"Hey!" she yelled out.

"What's going on, Harper?" Ridge asked.

No other sound would come out of her mouth other than another strangled "Hey!"

The girls responded to the sudden threat by pulling their arms in tight, getting small, but staying locked into place.

Harper might have done the same if her legs weren't already in motion.

As she drew closer, Harper saw a bright pink backpack and a long ponytail.

The girls stretched their eyes wide in shock.

Their mouths hung open with lips drawn down their jaws, showing their lower teeth in horror.

While Harper's artistic brain was snapping and storing the images, she wasn't processing anything about the scene.

Harper's legs powered forward. Closer. Closer.

The impact of each footfall vibrated up her shin bones, to her thighs, into her hips.

The slap of her running shoes against the blacktop was the echo of her "Hey! Hey!" accented with a heavy exhale.

Her internal autopilot had turned up the dial of its own accord. She was sprinting. Flailing. Gasping.

She had no stop button and not a single thought. Impressions. Colors. Actions whirled and swirled through her mind.

Adrenaline set her system ablaze, giving her heartburn. An internal explosion of sensations took up too much lung space and stopped Harper from catching her breath.

The man was huge.

Muscled.

An angry snarl menaced his barbed jaw.

The gun.

Still, she powered forward.

She had no idea what to do against a muscle-bound man with a sneer and a gun.

Her body did. She ran to the open car and leaped into the seat.

With one foot still on the pavement, Harper jammed the idling engine into gear and stomped the gas.

Sweaty palms slid over the steering wheel as she dragged her foot in.

The door stood wide as the tires screamed at the sudden shift of physics.

The tread gripped. Held. Then screeched as Harper rocketed down the road.

At the first street, she yanked the steering wheel to the right.

The car slung around the corner.

The action forced the door shut.

"Ridge!" she screamed.

"What's happening, Harper?" Calm words didn't have a place in her turbulence. Then to the side. "Trip, load up stat."

"Ridge!" Her hands were shaking on the wheel so badly, the car swerved drunkenly over the pavement.

"I'm coming."

"Help them!" Her shocked brain grabbed at words.

"We're coming, Harper. Tell me what's happening."

"Gun! Girls! I... I... I stole the car."

Horror washed over her as she realized the ramifications of what she'd done.

She *stole* the car.

This might be the knee-jerk reaction that would end up getting her killed.

Chapter 2

Ridge

Ridge spun the SUV out of the parking lot, his head on a swivel, powering forward. He followed the directions Harper had given them a few moments ago.

Harper's ragged breathing was channeled through the Bluetooth and came out over the radio speakers.

"Harper, we're coming. Is someone chasing the car? I need you to pull off the road."

There were no words on her end, only panicked noises pressed through jackhammering teeth.

Both Ridge and Trip recognized the sounds made by someone in a life or death situation.

They'd heard the wheels squeal. It sounded like Harper was with that car and not still out on the street.

The shriek of the tires, the bang of the door, engine sounds.

His name.

Gasps.

Ridge stayed vigilant of children in the streets. Especially if they were frightened, children could dart out without being aware that his behemoth of a vehicle was firing toward them.

The school bus directly ahead of them slowed.

Ridge didn't want to make choices about peeling around if the bus's door opened and the red stop sign flipped out. He drove off the road into the ditch and pressed past the bus before swerving back into the street.

Trip swiveled in his seat. "Four girls, two boys at that bus stop. They look calm. The bus is stopping to let them on." He looked down at his phone. "That was the street corner Harper read to us."

"Harper, can you hear me? If you're still driving, if it's safe to do so, I need you to stop." He kept his tone even but commanding. There was a particular way of talking to someone in fight or flight that could sometimes wiggle the words past the part of the brain in overdrive. "Pull into the first driveway you see. Do you see a parking lot? Can you pull over? I need you to stop. You're not safe driving like this. Pull off."

Trip pointed ahead.

There, in the middle of the road, were parallel skid marks.

Ridge came to a stop alongside them and opened his door.

The smell of burned rubber lingered in the air. Someone had taken off at high speed. It had to be Harper; she'd said she'd stolen a car. "Girls and a gun." He glanced toward Trip. "You heard her say that, right?"

"Roger that." Trip unhooked his seat belt.

"Harper, can you talk to me? I need to know what's going wrong here," Ridge said, switching away from the car's telecom system and back to his phone as he climbed out, rounding to the hatch. He opened the door, unlatched the crate, and snapped his fingers to get Zeus onto the scene.

"S-s-s-s-s," she said.

Ridge caught Trip's gaze. "I'm going to take a stab at this. Harper saw a guy pointing a gun at a student. Harper jumped in the car and deprived him of a getaway vehicle."

"I'll call it into Headquarters. You get Zeus's nose on it."

Zeus was the best ground tracker on their internationally renowned Cerberus Tactical K9 Team. It would help, though, to know what they were tracking.

Ridge didn't put Zeus on a lead. With a hand signal, Zeus swung to Ridge's side, flanking him as they crossed the street.

Tongue out, body primed, Zeus had his eye on Ridge, eager for his command.

Ridge stopped behind the tire mark. "Car stops. The guy gets out. He'd frighten the students into submission with the gun." Ridge turned to the side road. "The guy with the gun would have walked straight out from the car." He walked forward to reach the grass.

Ridge's focus sought along the edge of the road. He didn't see any tracks in the rain-softened soil. The girls must have been standing on the roadway.

The school bus lumbered sleepily past.

Ridge checked both directions then walked Zeus back to where the man probably exited his car.

Zeus's nose was in the air sniffing through wide nostrils, chugging the scent into his system, sounding like a train picking up speed.

His body froze.

His tail stood straight up and rigid. He'd picked up a scent he wanted to follow.

"Girls," Harper had said. Had they been kidnapped as a group? Was one girl the focus?

Ridge trusted his dog. "*Such*," (tsuuk) he commanded in German, "track."

Zeus took two steps forward with his head lifted into the wind, then lowered his snout to the road. Front legs wide, nose inches from the pavement, Zeus paced forward with Ridge on his heels.

Behind Ridge, Tripwire ordered his German shepherd, Valor, down from her crate, the hatch slammed, the fob chirruped, locking the vehicle.

Ridge scanned the neighborhood with a practiced eye.

A woman hunkered in a front window, her face stricken with anxiety.

Zeus stalled at that house, looked toward the front door, sniffed the air. He stepped onto the lawn, sniffed again, then went back to the road, his nose on the track he'd been following.

Ridge would bet good money that one of the girls had run home, and mama bear was guarding her den until the police arrived. Swiveling to see over his shoulder, Ridge caught Trip's gaze, then pointed toward that house.

"On it," Trip called out.

If Trip could gather intel, they might have a better handle on what was happening out here.

Sirens whirred a good distance away. Ridge called back to Trip. "Tell Bob to reach out to the P.D. and let them know we're on the scene with K9. We don't need any issues with mistaken identity." Ridge still had Harper on the phone. He didn't want to make the call to Headquarters himself and lose that connection any sooner than he'd have to.

"Wilco," Tripwire called back.

"Harper, Zeus is tracking. It would help if I knew what happened. Did you stop the car?"

"I stopped," she chattered. "I'm at a church. I don't know what happened. I'm… I can't recall. I… I was running. The man was big. Really big. Like *you* big. And he had a gun."

"Breathe."

Zeus was hard on the scent and moving fast. Ridge just hoped it was the guy with the gun that Zeus had latched on to. In their two years working together, Zeus had seemed to suss out the chemical composition of "bad guy." He hadn't been wrong yet. That was just one of the reasons why Ridge always trusted his dog.

"I…a girl with a ponytail. A pink backpack. I have pictures in my head." Her voice trailed off.

Shock. It was common.

Big guy with a gun. Pink backpack.

Zeus had led Ridge off the road and into the wood line.

"Harper, I'm putting you on hold for a second."

"Oh. Okay." He could hear the fear ratchet up in those three quick syllables.

"Are your doors locked?"

"Yes."

"Stay in the car."

"Okay."

He hated to do it, but there were protocols in place. And too, Harper didn't need to hear what was about to happen when Zeus found his target.

Ridge rang through to Cerberus War Room.

"Go for Bob." Bob, their tactical operations commander, answered on the first ring.

"Ridge here. You spoke to Tripwire?"

"Affirmative."

"Zeus is tracking. By his body language, we're on the target's heels. We came to the end of the cul-de-sac and are entering a wooded area."

"I have both you and Zeus on the GPS board and am following your progress. The wooded area is approximately ninety acres square. There are highways to the north and east. There are neighborhoods to the south and west. That puts cars to carjack and homes to break into in those directions. We want to get to the unsub prior to his finding shelter or another escape vehicle." Bob used the term "unsub" to indicate an "unknown subject." It was a term Cerberus used interchangeably with "tango" or "target" once an unsub was determined to be the person that Cerberus operators chose to get up close and personal with. "Have you got eyes on anyone yet?"

"Negative."

"P.D. knows you're on scene with K9. They've agreed to amass near your vehicle to protect the scent trails. Tripwire is heading your way. From Tripwire's interview of a witness, you're looking for a single, underaged, endangered female along with the unsub—stranger, not kin. The witness described the man as a 'hulk.' There's a gun involved."

"Roger."

Ridge was jogging on a carpet of pine needles and deciduous leaves, packed down with the recent late-season rains.

He softened his focus and tipped his head. Like this, he could now see the faint trail of debris dislodged by scuffling feet. Two tracks. A shorter gait track lay slightly ahead of a longer gait track. Ridge could picture a hand on the child's shoulder, propelling her forward.

Minutes passed as Ridge trailed Zeus.

Every second upped the child's danger levels. Surely, the kid had seen the guy's face. If the bad guy regretted hauling her off, if she became a liability to his escape, things could turn deadly fast.

Up ahead, Ridge saw a tiny speck of hot pink. It was directly in line with Zeus's tracking.

As they approached the backpack, Ridge pulled up his photo app that applied GPS coordinates and a timestamp to his images; he took several photographs.

Zeus's posture and intensity told Ridge he was on the trail of the guy with the gun. Zeus had a protective streak in him. When there was a bad guy and a victim, Ridge could see the cunning, strategic thought process of his dog. And today, as he'd noticed in past events, Ridge picked up what seemed like Zeus's moral indignation that one in power would harm someone unequal. In training, Zeus's attacks were aggressive in apprehending the bad guys. When facing true evil, Zeus brought righteousness to his violence of action, becoming a weapon of destruction, punitive in his takedowns.

Ridge could only imagine Zeus's behavior was borne out of his origins, his job before his rescue and placement with Cerberus.

Zeus's hackles were up. The bad guy was close. Zeus

was a force multiplier. They weren't going to let this guy get away.

Ridge bent his knees with each step, using the movement as shock absorbers to lighten his tread in the otherwise silent woods.

It would be easiest if the bad guy didn't know they were hot on his heels.

As he jogged forward, Ridge gamed this out. The guy didn't cut his losses and run. Instead, he grabbed a girl.

It meant the target was slower, clumsier, more distracted.

His taking a hostage meant the number of people and the quality of aggressive force coming after him would multiply.

Ridge knew this meant the target would be more likely to act violently because getting caught would lead to some serious time in the pokey. And prison for people who hurt kids was always more painful. The other inmates made sure of it.

Ridge shouldn't expect that the guy would turn himself in. Bodies in motion tend to stay in motion.

It described Harper, who was out for a walk; she'd sped that up and made her move. Taken the car. Boom.

They were already on the phone. Ridge and Trip already in motion to join her. Boom.

It probably described the guy with the gun. He was out looking for a victim to nab. His mind was on seizing the victim, and in his shock and stress, he didn't let go of his original idea. Boom.

Zeus slowed. He balanced his weight farther back into his haunches. He was an alpha dog if ever there was one.

Ridge changed his gait to match his partner.

Zeus's keen sense of sight had locked onto a briar patch so thick it looked impenetrable.

There were no tracks in—no place where someone would have forced a child onto her knees and compelled her to crawl inside.

Zeus froze, ears pointed forward. He rotated his shoulder bones. It was the stance he took in training before he got the command and went full fur-missile, shooting toward the guy wearing the protective suit.

Typically, Ridge gave three calls, warning that he was going to release his K9.

In this case, there was a gun possibly in play.

The surprise of his dog launching at the bad guy might distract him from pulling the trigger.

A snarling, chomping beast like Zeus coming full tilt scared away all rational thought. The person dissolved into a primal quiver. Ridge had seen it enough times to know what result to expect. And Zeus had been trained to drill his teeth into the hand with the weapon.

Zeus whole-body vibrated in anticipation.

"Packen!" Ridge commanded quietly with a hand signal. Zeus's favorite command, it allowed for a bite and a takedown.

Zeus took three massive leaps and dove into the briars.

If Zeus didn't have a perfect record for identifying the bad guy in real-world hostage scenarios, leaving the innocent unmolested, Ridge would never give such a command.

A high-pitched girl-scream of terror went up.

A man's howl of pain.

Zeus's deadly growls.

Ridge reached into the barbs, dragging them back to make a hole. A small hand pressed against the ground.

Reaching in, Ridge grabbed her wrist. "Good guy. Good guy. Good guy," he repeated so she wouldn't fight against him in the thick barbs. "I'm here to take you home." He pressed his forearm into the sharp briars, lifting them away from her face. "I'm here to protect you." He slid the child out. "Me and my dog. Did you see my dog bite the bad guy? Yeah. He's a good doggo. He eats the bad guys."

Not knowing what had happened to the gun, Ridge focused on getting the child safe.

She was covered in mud, and she had pissed herself.

Barking behind him pulled Ridge's attention.

Valor and Trip raced forward.

Ridge scooped the silent child into his arms. "We're the good guys. We're helping. Look, here's another good doggo. This here is Lil' Mama, and she's going to take care of you."

"Hi, Shawna. I'm Trip." Tripwire must have gotten the girl's name from the mom up the road.

When Ridge delivered Shawna into Trip's arms, he mouthed, "Gun."

Trip nodded and stepped behind a massive trunk. "I've got you, Shawna. I'm the good guy. You're going to be okay." With the shaking middle-school child cradled in his arms and Valor between his legs, Trip positioned himself there, protected in case the man in the bushes fired a round off.

"Do you know if she's the only one?" Ridge asked Trip as the hollering got louder in the bush.

There was no point in asking the girl. She was white with shock and non-responsive to anything they'd said.

"That's what the mother from the first house told the police. When the man grabbed Shawna—" he looked down at the girl then back to Ridge "—the others ran."

The hollering in the bush had turned to screams.

Ridge felt a sense of warm contentment knowing those screams, and the begs for help came from the excruciating pain of two-hundred-thirty-eight pounds of bite force.

Ridge called out, "Zeus, *bring*." It was the German command for fetch.

A dog butt emerged from the briars, tail waving joyfully. Zeus stepped back, pressing into his hind legs. Back again. Back. And now Ridge could see he had his teeth sunk into the man's calf.

Ridge reached down to the man's other ankle and gave a mighty yank until the guy was out of the briars.

The gun wasn't in his hands. Ridge would send Zeus in for it after the cops got the guy in cuffs.

Harper was right; this guy was a giant of a man.

Ridge commanded, "*Aus*." (owss)

Zeus immediately opened his jaw.

Blood flowed freely from the man's wounds.

"Sir, if you move in any way I don't like—" he patted the guy down for identification or weapons "—I'll command my dog to apprehend you again. Do *not* move. Is that clear?"

"Clear," the man sobbed.

"*So ist brav!*" Ridge praised as he gave Zeus a full body rub.

With a hand signal, Zeus lay down, his tail wagging, looking content with the way his day had unfolded.

It was always a good day for Zeus when he got to bite the bad guy.

Chapter 3

Harper

Harper knew that the police would be asking her questions. The truth was, she was much better at explaining details through her art. Everything in her memory over the last bit of time was a blur. She wasn't even sure how long she'd been sitting there, staring out the front window as if petrified in place.

Shaking herself free of the spell, Harper searched around the car's interior for drawing supplies. With a trembling hand, she opened the glove compartment then the console. She found a ballpoint pen, but no paper.

The engine was running in case Harper needed to make a quick getaway. She'd already pointed the car toward the grassy side yard that connected to a driveway and off to a different street. Maybe the bad guy, if he showed up to get her, wouldn't think of doing that.

Harper swiveled around in her seat. Out of the corner of her eye, she spotted a notebook on the back floorboard.

Lifting onto her knees to reach down, she snagged the corner and lifted. Underneath lay a handful of zip ties, a box of condoms, and a roll of duct tape.

Her stomach sloshed.

Holding the notebook out to the side to protect the pages, Harper leaned farther forward, puking up her emotions.

She filled the carpeted well behind the driver's seat. She coughed and puked again.

Buckets of angst left a bitter taste in her mouth.

She'd saved the pad, though. She sat back a little and rested her forehead against the cool seat.

The car stank. The kind of stench that roiled the stomach and…yup, here it came again.

Harper leaned back over, so it all landed in one area of the back, not that she was trying to save the bad guy with the gun time cleaning up, but for all she knew, this was a rental, and some poor minimum wage worker would be faced with the contents of her stomach. Or the cops would have to search through the slime to find a clue.

She didn't know anything about investigations, but Harper noticed she'd sloshed some of her bile onto the condom box and tape. It was going to mold if it went into an evidence locker somewhere.

She spun back around, her mouth hanging open as she panted.

Ridge told her to lock the doors and stay in the car.

She just couldn't. Nope.

Harper tapped the lock and pushed the door wide. For

a second, she imagined Ridge riding up on the scene, wrapping her in his arms, and kissing her full on the mouth, thrilled that she was safe, only to pull back in disgust when he met her puke lips.

So gross. What an image.

Right now, Ridge was doing what Ridge did best. He was catching the bad guy and saving the girl. That was the happy ending.

For her, no such thing existed.

Even if by some weird twist of fate Ridge could like her as more than a friend, romance with him—or anyone for that matter—wasn't possible.

Since she was thinking about romance, of course, she heard, "Harper, you okay?" Ridge's voice came through the line.

She shook her head. Even *now*, the trickster fiends were at play.

Harper had thought she'd been on hold, but nope, no such luck. Ridge had listened to her puke.

You're such a beautiful blossom. A delicate flower of womanhood. Harper rolled her eyes at herself as she scanned the empty lot.

"Zeus ate the bad guy. He's in cuffs. The little girl is on her way to the hospital for a once-over."

Harper gasped and gripped at her chest.

"Harper, listen to me. The little girl is on the way to the hospital because it's routine."

Harper's gaze searched the edges of the parking lot. They caught the man. But the feeling that the bad guy had his eyes on her was spooky.

"I vomited." Harper at the confessional. *He heard. He knows—no need to highlight it.*

"It happens. You're going to be okay. Listen, I need

to figure out where you are. Our lawyer, Sy Covington, is close. He wants to be there when the police talk with you."

The police.

She gulped and swallowed as her stomach churned again.

"Is there anything around you that would tell you where you are?"

She tilted her head back, taking in a slender cross hanging beneath the eaves. "It's a church. There's a sign, but it just says, 'Son screen prevents sin burn.' It's brick. There's a steeple."

"Okay, let's try this. Can you open your map app and tell me what it says?"

"The string of numbers?"

"GPS coordinates, yes, that would help."

Harper read them off as she walked toward the church steps. She could see a bench up there, kind of hidden from view. She'd feel safer over there.

"Harper, stay in the car." *How did he know?*

"I can't. The vomit is too much. I'm going to walk over to the porch. I think it's a good hiding place. There aren't any other cars here."

"Keep your phone on. Okay?"

"Yes. He's coming first? The lawyer?" Harper climbed the stairs then stopped to scan the area again, gripping the notebook and pen in one hand and the phone in her other. "He'll be here by the time the police come?"

"I won't give the police your location until Sy is there and has spoken to you. And I'll bring Zeus. That should make you feel more comfortable."

"Okay." She wiggled her knees. Man, she needed to pee. Right now. She looked longingly at the bushes but deemed them too sparse. "Can you bring me a breath mint, too?"

"I've got you covered." Ridge's voice held a smile.

Why he'd be smiling at a time like this, Harper couldn't imagine.

She appreciated him, though—his calm steadiness.

At the beginning of March, Harper had been doing her job as Berlin Tracy's personal assistant, making arrangements for a New York City appearance. Harper had had the TV on in the background, startling as the emergency system had blared. She'd anticipated them saying this was a test of the Emergency Broadcast System, but this time it had been an actual emergency. The first time in her life. A storm that had been out at sea had collided with another system and had created a storm of the century with almost no warning.

The Berlin Tracy crew were in the mountains of Virginia at the historical, five-star Wild Mountain Lodge, so that Berlin, who had zero experience in the woods, could do a Bear Grylls–like photoshoot in the bid for a TV role. None of her crew had any more of a clue than Berlin did about the forest. It was a pack of NYC videographers, stylists, and gofers.

All of them were out there, somewhere on the miles of manicured mountain trails around the lodge, clueless that they were in life-threatening danger.

Harper had dashed out of her room down the hall and burst out of the lodge door as if she could do something to help the situation.

Only when she found herself standing barefooted in the cold on the sharp gravel did she realize that she'd sprung into action, pelting straight out the door and into the steadying grip of a stranger.

Bob.

She had grabbed the Cerberus Tactical K9's head operations guy. He was at the lodge, making sure everything was set up as Team Alpha headed their way from a training mission called for the weather. Bob was so kind—that calm, serious professionalism. And there she was babbling out the problem because he looked like the kind of man who would have the skills needed for that kind of situation. He had his dog, Eve, there with him, and dogs were able to find people, right? "Can you help me?" she'd finally gasped out.

Luckily for everyone involved, the Cerberus dogs could actually find people.

Harper signed the contract, and Cerberus went into full swing.

The teams went out doing air scent searches.

Zeus was given Berlin's nightgown and put his nose to the ground.

Ridge and Zeus found the crew. Saved them. Brought them back to the lodge.

As a bonus, there were plenty of harrowing photos that Berlin could post to her Instagram account once connectivity was re-established.

She got her TV role.

It still made Harper shake her head. Some people led charmed lives.

Not everything turned out perfectly. Others that were out hiking those trails that day weren't as lucky. One woman almost froze to death. It was Tripwire and Valor who had saved her.

Berlin's crew and the Cerberus Alpha team had been snowed in for the next eight days. Some of the best days of her life. Safe from any dangers, she relaxed and enjoyed the tactical teams' company.

As the week progressed with them trapped in the lodge, a dozen handlers and their K9s, Harper learned that the handlers regulated their emotions because they impacted the dogs' emotions. Emotional energy runs down the lead.

If the handler was stressed, so was their K9.

Stressed-out dogs weren't good working dogs.

From the moment they met, Zeus seemed to take to her, so she got to hang out most of the time with Ridge. They'd become friends. Good friends.

That wasn't true.

Harper knew that their friendship was built on her lies. They weren't good friends at all.

Staring down at the open pad, the pen rested in the web between her thumb and index finger.

She needed to think about what to tell the police.

Harper remembered running. She remembered talking to Ridge. She didn't know what she'd said. She had the concept that there was a bad guy and girls and that she'd stolen the car—how else would the car be sitting here in the parking lot—

Nope. It was startling. Frustrating. Harper was missing a chunk.

Harper put her pen on the paper and told her brain to draw what she remembered last, and then she took her consciousness and stepped out of the way. Artistic meditation. She barely opened her eyes, just enough to make sure her hand was on the page.

And the next page.

And the next.

She let her hand go. Just let herself sketch to see what

details she had retained. It was an exercise that she'd done for years now, part of how she'd trained her artistic eye to capture moments for later. In her role as Berlin Tracy's P.A., she didn't always have the luxury to get images onto paper right away. Like these:

The car stopping.

The gun extending the length of a muscular arm.

The girls' horror.

Objects falling from their arms. A book. A phone. A jump rope…

His boot.

The anger that ran through his veins, bunched his muscles, altered his posture. It came from a deep, dark place. Vile and powerful.

Harper paused and exhaled, letting her lids shut. Thank goodness for Zeus and Ridge. Valor and Tripwire. My god! They saved that child from the beast. From an altered life. Now, that child would live with heightened vigilance, nightmares, and panic attacks, but she could carry on mostly okay.

Harper leaned her head back and gasped. *They saved her.*

But now, Harper was the one in danger.

Chapter 4

Harper

"Harper." The sound of Ridge's voice made her jerk, sliding her hand across the drawing she was working on. She had done a front-facing drawing of the man, and now she was drawing a circle, placing her measurement lines to render his profile.

She turned the page. She'd start again. Harper hoped to develop the drawing, as photoreal as she could manage with a ballpoint pen, to be used as evidence if necessary.

For reals, Harper wouldn't be showing up at any kind of trial. No way. She had to do what she could to keep that guy behind bars before she moved on.

"Harper?"

"Yes," she exhaled. "I'm here."

"A car is about to turn into the parking lot. It's a charcoal gray SUV, do you see it?"

She looked up, and an SUV idled out on the street with its blinker on. "Yes."

"That's Sy Covington. He's an Iniquus lawyer. He's going to represent you when you talk to the police. He has some breath mints for you and a can of ginger ale for your stomach."

"He travels around with ginger ale in his car?"

"His kid has a stomach bug. When I called, he'd just stopped by the store. He has some crackers, too, if that'll help."

Harper felt tears well up in her eyes. She gulped down a sob, and that made her burp.

Lovely, she thought sarcastically.

This was a nightmare.

"He's turning in. Should I hang up?" Harper asked.

"Yes," Ridge said. "I'm going to give the two of you five minutes to talk, then I'll come along with the police."

"And Zeus." She pressed down hard on his name. Harper would feel safer with her hand on Zeus's fur.

"Definitely with Zeus."

"Ridge?"

"Uh-huh."

"Can you come now?" She hugged the notebook to her chest.

"I think it's best if I give you that time with Sy. The cops will follow me, and anything they hear is part of the record. You're fine. You did nothing wrong. Your actions were heroic. It's an abundance of caution, which is how we handle our clients."

Clients. She wasn't a client. She couldn't afford someone of the caliber that Iniquus would hire.

"He's a nice guy, Harper. He'll take care of you."

Maybe. This was going to be a maze to navigate.

The lawyer had pulled up to the steps. He ducked his head and reached around in his cab. When he climbed out in his bespoke suit, she just shook her head. These people lived in a different world than she did. A year ago—before she met Berlin—she had been living out of her van. "I can't afford your services" was the first thing that sprang out of Harper's mouth.

His brows drew together. "Harper Katz?"

"Yes."

"I'm Sy Covington with Iniquus. I'd like to extend my warm regards," he said from the bumper of the SUV. His voice sounded like southern gentility, like old money. He lifted the bag toward her. "Might I come to have a chat? I understand you're not feeling well."

He was asking for permission to come up the stairs. There was something very *To Kill a Mockingbird* about this scene.

She nodded.

"Iniquus is very grateful to you and your bravery this morning. My services, if you'd like me to represent your interests here, are an honor and come with no fee."

Harper swallowed.

"If you don't want that, then perhaps I could offer you some saltines and maybe sit with you until the others arrive."

She held out her hands for the bag. She really could use some ginger ale. "Will they arrest me for stealing the car?"

"No, ma'am. They'll want to know the reason why you drove away in the car." He hiked up his pants just above his knees as he sat on the stair, right where everyone put their dirty feet. It must be at least a thousand-dollar suit. "What will you tell them?"

"I don't want to tell them anything. Here." She held out the notebook with the pen shoved into the coil of the binding wire. "I drew these."

As Sy flipped through the pages, his frown deepened.

Harper opened the bag, pulled out the cold can of soda, and popped the top.

"These are very emotional. I can feel the fear and horror of the people in each scene. You're extremely talented." He turned to the last page, staring at the image. "I saw him. This is exactly right. Right down to that mole by his nose." He caught her gaze. "It's surprising you could pick out such fine details under such frightening circumstances."

"I didn't." She tapped beside her eyes. "I've trained my eye and brain to see quickly. It's part of my process. I step aside and let my brain do its thing. I actually don't remember anything beyond that first picture until Ridge was telling me to stop. I'm blank. No use asking me anything."

"The officers will want this as evidence. May I take pictures of them for our records?"

"Please." Harper tipped the can back, taking a slow sip, then letting it settle.

"Ridge said that he was on the phone with you." Sy laid the notebook on the brick stairs and hovered his phone over each page. "He said you witnessed the approach of the kidnapper, and you took the man's car. Ridge and Tripwire were just down the street and were able to capture the man." He stopped on one and pointed. "This picture here that you drew of the zip ties, condoms, and duct tape, that's in the back of the car?"

"Yes, sir."

"And you never saw this man before?"

"I'm from California. I'm staying at The Lily on business and was out for a walk. I don't know anyone other than some Cerberus people in this area."

"Okay, I—"

"Mr. Covington—"

"Sy, please."

"Okay, Sy. Listen." She squirmed around on the bench, grabbing the cloth between her boobs and pulling it away from her humid skin. "I don't want my name, address, employer, or any identifying information to be given to the police." Her head turned toward an engine noise.

An SUV trailed by a police vehicle turned into the parking area.

"Is there a reason for that?" Sy asked.

"It'll be public record. He's a horrible—I'd guess from my pictures—a disturbed man. I don't want him to have any way of knowing who I am or where I can be found." Her teeth began to chatter. "My understanding is I don't need to tell the police anything at all unless I'm under arrest."

"Well—"

Her hands came up, encircling her neck. "Will I be arrested for taking the car?"

"Highly doubtful." He pushed to his feet, notebook in hand.

"Sy." Harper lowered her lashes with a frown. "Thank you for coming to help me when your child is sick." Her voice was soft and sad. "I appreciate the ginger ale and your time."

He looked at her for a long moment, pressing two fingers to his lips, thought lines deepening across his forehead. He dropped his hand with an exhale. "When they ask for your name, say, 'Call me Harper.' I'll take it from there."

Chapter 5

Ridge

Tripwire would stay with the SUV. The fewer people on scene here in the church parking lot would mean less confusion. Normally, with a lawyer on site, Ridge would hold back, too.

But this was Harper.

Luckily, he had the excuse of delivering Zeus to her as he'd promised.

He slid the gear shift into Park as his eyes caught on her and held. Pushing his door open, he climbed down from the cab.

Sy and Harper walked down the steps to stand on the sidewalk in front of the church.

She was obviously in emotional shock—her lips were colorless. Her eyelids held too wide.

Harper's gaze found his.

Ridge offered up what he hoped was a supportive smile.

As he circled around to the back hatch to get Zeus, Ridge slid his attention to Sy Covington.

Sy dwarfed Harper as he stood beside her, holding what looked like a school notebook. Something about Sy's expression was off. Something worried him. It wouldn't be evident to a stranger, but Ridge knew that was an expression Sy got when the situation took an odd turn—when his brain churned busily behind his cool gaze. It was the riptide intelligence Sy used to drag the bad guys under.

All Iniquus employees were tracked by the computer system. This was for their safety, but also—should there be an immediate need for action—the computer could pinpoint the closest possible teammate with the needed skillsets—like the Cerberus teams with their K9s.

Yeah, sometimes it put a spin in Ridge's plans. He'd be out. His vehicle speaker system would spark with the warning buzz followed by an operations manager redirecting him to an operator or situation in need of assistance. It cultivated the "all for one and one for all" mentality of the Iniquus family, knowing that someone always had your back.

If Ridge didn't have anyone in the cab with him, he'd redirect.

Certainly, Headquarters never wanted to put those not contracted to Iniquus in harm's way.

It was good that Sy wasn't transporting his kids and was only a few miles away at the grocery store. Ridge was glad that it was Sy who showed up in the computer system.

While Iniquus only hired the best of the best, and any of their lawyers would do, Sy had a fatherly, low-key vibe Ridge had found missing in many of their Ivy League sharks.

Granted, the sharks had their place. They were highly effective.

In this circumstance, it was Sy's low-key demeanor that would help Harper best.

Lifting the back hatch, Ridge released Zeus from his crate.

With Zeus's collar attached to a lead, they headed over to the sidewalk to join the two.

Zeus turned his head and caught Ridge's eye, and Ridge got the message instantly. When he released the lead, Zeus dashed toward Harper, who squatted down to wrap her arms around Zeus's neck and bury her head.

Sy reached down to retrieve the can of ginger ale from her hand.

A police officer had trailed Ridge from the crime scene to the church to get Harper's statement and secure the bad guy's car. He stood watching the scene play out as he adjusted the hat on his head and squared his shoulders.

As Harper rose to her feet, Ridge moved to her side, sandwiching Harper between her allies.

When Harper tipped her face up to him, Ridge swiped away the tears that clung to her lower lashes. He tried to imagine what it would feel like for a civilian to be so far out of her element—far from home, away from her support circle, and enmeshed in such a violent and hor-rific crime.

It could have been so much worse.

Ridge opened his arms, and Harper rolled into his embrace, trembling. He lowered his cheek to rest against her hair and whispered, "We're here. I've got you."

She nodded against his chest. Ridge thought it was telling that she hadn't wrapped her arms around him like she had Zeus. She pulled her elbows in tight to her sides and posted her fists under her jaws.

Friend zoned.

There was no mistake that Harper wasn't reaching for him as a man who would gladly share his heart with her, or even as her protector. He was a pal—her long-distance phone buddy.

Could she hear his heart racing?

With the first call of "Hey!" that had come over the phone, Ridge had picked out the specific sound that people use in life-changing moments. A "call to the ancestors," a "connection to the universal breath" were the pictures he had formed about the tone which could vibrate through his cell structure. He'd heard mothers in childbirth cry out like that just before the baby crowned. He heard people just before death use it. When he heard it, it always raised the hairs on the back of Ridge's neck. When Harper used it, his body dumped adrenaline in a way he had never experienced before. He'd had to wrestle his way through the sensations like a man swimming against white water to find the calm needed to be helpful to Harper. He'd done his duty. But now that Harper was in his arms, the near-miss of it all, the pictures of how things could have turned—like the gun aiming toward her yells, the trigger being pulled, the bullet that could have silenced her. He could have lost her. Yeah, his heart was racing.

Mixed with that adrenaline was respect.

His team had saved the young girl. It wouldn't have

been possible without Harper. Without Harper, that child would have been long gone down the road and out of reach.

Statistically, it wasn't likely that the girl would ever be seen again.

Harper had saved not only herself but had done absolutely the most genius thing possible to thwart the crime.

Ridge was so *damned* proud of her.

But, even with all those other thoughts boiling, he couldn't stand here with Harper vibrating against him and not have his body respond. And *that* would be wrong on so many levels. She'd run so fast in the other direction if her "friend" started acting like a creeper. Especially now.

Shifting his foot, so his left hip touched her right side, Ridge tucked her in a tight embrace but kept things platonic. Seemingly platonic.

Truth was, he was falling in love.

For Ridge, every time he talked to Harper, the deeper his feelings grew.

He'd liked her right off. They'd met in the Virginia mountains at the beginning of March when a massive storm pinned them down for eight amazing days.

From the beginning, Zeus had taken to Harper.

Zeus was an aloof dog. He had bonded to Ridge over time. But he was indifferent to others. Definitely an alpha dog. A king. There were three people that Zeus allowed into his regal sphere. Lynx Sobado, who had helped save Zeus from his abusers. Ridge was second in Zeus's pecking order. And right away, and very surprisingly, Harper.

Ridge always trusted his dog.

If Zeus made this exception and treated Harper as part of his pack, then Harper was special.

Ridge, of course, knew that...without Zeus's opinion. But the input was a confirmation.

Even now, Zeus had moved to Harper's back and was sitting between her legs, watching her six. Ridge had never trained this behavior. He'd asked Lynx if she had trained that behavior—and, no. It was the position Zeus took when Harper was anywhere where her back was exposed, sitting between her feet, his head up, looking fierce.

"You must be my witness," the officer said, clicking his pen against his chest to get the writing tip extended. A notebook was poised in the other hand. "Can I get your name, please, miss?"

"You can call me Harper," she said.

"Okay, Harper, I need you to tell me, as detailed as possible, what you witnessed."

"I took the car." She pointed at the Honda, sitting parked at an odd angle.

"Being a good citizen?" the cop asked.

"Being a human being, I'd imagine," Harper returned. "I don't remember any of it. I was jogging and talking to Ridge, then next thing I knew, he was yelling at me to pull over and stop."

"Who is Ridge?"

"Me, Caleb Hansen, Ridge is my call sign."

The cop looked his way with a warning glance. The officer already knew that. He was verifying Ridge's version of things.

Ridge needed to keep his mouth shut, or the officer would ask him to walk away. Ridge couldn't do that and leave Zeus alone with Harper, and there was little likelihood that Zeus would willingly leave Harper when she was upset like this.

Call Zeus off the bad guy even though Zeus loved the bite? Sure.

Call Zeus off guarding Harper? Ridge didn't want to test his command over Zeus that way. It could affect their partnership if Zeus tried to display dominance over Ridge by disobeying a command.

"All right. Let's start with when you first noticed something was wrong. What led to your taking the car?"

Harper sucked in a deep breath and pulled her shoulders back. "I have no idea what the reasons were in the moment. I was simply reacting. As I waited for everyone to arrive, looking back, I could guess."

"Let's hear that," the cop said.

Sy shifted his weight.

"I had no weapon. I have no skills. If the guy made the girls get into the car—isn't that what they always teach you? Never get into the car?" She looked up at Ridge, then over to Sy.

Neither of them responded.

"Getting taken to a secondary location." She stopped and coughed, turning a greenish pallor.

The cop took a step back. Cops had vomit radar; they were quick at the backward jump.

Sy lifted the ginger ale can toward her.

She stared at the label, taking in a stuttering breath that flared her nostrils. A poof of air seemed to signal her control over her stomach. "They say going to a second location is always worse than what would happen to you if you fought it out at the first location. The bad guys have privacy to do what they want once they get you away from help." The tone of her voice sounded almost like she was quoting someone.

Zeus let a growl rumble quietly into the space. He

came around the front of Harper, wedged his bottom between her legs, facing the same direction as Harper. It was his warning that he was on guard. Something had signaled Zeus that the stakes had been raised, and the threat was in this direction.

Ridge wondered if Zeus heard the echo of something from Harper's past in her words. He'd have to process that later.

The police sent a wary eye toward Zeus. His lips pressed together into a tight line.

"Harper," Sy said, "you don't know any of that to be factually correct, right? This is conjecture?"

"Exactly." She dropped a hand to Zeus's head. "I'm babbling. Saying that I'm stressed out would be a gross understatement. Look." She focused on the officer. "I don't know what happened back on the road. I drove. I stopped. I vomited into the back seat. Sy showed up. Then you all."

"The brain is a curious thing," Sy said as he opened the notebook. "Harper is an artist." He nodded her way and sent her a fatherly smile. "While she can't recall what happened to walk you through the step-by-step of her thought process and actions, she was able to imprint scenes. She's drawn them out for you."

Sy turned page after page of art done in blue ink across the lined paper. They showed the emotions of the moment as much as the positions and actions of the people involved. The last one, the one of the man's face, was spot on. It could have been a photograph. Sy closed the notebook and handed it to the officer. "These are for you." He turned his head to Ridge. "I'll forward the photographs to you and Tripwire for your reports."

The officer accepted the notebook, flipped slowly

through the drawings, then tucked it under his arm. "You happened to be out with a pen and notebook?"

"No, sir, I took them from the guy's car." She shuffled her feet. "When I turned around to reach in the back seat to get it, I puked. I tried to keep it all…in one area. It's pretty gross. I'm sorry."

The cop stared at her. Closed his eyes and gave a little shake of his head. When he focused back on Harper, he asked. "Do you work for Iniquus?"

"No."

The officer looked from Ridge to Zeus to Sy. "What's your association with them, then?"

"I just met Sy a few minutes ago. Ridge and I are friends."

Yeah, friends. It's not what Ridge wanted. But if Harper wasn't feeling the sparks like he was, he still wanted to be in her life. Still wanted to talk through his day—well, what wasn't classified about his day. Still wanted to hear her laugh. To know she was in safe for the night. To hear her bitch, and hear her gush, and, hell, hear her read the recipe she was making. He didn't care. That all made him happy. And happy wasn't something Ridge remembered being for a long time. He'd get what he could in the way of a relationship with Harper without any expectation that it should, would, or could be more.

But what he wanted most was to be by her side when she needed him to keep her safe.

"You don't work for them or with them?" the officer pressed.

"No."

"All right." He poised his pen to his own pad of paper. "I need your full name, address, and best contact phone number." He glanced up when she didn't answer him.

Harper swayed on her feet, sending a wide-eyed un-blinking glance toward Sy.

Sy reached into his back pocket and produced his wallet.

She nodded, then shook her head, then nodded, then wobble it around. It was cartoonish, and the only thing that Ridge could figure was that she was so stressed that her brain was misfiring. This wasn't a side of Harper he'd ever seen before. She was usually self-possessed, had an equanimity under stress.

It made him feel protective of her.

Zeus must have felt the same way because he stomped the ground with his paw and let out a second rumble of warning.

The officer took another step back. He visibly swallowed. "We need your contact information."

Harper still had her hand on Zeus's head. Her other hand went to her chest. Her exhale extended so long and hard, it doubled her over. Ridge realized his hold wasn't enough. Harper's knees were buckling under her. He dragged her into his arms, keeping her upright as she swayed.

For a moment, she dropped her head to his chest as she exhaled, "Thank you."

"Your information, ma'am?" The officer's tone changed to commanding.

Sy pulled a black card with the silver Iniquus emblem from the wallet slit.

"You can contact me through my lawyer." She pointed toward Sy.

"I'd like to include it in my report." His tone sharpened its edge.

"Here's my card." Sy held it out. "If you'd be so good

as to give me one of your cards, officer." Sy put a hand on Harper's shoulder.

Zeus allowed it but kept his eyes on Sy.

Sy must have noticed even though his gaze held on the officer. "My client is overwhelmed by the circumstances of the day. She needs to rest." They exchanged cards, and he slid the officer's information into his pocket. "If you need anything, please contact my office. Harper—" He bladed his hand toward the Iniquus SUV that Tripwire had kept running to keep the interior cool for the K9s.

Ridge supported most of Harper's weight as he wheeled her around and headed her toward the privacy of their vehicle. When they got there, Ridge didn't even try to put Zeus in his crate. The three of them climbed into the back seat.

Tripwire glanced around at them. Then, without a word, he put the SUV in gear and headed them down the road.

Chapter 6

Harper

"Weird. So weird what the brain does. I thought I was sitting there at the church for a very long time. And it also seems like a blink of the eye. Like I was telling you where I was on the road for you to do the search practice, and now I'm here. Like a wormhole. Or a pleat of fabric. Something… Strange."

"Where are we heading?" Tripwire asked as he pulled to the top of the parking lot.

"I need a shower and to brush my teeth. Can you take me back to my hotel?" She glanced over to Ridge. What must he think of her?

Fear sweat smelled differently than exercise sweat. She was grossing herself out, and yet here he was, acting like nothing unusual was happening.

He never talked to her about his job assignments.

Maybe this was what his day was like every day: saving victims, supporting the bit players, being a hero. "I'm just going to ask. It might be wimpy, but could someone stay with me? I'm…yeah. I guess I'm pretty shaken by this morning's events." Events—that was a nice emotionless word. Harper needed to keep the pictures from this morning at arm's length, as far away from her psyche as she could, for sanity's sake.

"The dogs can't go in," Tripwire said, turning down the road she'd swerved over in the stolen car. "I'll stay in the SUV with them, and Ridge can go up with you. When you're all cleaned up, how about you come back to Iniquus with us? You were heading there anyway in a little bit to help us get security planned for Berlin. You might feel better if you stayed tucked in tight with us until you're steadier on your feet."

"Oh." Harper's anxiety was short-circuiting her brain, but not so much that she didn't recognize how difficult it would be to lie on her bed, staring at the ceiling and revisiting the pictures in her head. "Yes, please. That would be great." She turned big brown eyes on Ridge. "Would you mind?"

"Sounds like a plan." He was holding her hand and turned it to lace their fingers. It was a tether of safety for her. A connection to goodness. She took advantage of the situation and laid her head on his shoulder.

He reached over to smooth a hand over her auburn hair and lay a brotherly kiss on her forehead. If Harper closed her eyes, she could pretend this was their relationship, that they belonged to each other, and this was a loving gesture of connection that went beyond their friendship to something with a deeper meaning.

She always had had a vivid imagination.

But it was *only* her imagination, she reminded herself.

For her safety, and possibly Ridge's, any connection would have to stay friendship zoned.

Zeus lay on the floorboard, his head resting on her knee. "Zeus, you ate the bad guy?" Her fingers tickled into his fur.

"He did and then some." Tripwire laced his words with laughter.

It was good that Tripwire could shake this off so easily. He'd been a SEAL. This was probably what he did before breakfast every morning and not the big deal it was for Harper.

She was grim enough for everyone. She wriggled her fingers behind Zeus's ears the way he liked. "But not the girl? She was okay?"

Zeus lifted his nose and closed his eyes, enjoying the sensation.

"Zeus only bites bad guys," Ridge said. "The dogs know the difference."

"They can smell bad guy," Tripwire said.

"I'm so proud of you. Thank you, buddy." She leaned over and kissed Zeus as they drove by a line of police cars parked on the side of the road, past the tire smears she'd left when she'd peeled out.

The Lily Hotel was a short drive away.

They'd arrived too quickly.

Harper preferred the protective cocoon of the SUV. The dogs. Ridge pressed up against her. Tripwire, whom she trusted deeply, at the wheel.

Before she was ready, Tripwire pulled up to the roundabout, and Ridge opened the door. "Wait here a sec. I'm going to load Zeus into his crate." He got out, shut the door, circled the front, and opened the door, waiting for Zeus.

Zeus gave Harper a once-over before he deemed her safe and spun around to jump down to the blacktop.

Harper pulled his door closed, then slid across the seat toward the hotel side to get out. "Thanks, Trip. I'll be as quick as I can."

He swiveled toward her. "Take your time. I don't mind being here. I have paperwork to fill out anyway. And Harper—" He waited until she looked him in the eye. "I'm so damned proud of you. You did awesome today."

She wanted to smile, but his kind words made her chin wobble, and tears glaze her eyes. She pressed her lips together.

Trip reached over the seat and patted her knee.

Ridge was at her door, pulling it open. His hand rested on the frame, his head on a swivel. It was part of what Ridge did by habit. There was no threat here at the hotel.

He held out his hand to her as if she were royalty.

She kept hold of his hand, pulling his arm in front of her and wrapping his forearm with her other hand. She held his arm like a shield as they moved through the electric sliding doors. He didn't seem to mind, so she didn't let go once they were inside.

I'm such a wuss, she thought.

"Good?" he asked as she headed them toward the elevator bank.

"Yes." Not really, but better than she had been. Man, did she stink, like for real. Puke and fear-sweat were a nauseating combination. But Ridge didn't even wrinkle his nose. She couldn't wait to get herself cleaned up. She'd just throw these clothes away. She didn't need the visual reminder of today.

"After exercising this morning, what had you planned for your day?" He tapped the up button, and the gears whirred as a car descended to the lobby.

"I planned to chill, do some art until I needed to head

to Iniquus with Berlin. What about you? What is all this keeping you from doing?"

"I don't have anything on my roster until noon. Zeus and I were scheduled to do a training evolution. I already called Didit to tell her to take over for me."

Harper reluctantly let go of Ridge to drag her phone from her leggings' pocket and tap the screen, bringing up the key card. "You were doing search and rescue?"

"A bit of search and rescue, a bit of close protection." He caught her under the elbow and steered her into the car when the doors slid open.

She held up the key to the scanner, the doors shut, and up they went to the top floor. "Do those two things coincide?"

"Only on a very bad day." They were looking at each other in the mirror. "Harper, why didn't you want the police to have your name?"

"Public records," she mumbled.

"All right." He tilted his head to let Harper know that wasn't an answer.

"I'm personal assistant to Berlin Tracy. *The* Berlin Tracy."

"No one would make that connection."

"Berlin will make the connection." She crossed her arms over her chest. "Give it thirty seconds from the time she hears this story, and she'll go public with her involvement. If I were to get more publicity than Berlin, it would make for tenuous job security. I need to stay on her payroll."

He looked at her for a long moment, processing. "You saved Berlin's life, her whole crew, in fact. When you were proactive about hiring our search and rescue team ahead of the storm, we got a lot of publicity for that rescue."

"Yes."

"But you were never mentioned."

"Exactly." The elevator car chugged to a stop; the doors slid open.

"The story is that we just happened to be out in the woods searching?" he asked.

"Iniquus discovered—" she put the "discovered" into air quotes as they moved down the hall "—that Berlin and her crew were endangered when Cerberus Team Alpha arrived at the lodge."

"And we took it upon ourselves to go searching the woods?"

She nodded as she stopped at the door and held the phone up to the scanner. "Out of adoration for Berlin—" the lock released "—you put your very lives in danger to go and save her." She pressed the door wide and went in, heading toward her suitcase.

Ridge stopped to turn the lock and swing the security latch into place before following her into the room. "Had we discovered people were in danger, we wouldn't have sat on our hands. Tripwire went after Dani. It's a stretch of the imagination that we would have just sat that rescue mission out. But still, credit where credit is due. We wouldn't have been out there looking for Berlin and her crew before the storm hit. They would have died. She gets that, doesn't she?"

"I don't think she does. But that's not important. I don't need or want that kind of recognition from her or anyone else. I prefer being as under the radar as I can manage." She was rummaging through her case for a change of clothes. "Look, I've been with Berlin for a little less than a year. She has drama running through her veins. She loves it, licks at it, savors, then gobbles it up. She can have all the glory. I want zero people to recognize me and associate me with anything, including, *es-*

pecially, Berlin." She hugged a pair of black slacks and a black blouse, bra, and panties to her chest as she stood up and faced Ridge.

"Why's that?" His voice was soft and coaxing like he wanted to convey that it was safe to tell him the truth.

But she couldn't trust him with her story.

She couldn't trust anyone.

"First, I'm not a public person. I'm not interested in tell-all articles people would want from me. Along those same lines, there's my contract and NDA." Yeah, that nondisclosure agreement was a serious deterrent. Not that she needed one. Harper sidled past Ridge, moving toward the bathroom.

"And what else?" That was probably an interrogation trick he used. She'd ignore it.

Did she feel interrogated? Like he was the other side, the one that wanted to manipulate her? Pry loose her secrets?

No. They were friends. Long-distance hang-out buddies. She'd kept things light. And it wasn't like he was pushing for more. She wouldn't allow *more*. Couldn't allow more.

"I want to make sure the bad guys don't know how to find me." She pointed toward the pale pink slipper chair. "The chairs are attractive but hard as rocks. The bed isn't bad. Make yourself comfortable. I won't be but a minute."

She shook her head as she closed the door. Yeah, she'd just invited Ridge onto her bed, Harper realized. As she started the sink faucet to brush away the vomit scum, that she'd chosen not to lock the bathroom door behind her. *Girl! You are going to get yourself in so much trouble!*

Chapter 7

Harper

"Harper." There was banging on her hotel room door. "Harper!"

Harper emerged from the bathroom, wet toothbrush in her hand. At least she didn't have puke breath anymore. But she hadn't had time yet for a shower. She threw the locks and grabbed the knob to pull the door wide for her boss. "Hey, you're up early." It was nine o'clock.

As she pushed her way past Harper, Berlin's gaze swiped over her assistant. "Why are you dressed for Halloween? You look like a pumpkin."

I'm aware, and now Ridge heard that.

Harper *liked* her body. She loved how voluptuous and sensuous her curves made her feel. She preferred looking at Rubens's Renaissance body types over Picasso's.

In her own work, Harper enjoyed exploring the wide variety of body types that women came by naturally.

She hated the ease with which people said outlandishly personal things to her that exposed their own biases as if their preference was everyone's preference.

From Harper's previously active dating life, she knew that one size did not fit all. And men loved her body, too.

"I was out for a walk, Berlin. I'm showering and changing to head over to Iniquus, you know, to get the ball rolling on your security intake." Harper trailed Berlin around the corner to the main room. "Ridge and Tripwire were nice enough to offer me a ride. Tripwire's down in the parking lot waiting with the dogs." *And I'm babbling.*

"Then I bet you didn't hear." Berlin bounced into the room. Her raven black hair was caught up in a messy bun. She had no makeup on. Wearing her nightclothes— oversized sweatpants that hung low on her hips and an undersized tank that barely made it over her bra-less boobs—she was gorgeous.

"Hear what?" Harper asked, sending a glance toward Ridge, who was stretched out on her bed with his back leaned against the headboard, his fingers laced behind his neck.

She blinked at him. It was one of Harper's fantasy images. She might have even drawn that one into one of her sketchbooks. Easing past Berlin over to the lowboy, Harper scooped the pad into a drawer, just in case Ridge idly leafed through while she was showering. 'Cause there were a few examples in there of poses that she'd imagined Ridge striking. And most of them didn't in- clude clothing. Just studies of the male form and muscle structure. It was the lie she liked to tell herself, so she felt less like a creep.

"Oh! Ridge." Berlin stopped on a dime and swung back and forth. "You have the shower water running," she said to Harper. "And look at you all comfortable on Harper's bed." She swatted at Ridge's Vibram-soled boots that hung over the edge of the mattress away from the comforter. Berlin swished her hips left and right. "Were you two about to do the nasty? A little early morning nooky nook? Did I interrupt?"

"Berlin, stop. That's inappropriate." Harper blushed so hard the extra blood circulation lifted the hair up from her scalp.

"Do you hear her, Ridge? She's such a scold," Berlin said. "Can you imagine I *pay* her to be my mother?"

Ridge was stone-faced. Berlin put him in a bad place. Berlin was, after all, an Iniquus client.

"I went for a walk this morning." Harper changed her tone to personal assistant running down an action list. "Now, I'm getting dressed for the day. It's not time for you to leave yet. You're due over at Iniquus at one. I had a wake-up call scheduled for eleven. Your lunch was ordered to your room at eleven-thirty, and a limo was ordered for twelve-fifteen. Why are you here so early? It's six o'clock west coast time. Was there something I needed to know?"

"Yes!" Berlin plopped on Harper's bed, legs wide, straddling the corner. "I got an alert from my emergency app. There was a kidnapping attempt right up the street. Up *this* street! It's on the news." She hugged herself gleefully. "I'm going to go up with DeWayne and have him take my picture where it happened!" Berlin always talked as if there was an exclamation point after her every thought.

It was exhausting.

Berlin turned to Ridge. "DeWayne's my photographer slash videographer for this trip. I'm traveling light this go-round with just my camera person, my stylist, and my Harper."

"What are they saying on the news?" Harper asked.

Berlin turned and stared at Ridge. "They interviewed a mom. Do you know what she said?"

Ridge raised his eyebrows as if asking what.

"That some *madman* stopped his car and pointed a gun at the kids waiting for their bus. But a woman—" she swung back and looked at Harper "—dressed in orange, stole his car so he couldn't get away. Then two men in uniforms—" she swung back to Ridge "—had security dogs." She pulled her brows up toward her hairline. "It was you!" She covered her mouth with both hands and sucked in a gasp of air as she bounced on the bed, her breasts bobbing up and down under her shirt, her nipples hardening.

Harper would hope that was a response to the friction. If not, she was finding Ridge and his heroism to be visibly arousing.

Ridge jerked his legs to the side to make room for Berlin as she flopped back on the bed, stretching her hands over her head, and started laughing.

Her shirt just wasn't up to the job. It slid up toward Berlin's neck.

Ridge's head snapped down to the side, and he refocused on his phone screen.

Harper reached out and pulled Berlin's shirt back in place, whispering, "You're putting Ridge in an awkward position. How about we keep our breasts covered?"

Berlin rolled toward Ridge, bending her knees to curl up cat-like, her elbow bent to prop her head. "Psh." She waved an erase-that-thought hand through the air. "Ridge has seen enough boobs in his lifetime. He's not going to lose self-control if he sees mine." She batted her naturally thick black lashes at him. "Are you?"

Ridge pretended to miss that question; his eyes were still on his phone.

Harper didn't think Berlin really wanted Ridge's affections. Berlin simply liked to collect men. She'd flirt with them with just enough promise, offered through her body language, that they'd be welcomed into her bed. Invariably, the guys gave Berlin enough emotional slack for her to wrap them around her finger. Acquisitions made her feel powerful.

Male attention was her fuel.

When Berlin didn't get the reaction she'd expected from Ridge, she turned a pout toward Harper. "You can be such a mother-scold. It's not a good look."

It shouldn't bother Harper that Ridge was hearing this, but it did.

Ridge lifted his gaze from his phone and let it rest firmly on Berlin's face. It didn't even look like it was a strain to keep his gaze level with Berlin's instead of dropping to her jugs.

What if Harper was wrong?

What if Berlin *did* want to start something with Ridge? If Berlin wanted Ridge, and they became a thing, man, wouldn't that just be all kinds of torturous to watch?

This was turning into a poor girl's version of Dolly Parton's *Jolene*, the one where "my man" was really just part of Harper's fantasy world. And no matter what, that's where Harper's sexual desire for Ridge needed to stay.

Berlin sat up cross-legged, leaning toward Ridge. "Tell

me what happened. Harper drove the car away, and you saved the girl, right?"

Ridge said nothing.

"Your silence is confirmation, you know." She swung her legs around until she was kneeling to get herself bouncing again and clapping her hands. "It was Zeus, right?" Bounce. Bounce. "Zeus took down the bad guy and saved the little girl?" Bounce.

Berlin reached into her waistband and pulled out her phone. Curled over the screen, her thumbs swirled over the keyboard.

"You can't use our names," Ridge said. "Are you posting to Instagram?"

"Of course, I'm protecting your names. And of course, I'm posting to Instagram!" Bounce. Bounce. Bounce. "I'm letting everyone know that *my* bodyguard is a hero. And that the same K9 that had helped me save my crew in March—" Berlin never acknowledged that she was in any kind of danger but had made it out that she was there protecting her crew and performing first-aid on them while the rescue team came to help her "—is the same hero who was out for his morning jog with his K9, saw the girls in distress, and jumped in to save the day. The bad guy is in the hospital before heading to jail!"

"You didn't include me in any of that, did you?" Harper asked.

Berlin batted her hand through the air without looking up. "Why would I include *you*?"

"That's not how things went down," Ridge said.

Berlin tapped the screen. "Oh, I'm sorry if I got some minor details wrong. But it's been posted. Ha ha! Nothing I can do about it now." She sent Ridge one of the smiles she used when she posted pictures of herself in sexy outfits, eating decadent desserts with captions like "This is so naughty, I think I'll need a spanking later."

Harper was pissed. She crossed her arms over her chest and tapped her toes on the floor, trying to dispel this unexpected emotion.

"Oh! And I attached a photo of you and Zeus, but it's the one taken from behind you. You approved it back when we were at the lodge. Besides—" her smile took on a wicked gleam "—your ass is one of your best features."

Berlin wasn't wrong about that. Ridge had a most excellent bu—

"Harper!" Berlin spun toward her.

"Hmmm?" Harper released her arms and concocted a "how may I serve you, my liege" smile. She couldn't imagine what was going to follow, but she knew from Berlin's tone that an idea had sparked, and it was going to throw a wrench in Harper's carefully aligned schedule.

"Make sure that when we get to Iniquus, they know I want Ridge and Zeus to be on my security team. And Tripwire with Valor. They match nicely. Same height. Same coloring. Similar dogs. My security set with K9s to frame me. I'll look amazing." Bounce. Bounce.

"Tripwire and Valor are search and rescue, ma'am," Ridge said.

Berlin shrugged. "Oh, I don't really care about that. It doesn't matter."

"Yes, ma'am, it does." Ridge ma'amed Berlin. That meant he addressed her as a professional and had stepped away from the familiarity they'd developed at the Wild Mountain Lodge. "Iniquus would never assign a team to perform a job they hadn't trained for and weren't a hundred percent able to succeed at performing."

"In Washington, D.C., at The Bradly?" She laughed.

"The most Tripwire and Valor would really need to do is search for the ballroom door for the congressional luncheon and wait outside."

"That's not how it works, Berlin." Ridge was far more patient in his explanation than Harper felt. "Tripwire and Valor are the team you want with you when you're over a cliff and need to get pulled to safety. Valor isn't bite certified. She won't do it. It's not in her nature."

"Zeus did, didn't he? I bet he bit the bad guy but good. Was it a bloody mess?" She pulled her knees to her chest and hugged them. "Did Zeus take off the bad guy's leg?" The glee that glittered Berlin's voice meant that she had never been in a situation where true evil threatened her. She thought this was a game. One of her TV shows where the wounds washed off with soap and water at the end of the day.

It was far from it.

Harper knew from experience that today was going to brighten her nervous system and fuel her nightmares for a long time to come. Just the smell of her skin, with the stench of dried adrenaline sweat, sent her memory back to…

Ridge's voice bit into her consciousness. "Harper?" He slid down the bed until they were face to face. "Harper, are you okay?" His hands steadied her shoulders.

Harper realized she'd folded over, with her hands gripping her trembling knees. She panted like she'd just finished a race. Swallowing hard to keep the extra saliva from drooling out, she managed, "Yeah, good. Thank you. My mind went back for a second." She stood and deliberately lifted the phone to read her notes, trying to switch her brain to another subject before this turned into a full-blown panic attack—the kind that made her feel like she couldn't survive. "Berlin, we already have two operatives assigned." She tapped her phone. "Their call signs are Blaze and Gator from Iniquus's Strike Force."

"Not Cerberus?" Berlin pulled her brows together.

"I know Blaze and Gator. Blaze is a former SEAL. Gator is a former Marine Raider," Ridge said. He hadn't taken his hands or eyes off Harper. "They're excellent at what they do. You'll be well protected."

"Oh! I have an idea!" Bounce. Bounce.

That was *always* a bad thing. Before Berlin said something that Harper needed to act on, Harper scooped up the panties she must have let tumble on her way to the bathroom. Yep, those were her lacy hip-huggers that snagged Ridge's attention. "I need that shower. I'll be out in a minute."

Ridge released his grip.

Her skin still sizzled from the electricity of his touch as Harper started down the short hallway to the bathroom.

Berlin was busily tapping at her phone. "Good. You stink, and that orange is a terrible color on you," she said without looking up.

She isn't wrong, Harper thought, stepping into the bathroom. The blaze orange was a safety choice, not a beauty choice. She wasn't in a place in her life where attractiveness needed a toehold. She was in a place in her life where she needed to dress in black, slide into a secret shadow, and stay there until January.

January and she could feel the sun on her face, again.

Chapter 8

Ridge

Harper sat to Ridge's left on the back seat of the SUV while Tripwire drove toward Iniquus.

This time, Zeus was in his crate; and because Harper shoved her hands under her thighs, Ridge didn't reach for her.

The drive had been silent.

With her hair still wet from the shower, Harper had tied it into a ponytail and threaded it through the back of a black baseball cap. The brim cast a shadow over her face, making it hard to see her eyes, hiding her expressions.

Ridge wondered if that was by design.

Was Harper overwhelmed as she tried to continue with her job today?

Was the hat how she gained solitude or privacy for the feelings that had flashed over her face at the hotel?

She'd wrestled her emotions down. Hidden them, for the most part. He wasn't sure why. Maybe she didn't want to look incompetent in front of her boss. Maybe she thought her feelings weren't valid or that if she gained the upper hand, she wouldn't have to deal with them. Her anxiety sparked out of control a couple of times. She'd almost collapsed, but she'd swallowed hard and righted herself.

Ridge wasn't convinced that was the best strategy.

Today wasn't a normal one in Harper's life, and she shouldn't treat it as if it were. He'd make sure to ease Harper into a discussion about PTSD later and offer some techniques to help.

Trip had already updated Bob and sent their pictures over, ones they'd taken at the scene, and those Harper had drawn. With his phone down by his side, Ridge texted a brief message about his concerns over Harper to Bob.

At Wild Mountain Lodge, Bob had been Harper's first point of contact with their team. She was the one with the forethought to hire Iniquus to go find Berlin in the woods. Bob had set up the TOC—tactical operations center—in the lodge's ballroom, ready for when the team arrived. During the search, Harper and Bob had obviously forged a bond. Ridge always picked up on the affection Bob displayed around Harper. Avuncular was the term that came to his mind.

Bob would want an update on Harper's well-being.

From watching her at the Wild Mountain Lodge, Ridge thought Harper would try to wrap herself in the invisibility cloak she liked to don in front of others, keeping to the background.

At first glance, Harper had a Teflon exterior; bad things slid off.

Since March, as they got to know each other better, Harper allowed him to see how empathetic and emotionally engaged she really was.

He'd loved the journey and the discovery.

Man, she needed the day off.

Several days off.

Harper wouldn't ask, and Berlin didn't have enough awareness of others to offer.

Tripwire and he had a professional relationship with Berlin now that she'd signed Iniquus contracts. They had no business butting into Berlin's employee relationships.

It was a fine line he had to walk here.

Ridge had decided not to whisper something in Berlin's ear while Harper was showering. He didn't want to leave Harper alone at the hotel. Tripwire and he had to submit paperwork from the incident and do a debrief with Bob about the morning's events. Protocol. No wiggle room there.

He rubbed his thumb and forefinger over his eyelids, then pulled his hand down his face.

Watching Harper, sitting there next to him with her shoulders up around her ears, was tough.

That she was wearing all black sent up a red flag for some reason. He wasn't sure why.

Could be nothing.

She might even be wearing black as her work uniform, he reasoned.

At Iniquus, they wore charcoal gray. The distinction between jobs was through wardrobe choice. It was tactical pants and compression shirts for operators, charcoal gray dress pants and light gray dress shirts for the technicians and support staff, suits for the Command wing, and those who had offices—lawyers, like Sy, personal assistants—all wore charcoal gray, with one exception: Lynx.

But Lynx played a unique role here at Iniquus. Ridge thought of her as part of their psychological operations. It was important that she stand out as the antithesis; it was part of her job.

Lynx might be the right person to talk to Harper. Lynx had a renowned aptitude for reading people. He'd have a good reason to take Lynx aside and ask for her impressions since Harper had said that Gator and Blaze from Strike Force had been assigned to Berlin as her close protection operators. And Lynx was attached to Strike Force. It wouldn't be a stretch for Ridge to quietly tell her today's story.

With a nervous lick at her lips, Harper reached back to the pocket on her black pants and patted her phone, reassuring herself that it was there.

Black pants. Black phone. Ridge was back to wondering if Berlin required Harper to wear all black as a uniform, if this was part of Harper's artistic styling, or if there was some other reason. And why was it making him uneasy?

He thought back to the times she was on video chat with him over the last three months. They usually happened late nights East Coast time, three hours earlier in California. But Harper and Ridge went to bed about the same time when he didn't have night evolutions. Harper went to bed early because she liked the twilight hours before she was on duty with Berlin.

When Harper was watching a movie with him over a video chat or they were playing a game of chess, puttering around the kitchen… Yes, she'd been in black at the lodge but had more colors in her "lounge around the house" wear. Was it black for public, color at home? Was it black for work, color for her off time? Was it a choice for today alone?

He could ask.

But again, his warning radar was pinging. He'd tuck that aside for now.

Harper leaned forward. "Trip, have you heard from Dani?"

Dani was one of the lodge guests Cerberus had searched for during the storm. The four of them had often eaten at the same table when they were snowed in for the week following the bomb cyclone that made the roadways impassable with downed electrical wires, trees, snow, and ice this past March.

"Yeah, she's back in Afghanistan now, doing her thing, taking care of the operators' K9s."

"Is she doing well?"

"She has new staff. Dani says they work efficiently, but they haven't formed the bonds that she's had in the past, yet."

"That sounds lonely."

"It can be." He clicked on the turn signal and looked left to take the corner.

"I was thinking about her the other day." Harper leaned back. "Do you remember at dinner one night we were talking about forest bathing? *Shinrin-yoku.* I looked it up once we got back to California, and I had dependable Wi-Fi again. Dani was right. It's a thing. I decided to develop an art project around that idea. As I've traveled around with Berlin, I've made an effort to find time in nature—or close to nature. Sometimes the best I can do is suburban landscapes, but usually, there are trees somewhere nearby. Like this morning, I was heading toward the woods when everything went nuts."

"Dani would be interested to hear about that. She liked your art." Trip twisted his head to the right and sent a brief glance back at her. "So, what's this art project about?"

"When Dani was describing forest bathing to me, I thought about Carl Jung's theory of the collective unconscious. I had a whole semester working with those thoughts way back in my undergrad days, a class called Symbolism in Art."

"Undergrad days… Does that mean you have a graduate degree?" Tripwire asked.

"Masters of Fine Arts."

Which she had never mentioned before, Ridge thought. When he'd asked where she'd learned to draw, she had said that she started back in high school and was bitten by the bug. She liked to do a little art each day. From that, he had assumed she'd just evolved through practice. An MFA was another story. Had she meant to obfuscate? Maybe she'd just misunderstood his question.

"Yeah? Where did you do that?" Ridge asked.

"Virginia Commonwealth University, down in Richmond."

Trip nodded. "They've got a great basketball team. Are you from there?"

"I was there long enough for the MFA program. It's a nice place. Lots of parks, and there's the James River."

Harper rarely mentioned anything from the time before Ridge and she had met. Everything had been present tense with Harper. All along, Ridge had figured that was part of living in California and Harper's yoga practice. Living in the present.

He pulled out his phone, and holding it down by his knee, did a quick search for VCU, MFA program. It popped up as ranking fourth in the United States. That was impressive. How did Harper go from a leading art school to being Berlin's personal assistant? Those two things didn't line up in his mind.

MFA. That explained the art she'd been able to produce with a Bic and a college-ruled notebook at the crime scene.

"In the collective unconscious, Jung believes there are universal symbols." She turned her head and was talking to the window. "They're well known, but different people give them different names. The Wise Man. The Earth Mother." She turned back to Trip and leaned forward again. "I take some of those archetypes into the woods with me. The idea of the Tree of Life—Dani described phytoncides—the scents from the trees—when she talked about forest bathing. Did you know there's one study—so grain of salt, right?" She didn't pause. It was like she'd grabbed hold of the topic, climbed on, and was racing it out of the storm.

Sliding his phone back into the cargo pocket on his thigh, Ridge bet Harper was glad to latch onto something in the fact-based part of her brain, relieving the strain of her emotions.

In his time knowing her, he'd found her to be a fount of interesting facts. Ridge always hung up the phone after talking to her with something new to ponder. That had led him to guess she had a science background. In his career, though, he'd learned never to assume. *MFA? Huh.* He rubbed his hand back and forth across his chin.

"Researchers studied subjects who were assigned to take a long walk in the forest for two days in a row. When they did, the researchers collected blood samples and discovered…" She paused. "I can't remember. These are made up numbers," she plowed ahead, talking fast, "but these are close enough to make my point. The phytoncides increased good white blood cells that fought cancer and inflammation by fifty percent, and that those benefits lasted to a slightly lesser degree for a whole month. Anyway, that's not why I was doing the art study. Ha. My brain is kind of jumping around. But we were talking about art…" Her voice faded off, and she was silent for a long moment before starting in again mid-thought. "…focused on the idea of shared support—exhaled carbon dioxide, inhaled oxygen, the Tree of Life, the archetypical shadow created by the height of the trunk, the breadth of the branches, foliage. And too, as I watched the animals, I was considering Jung's thoughts about instinct, especially reflex." Her face flamed red beneath the brim of her hat. "Ha ha! I thought this was a good subject. You know, to pull me into my rational philosophical mind. I'm a little more balanced over in that section of my gray matter when I'm getting stressed out. But look what I did. I circled myself back to reflex, which is how I'd describe my behavior this morning. Reflex." She tensed, curving her shoulders like a protective shell.

"Exploring this morning through an archetypal lens could be helpful." Tripwire eased onto the brakes as they drew up to a stop sign.

"You already know art is a good way to get emotions out." Ridge lifted his chin, gesturing toward Trip. "Tripwire and I have friends who were injured during their time in the service. VA hospitals are starting to find mental and physical health benefits to art therapy."

Rubbing at the blue ink that she hadn't been able to wash off, Harper's gaze focused on the stains. "Yeah, there's a big push in worldwide emergency response work, especially trauma around natural disasters. Same reason. It allows survivors to process their emotions. It can be cathartic." She turned to Ridge. "Did I ever tell you I was on the team that went to Sri Lanka to do art with the kids after the last tsunami there?"

"No." As she was speaking past tense, Ridge wondered why he'd never paid attention to the fact that Harper never talked about her past, *ever*.

Maybe it was because he was glad Harper didn't dig around, trying to find out about his own past. He didn't want to share it with her. Ridge thought it was too much, too soon. If he wanted to build an intimate relationship with Harper, he was walking a fine line between the time it would take to build a relationship based on compatibility and the time when it was too late in that relationship for him to have told Harper about his past and how that affected his now.

The time had come when he should do some sharing.

He couldn't ask Harper to tell him about her past if he wasn't willing to reveal his.

"That tsunami was before my time at Iniquus," Tripwire said. "But I know we had the Cerberus Search and Rescue team there, pulling folks out of the debris. What was it like working with the survivors?" Tripwire sent her a quick glance through the reflection in his rear-view mirror.

"Heartbreaking. Demoralizing. And in the end, inspirational." Harper tucked her hands back under her thighs. "The first day we set up, I put out all of these pots of brightly colored paints, but the kids would only do art in black and white."

Ridge wondered if she realized she was gently rocking back and forth. Self-soothing. He put his hand out on the seat, palm up in case she wanted to reach for him.

"It's interesting that in all ancient languages, the colors of black and white exist even in the absence of vocabulary for any other color."

"Huh." Tripwire's tone encouraged her to tell them more. "Like they don't have a word for purple? Only black and white?"

"It starts out that way in all known languages. As a language develops and becomes more descriptive, all languages add the color red to their vocabulary next. The next color they add is yellow, then green."

"All languages, no matter where on Earth or what the landscape?" Ridge asked, and she slid her hand in his. Her fingers were ice cold.

He pulled her hand toward him and wrapped it with both of his.

"Yup, all of them, exactly that pattern."

"That's wild," Tripwire said.

"But why were the children only painting in black and white?" Ridge asked.

"My question, too. And this was so interesting to me that later, in grad school, I studied color psychology. When people are deeply depressed, frightened, or traumatized, the color goes out of their world. Literally, they often lose their acuity for color. If you ask a depressed person about the colors around them, they'll describe the room they're in as cloudy gray—their perception changes.

"I didn't know that at the time. We tried cajoling the kids into using the bright, kid colors. They wouldn't do it. We didn't want to stress them out, so we stopped trying to force the colors on them and just worked on themes instead. Little by little, color started creeping into their art. And guess how that worked."

"Red?" Ridge offered.

"Exactly. That's exactly what happened. They went from black and white pictures to painting black and white with red, then they added yellow and green, and eventually blue. By the time we left, they were painting paintings like you'd expect a kid to do." She clutched her free hand to her heart as she turned to look out the window. "It was one of the most gratifying experiences."

"Nice," Tripwire said.

She focused on the back of Tripwire's head. "Would you tell Dani, next time you speak, how much I appreciated her telling me about forest bathing?"

"I will. She'll get a kick out of it that you're doing something unique with it. Are you liking the work that's come out of the forest project?"

"The connection to the trees part was the thing that I landed on as the most important. Sometimes, when I'm doing an image of a person or an animal—" she turned in her seat to look at Zeus in his crate; he stared straight back at her "—like I did when I started painting Zeus at the lodge." She smiled at Zeus. A small, sad smile.

Zeus stuck out his tongue and yawned. He was definitely picking up on Harper's stress.

"I connect with my subject. Things that I didn't know I knew, or didn't know I'd noticed, showed up in my rendering." She blew a kiss to Zeus and turned to Ridge. "Like the pictures I did for the police."

"Ridge texted those to me," Tripwire called over his shoulder. "Those were phenomenal."

Ridge remembered back at the lodge. Harper had asked his permission to use Zeus as her subject.

At the fire circle the night after the storm, Harper had let Ridge look through her sketchbook. The whole thing was pen and ink. Black and white.

Another red flag went up for him.

A prickle sparked across the back of his scalp.

The first time she did what she called a "rendering" of Zeus, she had done it in pen and ink. Ridge had assumed that was her medium of choice, or that was all she had with her by way of art supplies when she traveled. But over the days they were there, with Zeus training to find her during the day and lying near her in the evenings, Harper had started adding some watercolors, faint washes of pink, brown—that was in the yellow family, wasn't it? That's what she said happened with the kids, red then yellow. Eventually, she'd asked to add Ridge to the pictures. He remembered now, though it had been a subtle thing at the time, that over the days they were there, she'd added more colors to include the background of the lodge.

Ridge had had no idea that what he'd been observing, based on what Harper was now saying, was Zeus healing Harper. Or Harper feeling safe at the lodge with Zeus and him.

She had stuck close the whole time.

They'd forged their bond.

Now, Ridge wondered what could have happened to Harper that had drained the color from her art.

Chapter 9

Harper

"Predictable," Tripwire said with a grin as he turned into a parking space outside of a building that looked like a one-story McMansion and not at all like the office park–like structure that Harper had imagined.

Nothing here at Iniquus, after they had been badged through the security gate, had been what she'd envisioned. The Headquarters, that Ridge had pointed out, looked more like a country club than an office. Harper assumed it would be like the Pentagon or a military base.

As they drove down the street, Ridge had pointed to a high rise off to the left. "That's the barracks where Tripwire and I live."

There were woods and park-like stretches. Harper could make out flashes of what had to be the Potomac.

Now, she was following Tripwire's point toward a woman standing on the brick sidewalk, looking their way, seemingly waiting for them.

She was young, maybe early twenties. Her long blonde hair was pulled back into an elegant ponytail that went beautifully with her rose-colored nineteen-fifties styled dress with its boat neck, fitted bodice, and flared skirt. Her kitten-heeled pumps matched the color of her dress perfectly. She looked like she fit into a man's world in a retro-feminine way. And when Harper thought that, based on the high-esteem vibe she was picking up from both Tripwire and Ridge, she also thought, *She's their secret weapon. No one would see her cunning.*

"Who is she?" Harper asked, fully aware of how dowdy she felt in comparison.

"That's Lynx," Tripwire said.

"Oh. Is she part of the intake? Did she know we were coming early?"

"I'd imagine this has something to do with Zeus," Ridge said.

Tripwire pulled into a spot, and Ridge pushed his door open.

"Hey," Lynx called, raising her hand. All perky and smiley. "Zeus told me you needed me."

Harper turned her attention to Ridge to see how he interpreted what Lynx had said.

"Yeah, thanks." He turned to Zeus. "Good thinking, buddy. *So ist brav.*" Ridge squeezed Harper's hand, then released his grip. "I'm going to let Zeus out of his crate. Two seconds."

Zeus had his nose pressed up to the crate wires, making high-pitched noises in the back of his throat. Harper had never heard him do that before.

Harper climbed from the vehicle behind Ridge and stood there unsure of what to do with her hands. She reached down to her pocket to reassure herself her phone was with her. She felt a little lightheaded and attributed it to not having had anything to eat yet that day.

"Hey there, I'm Lynx," the woman said, walking forward with her hand extended. Okay, not perky and smiley—that wasn't right. Now that Harper could see her eyes, she picked up a kind of sisterhood vibe from Lynx. An inclusion and familiality that was confusing.

"This is Harper Katz," Ridge called from the back.

"*The* Harper Katz?" She smiled. "I'm so glad to finally meet you."

Cold and distant might have felt better. Easier. Harper wanted to be in her own little box, still and quiet. She'd been too far out of her element for too long today. Harper extended her hand, mechanically accepting Lynx's shake.

"You're the heroine of the great bomb cyclone." Lynx held Harper's hand between both of hers. Not a shake. Something warmer…and more tingly. "I've wanted to meet you."

"Oh?" Warmth snaked up her arm. "But why?"

"Because Zeus—"

Zeus circled behind Lynx and head-butted her forward.

Lynx took a lurching step with a laugh and put her hand back on Zeus's head to stop him from doing it again. "Zeus wants me to give you a hug. Is that all right?"

Harper held her hands out to the sides, not sure what was happening here, but sure, a hug, why not?

As soon as Lynx put her hands on Harper's back, Harper felt deeply penetrating heat and a tingling effervescence where Lynx placed her palms.

"Reiki," Harper said, arching back. She didn't want that.

"Sorry. There's no control button." Lynx dropped her hands to her sides.

Tripwire tilted his head.

"Reiki is energy healing," Harper explained, then turned a frown toward Lynx. "You're quite strong with it, aren't you? I mean, back in California, it's a thing. I go to a Reiki practitioner once a week if I'm not traveling. Therapy for anxiety attacks. But that was…" Had she just offended this woman by pulling away? "Normally, I like it. But today, my own energy is sparking, and I can't handle any more. Sorry."

"Not at all." She looked up at Ridge. Messages seemed to flash between them.

"Bob told me you guys had quite the morning." She spoke to Ridge when she said, "I was going to take a walk to the rocks. Care to join me?" She turned to Harper to include her in the invitation. "I thought I could use a little time beneath the trees. It's a nice walk. Pretty short. There's a boulder by the river that's perfect for sitting on. A lovely view."

Harper didn't answer. Funny that Lynx said that when Harper had been thinking, ever since they were talking about forest bathing in the SUV, that time beneath the trees would help her regain her equilibrium.

"Great idea. Zeus would like it, too. Harper, do you want to go?" Ridge held out a hand.

Harper nodded. She wished she could go alone, though. What Harper really wanted was to be in her bed with the curtains drawn and a pillow over her head. She wanted to pout and have her own sucky birthday, shoving cake in her mouth as fast as she could chew it.

Today had been a reminder. Life can change in a snap of the fingers. It can all go to hell in the blink of an eye.

Ridge turned to Tripwire. "Do you want to start with Bob? Tell him I'll catch up in a few."

Tripwire was clipping a lead to Valor. "Wilco. Hi, Lynx. Bye, Lynx."

"Later," she said with a finger wave.

"Harper, I'll see you when you get back." He held his hand up in a salute, then he and Valor took off at an easy jog toward what she assumed was Cerberus Headquarters.

"Harper?" Ridge must have said something she'd missed. She blinked at him.

"I was asking if you need to go to the clinic to our doctor for help. You said you're being treated for anxiety attacks. They're no joke."

"The trees are good for that, I think."

Ridge signaled to Zeus, who fell in step between them. "I don't remember you mentioning anxiety attacks before. I've never seen you have one."

Harper said nothing, just licked at her lips.

"Today would be a trigger, though. Have you had them for a long time, or were they the result of the near-miss on the mountain?"

"They started when…" She stopped herself, shocked that the words almost flew out of her mouth. "It's been about a year and a half. Exercise helps. Meditation before bed. Tree time. Reiki once a week." She turned what she hoped was an apologetic face to Lynx. "Today, though, my nerves feel like I'm standing in a puddle of water with an electrical current running through. I can't…"

Harper looked toward the trees. Far from that snowstorm at the lodge adding to her woes, she thought of that time stuck at Wild Mountain as one of the best times of her life. She'd felt safe there. She'd loved the evening fires under the stars. Zeus lying on her feet. A mug of mulled wine. Ridge's deep laughter.

It had been a moment in time.

A cease-fire in her survival war.

They walked in silence down the wide path. Light filtered through the canopy of green leaves overhead. She should feel better here instead of worse. Harper realized with a rumble in her stomach that some of her emotions were because she was hungry. Maybe there was a dining room back at Iniquus. The walk couldn't take but so long.

She looked down when something pressed into her hand. It was a bag of trail mix, the kind that you get from a vending machine with nuts, dried fruit, and M&Ms.

"Zeus says you need something to eat." Lynx looked past Harper to Ridge. "Not too long out here. Just to the water and back. Harper is bound to be starving. She hasn't eaten yet today."

"You *talk* to Zeus?"

"He and I go way back."

Harper looked up at Ridge. "Do you talk to him, too?" She put the talk in air quotes. Harper had met some folks out in California who were friends of Berlin's who had an animal communication gig. They'd come to talk to your dog to figure out why he might be depressed and pooping in your shoes while you were at work. Harper had thought of it as part of the smoke and mirrors world of Berlin Tracy.

But then again, she'd seen the Cerberus team members also speak through a glance. They seemed to make a practice of communicating without words. All it took was the tilt of the head, an arch of the brow, a lift of the chin.

Sometimes even she could detect a slight shift in their facial features. And Tripwire's K9 Valor had a comically expressive face.

Zeus was more stoic.

Ridge nudged her with his elbow. "Eat. Zeus and I communicate, but I can't do what Lynx can do."

"You said that you were down in the parking lot because Zeus said to go down there?"

"It's true. And he said to bring you something to eat. I don't normally have trail mix in my pocket." Her laugh was light. It reminded Harper of field flowers and butterflies—the good kind, the pretty, graceful, beautiful kind. Not the kind that were in her stomach right now.

"Distance doesn't matter very much when it comes to Zeus and me communicating. It's not like words. It's pictures and impressions. Think about it like wolf mentality. The pack is circling caribou. Sometimes there are miles between them. They can't howl to each other. It would get their dinner running away. So they send each other pictures, *knowings*, if you will. Zeus and I are family, the same pack. With Ridge and you. When he sent me a picture of you in the car, I recognized you right away except for the hat you're wearing. I've seen several images of you from Zeus. He liked it when you drew pictures of him."

"He knows I was drawing? I mean…a dog can conceptualize making art?"

"He showed you with a pad on your lap, a brush in your hand, colored water, and that you were looking into his eyes. My fiancé paints, so the images Zeus sent me made sense. It wasn't the art that he saw and liked. What he liked was that you were looking at him in a way that—" she tapped her chest "—mmm, I'm not sure I have the words for this. Like…like you were experiencing him. Maybe that's the best way to put it. And the way that you looked at him meant he could see you back. And he liked what he saw." She smiled. Then a frown tugged the smile away. The sparkle that had lit her eyes ducked behind a shadow.

Or maybe Harper was imagining things. "I'm intrigued. How did you get this ability with Zeus? I imagine you were his trainer."

"Well, as usual with dogs and humans, Zeus and I trained each other. The story goes like this. A couple of years ago, I was the victim of a kidnapping."

Harper put her hand around her throat and searched out Ridge's eyes. They caught, held. He reached for her hand.

"You've had a scary day. I don't want to add to your angst with this story. I'm fine. So there's a good outcome that includes Zeus."

Harper was too curious not to hear it. "No, I'd like to know—Ha! That sounded prying, snooping, something… I'd like to know how you grew close to Zeus, not necessarily about the crime." *Blabbering. It sounded like blabbering.* She shook her head. And sucked in some air.

"Zeus is definitely part of this picture. He saved my sanity and my life. The kidnappers knew I was connected to Iniquus. Iniquus is fiercely protective. The bad guy— was actually a woman—bad gal just sounds wrong. She flew me to Honduras, where a private prison held political prisoners and others, like myself, who were held for other reasons."

Harper nodded.

"Zeus was a guard dog there. The alpha dog. And that's what I called him in my mind, Alpha. Eventually,

Iniquus helped the Honduran soldiers take control of that prison and freed the prisoners."

"You?"

"No. I was already gone. But Iniquus rescued the K9s and brought them back here to Washington. They renamed Alpha as Zeus because they didn't want to confuse him when they talked over the radio. The military alphabet starts Alpha, Bravo, Charlie."

"He didn't go work for you?" Harper asked.

"I already have two working Dobermans. And Zeus likes to do fieldwork. I work in an office."

Harper nodded; she could see that being true. Zeus wasn't a lay around the office kind of dog. He needed to be working through a puzzle, always learning.

"Once Iniquus rescued the prison dogs, the dogs were sent to a training kennel where they were evaluated and given veterinary care. They were all in pretty bad shape. The guards didn't feed them much or care for their health. Granted, there weren't many resources where we were. Also, they liked the dogs hungry and mean."

"Zeus got renamed and assigned to you, Ridge?"

"He was assigned to a guy over on Cerberus Team Bravo."

"Zeus wasn't having it." Lynx chuckled. "He told me that he was Ridge's K9 partner, not that other guy's. So I intervened."

"Wait—" Harper's brows pulled together "—you told people that they needed to reassign Zeus because Zeus said he wanted to work with Ridge? And people didn't think you were nuts?" Harper was horrified once again at her lack of constraint around this woman. She should have just said, "That's nice," and moved on.

Day after tomorrow, she'd be back in California, and none of this would matter at all.

"With anyone else, they might have," Ridge said. "But Command trusts Lynx's intuition. We all do. It's part of her job. She's a people reader. An occasional K9 whisperer."

"And you were reading and communicating with Zeus when you were at the prison?"

"Exactly, it was how I occupied my days. You know about Reiki, do you know you can send energy healing at a distance, you don't have to put your hands on someone?"

"Yup. I do. I've experienced that."

"That's how it started. I was standing at my cell window, and I saw Zeus limping. I started sending him Reiki. And we progressed from there."

"And how did he save your life?" She stared at the ground with a wince. "Is it okay if I ask that? You don't need to tell me." Harper knew that she had zero interest in ever talking about today ever again. Getting kidnapped and stuck in a foreign prison?

Who would want to dredge up those memories?

How does someone right themself after something like that?

Her mind flashed back a year and a half ago to the image of the man crouching in the mud, naked, zip-tied to the fence. Had he recovered? Or was he as messed up as Harper was—still?

Zeus moved from walking between Harper and Ridge to walk between Harper and Lynx. Bumping into Harper, pressing her up against Ridge.

Ridge wrapped his arm around her, and it felt so good she hoped he wouldn't stop.

She slipped her arm around his waist, tucking a finger into his belt loop.

Lynx had crouched as she walked, rubbing Zeus's ears. "How did I get out? I bribed a guard to let me hide in his truck under a tarp. It was Zeus's job to check the trucks to make sure escapes didn't happen. I asked him not to alert on me, and he didn't. I was able to get out of the jail gates that way. And I promised Zeus I'd help him in return." She stood. "We're family. I love him."

Zeus pushed his head under Lynx's hand. They looked at each other like Harper had done with him when she was working on watercolors of him. There was an exchange. She saw it.

"What did you tell him?" Harper asked.

"He wants you to know you're safe here. He said, 'Ridge and I won't let anything hurt you.'"

"Oh." Harper swallowed.

Ridge and Zeus would protect her? Harper didn't believe that was possible. Her enemy was too powerful.

The only thing that could save Harper was Harper.

Chapter 10

Ridge

They'd reached the end of the path.

Harper had wandered out to the boulder's edge, where she sat cross-legged with the swift turquoise water of the Potomac flowing past.

Ridge and Lynx found a place on a fallen tree, giving her some space.

Zeus paced the area, tongue hanging out, dripping saliva.

"He's stressed." Ridge used a tone that wouldn't carry to Harper. If Zeus had been sending pictures to Lynx since the lodge, she might have some insight to share with him. "I'm glad you came down to meet us, thank you."

"Oh, I've wanted to meet Harper. I would have come anyway. Zeus has been worried about her."

"Recently? Or just today?"

"The pictures he's sending me say the thing that makes him feel 'all alpha' for lack of better term around her—mmm, protective instincts might be better—it seems like his worry is about something older than when they met. Right now, though, he's mad at you."

"Me? Why?"

"He wants you to take Harper to your apartment to be with the two of you. She shouldn't be sleeping anywhere else. He's actually told me that since you got home, and Harper wasn't in your apartment where he expected to find her."

Ridge tipped his head back. "I remember that. When we walked into my apartment, he went to each room, sniffing around, then came back and stomped his foot at me. I had no idea what he wanted, so I took him out to throw his Kong and burn off his stress." Ridge rubbed his hand back and forth across the back of his neck. "You've explained to him, Harper isn't my—we're not..." Ridge looked over to make sure Harper hadn't heard that and adjusted his tone to a quieter one. "That we're not a thing."

"No?" Lynx asked.

"Between you and me—and Zeus, apparently—I'd like nothing better than to be in a relationship with Harper."

Zeus wandered over, and Ridge scrubbed his fingers into Zeus's fur.

"Zeus isn't buying it that you're not a 'thing.' Have you talked to Harper about the way you feel? Have you asked if maybe she feels the same as you do?"

"No."

"Have you invited her on a date?"

"No."

"What's the hang-up?"

"We've become good friends. I'd like more, sure, just

like Zeus. You know how it goes—unrequited love. I just eat ice cream straight out of the carton. Write her name with little hearts on my notepads. Sob into my pillow. I figure I can put this pain into my music. Make it *real*." He put his hand on his chest. "Touch the hearts of my fans."

"Ridge, I've heard you sing in the shower. There are no fans," Lynx said sardonically. "There's barely a tune."

He balled his hand into a fist and tapped his chest. "I'm hurt, Lynx." He lifted his chin toward Zeus, who had wandered to a place equidistant between Ridge and Harper and lain down. "It looks like he's moping."

"He's unhappy. But I told him he's about to be deployed with Harper, and he'll get to spend time with her over the next two days."

"Berlin is assigned to Strike Force."

"She's insisting on you and Zeus. She talked to Command and worked something out. I haven't heard what yet. There's a second principal, one of Berlin's friends is coming in." She closed her eyes then blinked them open. "Zeus wants to know if he can stay in her room. She smells better than you do."

"Funny."

"You think I made that up?"

"What is Harper doing, rubbing bacon behind her ears or something?"

Lynx rolled her lips in as she stared at the ground. "The picture he's sending is him as a puppy and a young woman—the woman who took care of him. And I see a picture of her bloody on the ground. Zeus gets that same sense from Harper and wants to be near her to keep her safe. Those protective instincts I mentioned."

"Oh, and here I thought maybe he sensed Harper and I would make a good couple and was picking up something from her."

"Could be. I'm not saying that isn't true."

"But…"

"Yeah, it's hard to say. Zeus is a thinking dog. He figures things out. He did when I was in the prison. I mean, there were some very complicated things that happened. Things that are difficult for me to explain, and frankly, things I won't even try to explain to you. Understand, Alpha… Zeus. Zeus is a strategist. He's picked up his understanding, and he's come to some conclusion. His solution is that he wants Harper to sleep in your bed, where the two of you can keep her safe."

"You know, Lynx, that has major implications both personally and to our work. I'm thinking about Harper's anxiety attacks. She's never mentioned them to me before. I've certainly never witnessed one before today. It's possible there's a chemical something that's off in her system that Zeus smells, and he's identifying with his puppy picture of that same scent. When we were at the lodge, Harper seemed to be comfortable when she was around us. That might change when she's out in the wider world. But let's try a different scenario. What if there is some shadow chasing her? Is it possible that it becomes a security risk for our client? It's our job to find out."

"If she's part of the dedicated team on-site with Berlin, each member fills out an intake questionnaire. We'll have the basic data I can run through the computer system. It's a start."

Ridge was processing the tightrope on which he'd need to balance. His work ethic required him to explore every possible avenue to keep his client safe. But looking too deeply into Harper might agitate some situation.

If there was something personal Harper was dealing with, any little thing could be a tipping point.

Chapter 11

Ridge

"Harper." Ridge waved to catch her attention. He cupped his hands around his mouth to help project his voice past the strengthening breeze. "Come on. Let's get you something to eat." He was reticent to walk over and loom while she was in her private headspace. When she didn't seem to hear, Ridge looked down at Zeus. "Go get Harper. *Bring.*"

Zeus trotted up to Harper and exhaled loudly on the back of her neck. Zeus's playful side on rare display. She turned around, laughing. She fell for it.

Lynx was right; Zeus was a strategic dog.

Harper's hands rubbed over Zeus's chest and belly, then she cupped her hands around his snout and kissed him. If she had seen the savage way that Zeus had torn into the kidnapper this morning, she might not be as comfortable putting her lips near Zeus's sharp teeth.

Zeus had a thing for Harper, just like Ridge did, in the protective wanting to be around her way. Only Zeus got the snuggles and rubs. The kisses and hugs. And Ridge was not about to be jealous of his dog.

She turned toward Lynx and Ridge. "Time to go?" She got her feet under her and pushed up. "It's a gorgeous view," she called over, brushing at her pants.

Ridge watched her hands petting over her voluptuous curves.

"Thanks for sharing." Harper seemed to be back to her normal self again. Her shoulders had relaxed, her smile was genuine.

It was good they'd taken a time-out to come here. He'd always liked this spot. The perpetual breeze and the flowing water carried away his stress at the end of the day.

Zeus liked to hang over the edge of the rocks and watch the fish swim by.

When Harper joined them on the trail, before he could reach for her hand, Lynx hooked her arm through Harper's like he'd seen women do in Italy as they strolled down the street, licking gelato cones, and listening to the sidewalk musicians. Good friends. Old friends.

Ridge stepped to the side a bit. Obviously, Lynx wanted to have a quiet woman-to-woman.

"You shouldn't get a zap of Reiki like this," Lynx said.

"I'm good." They started down the trail in a gentle stroll.

"It's fun that you know about energy healing. I guess it's more prevalent out in California than here on the East Coast. Though Harvard is doing a study, Reiki is making its way into the hospitals around here."

Harper nodded.

"Did your physician suggest you try it?"

"She did. I'm a transplant to the West Coast. The idea was new to me. She suggested it because I didn't want to take any pills."

"For anxiety?" Lynx asked.

"Right."

From his peripheral vision, he caught Harper shooting a glance his way. He was looking straight down the path; he didn't want her to feel judged, though why anyone would judge someone for having anxiety was beyond him.

"Because pills would stunt your senses?" Lynx asked her.

Zeus must sense that Harper was doing better, too. He was padding along out in front of them, leading the way, the alpha.

"Exactly," Harper said on an exhale.

"Not just for your art, but your intuition, I bet." Lynx's voice had a meandering quality to it that matched their gaits. Nothing pointed. She wasn't prodding. These were lazy thoughts.

Ridge knew better. Lynx was aces at getting the information they needed on cases by being genuinely kind and asking the right questions. It wasn't manipulation, Ridge had noticed; it was an opportunity for folks to get things off their chests.

"Hmmm. I hadn't thought it through that way. I don't phrase it that way in my own brain, but that's what intuition is, isn't it?"

"What's that?" Lynx asked.

"The brain picks up things, subtle things—even etheric things like—hmmm. Ridge and I were talking about

Carl Jung on the drive over here. So that's on my mind. Jung explored the idea of the collective unconscious. A shared energetic—for lack of better word right now—experience. All that goes into the themes I explore in my art, either consciously or not. Anything that would mute my perceptions on any level, like anti-anxiety medicines, would close that down. Art is like breathing to me. I can't *not* do art."

"I find intuition a fascinating subject. The way I communicate with Zeus, I label that as intuition."

"Pretty good intuition if you trust it enough to put trail mix in your pocket and go stand in a parking lot."

Lynx laughed. "I think things like that are fun. I call it my 'affirmations' when I follow my intuition, and it turns out to be accurate. I've found the more I lean on my sixth sense, the stronger it becomes. Is that true for you?"

"Maybe. Though, I'm searching for that middle ground—enough intuition that I can apply it to my art and still be safe."

Safe from what? Ridge wanted to ask, but he wasn't about to break the flow between the two women. He needed to keep his mouth shut and his ears open.

"Not so much that I'm picking up on other people's stuff," Harper said. "If I'm around anxious people, I tend to absorb their distress. It's one of the perks of working for Berlin. *Nothing* makes her anxious. She thinks the world conspires to make everything work out perfectly. She leads a charmed life."

"That must feel disorientating."

"A bit, yeah. Though not always." They walked in silence for a stretch, then Harper said, "I'm thinking about what you said just now, having your intuition affirmed.

And I used to like that, too. There was a time when I lived more in the realm of intuition."

When, Harper? What shut it down? Ridge's brain yelled.

Lynx reached out and tapped his arm. He took that as a warning to quiet his thoughts, and he pressed his lips together.

"Tell me" was what Lynx said instead.

"Okay, here's a silly example. Sometimes I would lose things around my apartment. If I looked and couldn't find the item I needed, like… I don't know—my wallet. Or… yeah, here's a good example. So I would lose something. In this case, it was my keys. They'd been gone for days, and I had to use my car. As an experiment—Jung, the collective unconscious—I asked on social media. I did that from time to time. Invariably, I found the lost item."

"Fun!" Lynx said.

"I might say, I can't find my #4 paintbrush, where should I look for it? People I'd never met in person, people who had never been to my apartment, would post what their intuition told them. I could just wait and find the theme. Like, one person would say, 'Do you have a green chair?' And another would say, 'It rolled near a vent.' Another person would say, 'It's near your books.' I'd go to my green chair, that sat with the bookcase behind it, and the vent to the side, and I'd fish around where it might have rolled and *voilà*! My brush." As she talked, Harper's voice became more lyrical, her hands more animated. "So there was that time I was looking for my car keys. Three people posted that the keys were hiding until it was safe—some variation on the theme."

"Interesting."

"That gave me goose bumps—safe from what? More

people weighed in. After I was told by a list of people that the keys were hidden until it was safe, I asked, 'What should I do to make things safe?' I was somewhere between put out that I didn't just get my keys back, curious, and to be honest, I found it spooky. That was strange, right?"

"Maybe."

"The next stream of suggestions had to do with my car. The theme became 'in the car.' 'Under the hood.' 'Beside the engine.' As if I ever lifted my hood and looked at my engine." She chuckled. "I knew the keys weren't there, but I went out to the car to look anyway. As I unlatched the hood, I remembered that my then-boyfriend had said he'd fixed some noise or other. Perhaps he had left the keys under the hood."

"Yes?"

"I lifted the hood, no keys. I fished around a bit, and I did find a huge aerosol can that my then-boyfriend let roll off the engine when he was doing the tune-up. It said on the label that it was under pressure and highly flammable. I called a mechanic friend, and he said where it was wedged would have gotten very hot from the engine, and probably the can would have combusted. He said, 'like a bomb.'"

"Ha! Awesome." Lynx grinned. "Then what?"

"I held up the can up to the sky and said, 'I found it! Thank you!' and went inside."

"Where you found your keys."

"I did. They were sitting on the entry table under the lip of my key bowl, just out of sight. I shouldn't have missed them."

"They were hiding from you until you were safe."

"Which shouldn't be a thing. Should it?"

"It's fun."

Harper's phone pinged. She tugged it from her pants' pocket. "It's a Berlin Instagram." She looked past Lynx to catch Ridge's eye. "It's a picture of the skid marks on the road." She held up the phone to read. "'I just want you all to know that my close protection guy is a hero. These tracks were from the getaway vehicle just a short distance from where I stood.' And the next one is a picture of a police car. 'I want everyone to know that I'm A-Okay. Safe and sound. Whew! Good thing for my security team! I'm taking them out to celebrate tonight. I'll be at the Cash Cow Night Club. Come and help us celebrate.'" She looked at the time at the top of the phone. "She'll be on her way soon."

"Okay," Lynx said. "We can get you going on the intake."

They could see Cerberus Headquarters now between the leaves.

"What does that include? There wasn't much to it when you all were doing the search and rescue. I was asked what kind of experience Berlin and her crew had in the wilderness and with weather events. That was easy enough. None."

"Strike Force will be—" Ridge started.

"Berlin insists on you and Tripwire with your K9s," Lynx said.

"Not at a night club she doesn't. Besides, Tripwire isn't on the schedule. He's teaching the chicken school tomorrow."

"What?" Harper laughed. "Chickens can't be trained."

"Care to wager?" Ridge waggled his eyebrows.

"Are you serious right now? Tripwire trains *chickens*?"

"He teaches the chicken training class. It's a four-day

course for people who are training K9s. Usually, they're civilians who are working with volunteer-force search and rescue. Sometimes, military or police departments. Training chickens teaches the concepts quickly and clearly. The ego is taken out of it. It's not the handler's dog getting judged against others. And honestly, no one's going to think worse of you if your chicken is misbehaving."

"That's hysterical. I'd love to see it."

"Are you here long, Harper?" Lynx asked.

"No, tomorrow—" Her phone pinged. "Hang on." She swiped the screen. "This is Harper. Hi."

"Wee!" Even with the phone not set to speaker, Ridge could hear Berlin's distinctive pitch. "Guess what! Guess what!"

"What?"

"CiCi is coming in this afternoon on Matteo's private jet. Matteo said that CiCi has the jet for the whole week! We'll fly back with her instead of having to be on a commercial flight. A wonderful opportunity to take some great photos on the tarmac, right? CiCi and me getting out of a limo to board a private jet. Very A-list—" there was a clinking sound then "—it's just CiCi, though, coming alone. She's going to use DeWayne and Carlos for her stuff, too."

"She's coming to Washington, D.C.? Does she need me to organize anything for her?"

"She's staying at The Lily Hotel with us. Matteo isn't coming at all. He has a meeting coming up. CiCi is going to give his speech tomorrow for the congresspeople with me!"

"Okay."

"And I called Iniquus because CiCi will need security too, and I want the pictures to match because that looks best. CiCi agrees."

"Okay."

"So Striker is the Strike Force guy. I guess they named Strike Force after him."

"I guess."

"And he said since those guys Blaze and Gator are already on the schedule that we can keep them and add Ridge and Tripwire."

"Not Tripwire. He's teaching a class."

"Oh, boo. He can't change that for me?"

"It's a whole class, Berlin. He can't change it. Don't you think three is enough? You're not really in any danger."

"That girl was almost kidnapped today, not two miles from our hotel!"

"Okay. Fine. I saw how you're dressed in your Instagram photos. Can you please have Carlos style you in something a little less revealing when you come here?"

"You don't think the men can restrain themselves?"

"This is a business. Talk to Carlos, tell him the look you're going for is 'respectable businesswoman.' Remind him no photographs are allowed on campus. No need to bring DeWayne or Carlos with you."

Lynx put her hand on Harper's arm. "They need to fill out the intake paperwork. If they don't come here, then we'll go to them."

"Can you send the papers back with me?"

"I'll handle it," Ridge said.

Harper nodded. "Berlin, your lunch will be up soon. Are you in your room?"

"Yes, well, I will be in two seconds. I just came back from the photoshoot at the crime scene."

And just like that, the pall from this morning slid across Harper's face.

Chapter 12

Harper

Berlin perched on the back seat of an Iniquus SUV with her arms crossed over her chest.

"She's not happy." Harper stepped off the porch.

Ridge and Harper had been back from lunch at the Iniquus cafeteria for a good while. Berlin was late because… she was Berlin. She liked to keep people waiting. In her mind, it made her seem like she lived a busy life, and she could *just* squeeze you in. And on occasion, that was true. It wasn't true today. There were zero reasons for her to be this late.

At the beginning of her employment with Berlin, Harper had accounted for this. Posting on Berlin's schedule and sending the limo a half-hour in advance, Berlin could be the queen, and other people weren't inconvenienced. A win/win in Harper's books. Unfortunately,

Berlin figured it out when she said one too many times, "I'm sorry I'm late," only to be met with a confused look and a glance at the watch, followed by reassurances that she was exactly on time.

On-time wasn't Berlin's goal.

Harper went to open the car door.

"They wouldn't let my limo up the driveway," Berlin grumped before Harper could even get a greeting out of her mouth. "They made me ride in *this*." Scorn dripped from her voice, making it sound like she'd had to ride in the back of a septic truck instead of this top-of-the-line SUV. "The limo has to wait by the guardhouse." She climbed out and stood next to Harper while Harper closed the door.

Berlin's hand smoothed over her sunflower-colored mini-dress. Made of soft T-shirt material, it hung wide and comfortable from two spaghetti straps. Not the businesswoman attire Harper had suggested. Poor Carlos. Harper could just imagine what he'd gone through. At least Berlin was covered from clavicle to mid-thigh.

"It's like a concentration camp here."

"It's nothing like a concentration camp here." Harper kept her voice smooth and non-confrontational. "This is a secure campus. Think of it more like you get to see behind the scenes at MI6. Like a Bond film."

"I could do a Bond film." She stuck out her hand to Lynx, who came up to them. "Tracy. Berlin Tracy."

Lynx smiled warmly. "I recognized you right away. I'm Lynx with Strike Force. Shall we go in?" Lynx gestured with an open palm.

"Hey, you said I couldn't have Tripwire on the team." Berlin glanced over her shoulder to Harper. "I saw Ryder on the way in. He's jogging with a dog, but it's not Voodoo. I want him to be on the team. He's got the same build as Ridge. Same brown hair. Mmm, not exactly. Ridge is more honey-blond, and Ryder's hair is more chocolatey-brown. Sable." She pushed her Jackie O–styled glasses to the top of her head and popped her eyebrows to emphasize that she'd used a color description that Harper would choose. "They both have yummy brown eyes. They'll look good together."

"No one will see the color of their eyes." Harper took a quick sidestep to evade Berlin's huge mahogany hobo bag. "Their faces can't be photographed."

"I've read about that. The Aboriginals think it steals their souls. Poor Ryder." She placed a hand on her heart and sent Harper a sympathetic frown.

"That… What? No." Harper closed her eyes and took in a breath. "In the contract, it says very clearly, no pictures of the security forces' faces. It's important they stay anonymous. Besides, Ridge already tapped Didit for your team."

"No." She slid her hobo sack further onto her shoulder.

"Why no?" Harper indicated the open front door to Cerberus Headquarters, where Lynx stood patiently. Harper tapped the back of Berlin's arm and got them walking again.

"Didit's a girl. I don't want a girl."

"She's a woman. And she's a decorated war hero."

"I don't care if she's the Queen of Sheba. The look I'm going for is that I need big, strong men to protect me from big, bad, scary guys."

"Didit can protect you just fine," Harper insisted.

"That's probably true." Berlin climbed the two steps to the porch then waited for Harper to open the front door and hold it for her. "But no. Ryder is the one I want."

"Voodoo had a tendon injury," Lynx said, following them in. "Unfortunately, he's not working right now."

"Oh, but that's Voodoo. That shouldn't stop Ryder. He has another dog with him. He can use that one." Berlin turned to face Lynx. "Who are you exactly?"

"I'm with Strike Force," she said evenly. "I'm here to assist with your intake, so Strike Force can finish up their plans."

"About me?"

"Harper sent your schedule ahead. Mostly we needed to know where you're going and when. I understand there have been additions to your plans?"

"Yes!"

"We want to make sure to accommodate them." Lynx smiled as they stood in the spacious foyer with its cathedral ceiling. "We also ask questions about your security concerns, so we can develop our strategies to thwart any issues that might come up."

Biting her lip, Berlin's face had a strained look that Harper thought might be her trying to look worried. Apprehensive. Something—

"Fans are really the problem." She frowned as she nodded like Lynx would completely understand the struggles that Berlin went through. She pulled her sunglasses from her head with a flourish and hung them from an earpiece at the top of her dress.

Harper shifted behind Berlin because she was having trouble stopping her eyes from rolling, and that was unprofessional.

Sure, on occasion, someone recognized Berlin in public. And there was a time or two that someone had asked for a selfie or an autograph. But it wasn't like Berlin was getting swarmed or that she didn't like the attention.

Quite the opposite.

Berlin ate the public recognition up with a spoon. Berlin was hoping that having security would increase her need for security. Not in the cosmic, if I build it, they will come sense. More like, walking in with a security force would pull people's eye her way, let them know she was important, valuable, precious. She was worthy of asking for a selfie and an autograph. Unlike other autographs Harper had seen that were like checkmarks and squiggles or something equally thoughtless and tossed off, Berlin's were carefully legible. If someone thought she was important, they could get her autograph, look her up, and then post online, thus increasing her notoriety. More followers and fans meant more contracts. More contracts meant more money and popularity. She was on an ever-increasing upward staircase to everything Berlin ever wanted.

Honestly, Berlin wanting security was a marriage of her enthralling experience being saved by the Cerberus team at Wild Mountain Lodge and watching Whitney Houston in *The Bodyguard* on a long flight. Berlin told Harper that if she had a stalker, that would do wonderful things for her career.

Harper thought that if Berlin really did have a stalker, Berlin would change her mind about how awesome that was. Having someone actually coming after you? It made you willing to do anything to get away from them—uproot your life, your relationships, *anything* to self-preserve.

Harper tuned back into the conversation as they walked through the double doors into what Ridge had called the "Alpha war room." Bravo's war room was in the east wing of the building. That team was "downrange" right now.

Ridge had explained that Cerberus K9 had been developed like the Deltas. There were two spears. Alpha and Bravo. Ridge commanded Alpha. The teams took turns being on alert. One team would be here at Iniquus for a period, training, doing area assignments, and taking their R&R time on rotation. The team who was "up" were the ones who would be sent worldwide to "meet the need." Though Ridge never specified what that meant. Harper did know that their charitable arm sent the K9 teams out if there was a disaster somewhere in the world. Harper wasn't aware of any natural disasters right now.

Ridge had said *downrange*, which sounded very clandestine, bad-guy-whomping to her. She hoped Bravo stayed safe. Since Ridge hadn't told her what the away team was doing, she thought about GI Joe movies and maybe a new film genre—*Fast and Furious with Fur, baby!* Wouldn't Berlin just love a starring role in that?

Iniquus had contracts with world risk insurance companies that protected everyone from university students and faculty to corporate and government workers. If they were at high-risk, they might have kidnapping insurance. In those cases, Iniquus had teams that would negotiate, or go in and rescue, whatever would work to get the endangered person safe. Those same contractors had insurance covering everyone who might be a liability—that is, sue the entity for negligence—should something bad go down like a natural disaster.

When Harper had told him they were heading to the East Coast, Ridge had said it was good timing. The two teams would be changing roles in the next two weeks, and he might have missed his chance to see her in person.

That had made her heartbeat double-time as she admitted to herself that the *only* reason she had risked coming to Washington, D.C., was to get to see him in person again. Up until this morning's fiasco, she had felt confident that she could fly under anyone's radar.

Ridge gave her the right phone number to call to get the contract in place.

The next time they spoke, Harper had been feeling nervous about coming to Washington, D.C., Berlin hadn't let her wiggle out of it. She'd asked Ridge about that insurance. "Am I covered?"

"Our contract is with Berlin."

She'd laughed. "So I'm shit out of luck if there's a natural disaster? Do you have natural disasters on the East Coast?"

Ridge looked at her hard, over their video call. "As long as I'm around, there's no contract necessary. I'm here for you, Harper. You do understand that, don't you? You get it?"

Harper was taken aback by the intensity with which he had said that to her. All she could do was look at him and blink. She didn't want to misinterpret what he said as meaning anything deeper than that he was an alpha male who rushed into the fray as part of his DNA.

To think that he meant her specifically, *especially*, well—she couldn't allow that. So she tucked that into one of her recurring fantasies that kept her company in the middle of the night, where he'd say that, then kiss her, then pull her into his arms and stroke his fingers into her hair. "You're mine," he'd say in her imagination. "You're safe."

And the idea of being safe was the biggest, most wonderful, most fulfilling fantasy of all. Safe with Ridge?

It was never gonna happen because she'd never let it happen.

Even if he did want "them" to happen.

Did he want "them" to happen?

Chapter 13

Harper

When the group moved into the war room, Harper found Noah, their logistics guy, at the computer in the large open room's back corner. His beast of a Newfoundland stability service dog, Hairyman, was asleep with a little stream of sunlight from the window warming his up-turned belly. Noah held up a hand to acknowledge them, then turned back to his task.

In the center of the room stood a table like the one Harper had seen them use at the lodge for tabletop exercises. There, they set up 3D paper models of floor plans and moved plastic figurines—human and K9—through the model to try out scenarios, pinpointing where things could go badly.

There was a lot that could go badly, Harper had discovered as she'd watched them work.

There was a sense of competency to the décor: minimalist, clean lines; quality materials.

Like Berlin, Iniquus paid attention to the details of its appearance. Here, everything worked like a well-oiled machine. It all said: successful, competent, focused, wholesome.

Wearing her head-to-toe black, Harper had fit right in at their cafeteria of charcoal gray–clad employees.

On the other hand, Lynx absolutely stood out like a rose amongst the industrial cogs. Nothing here was done by happenstance. Lynx must look the way she did for a reason.

No clue what that reason might be, Harper thought once again, other than that Lynx looked soft and pliable against the hard edges of Iniquus.

Harper turned her head in search of a coffee station. Not seeing one right off, she considered asking. But no, caffeine was probably a bad idea. Her nerves were still jacked from this morning.

When she refocused on Lynx and Berlin, Harper found Lynx explaining, "...intake is a bit more complicated with the close protection than it is with search and rescue. With search and rescue, knowing your experience with the outdoors, what kinds of sports you do, age and health, are the major determinants of where the S.A.R. team looks." Lynx pointed at the table. "We put out maps and look at all kinds of things from where the vehicles might get bottlenecked at what time of day to what we should do to keep you safe if there was another 9-11-like event on D.C. We decide in advance how to handle communications. Safe routes. Safe places."

"The Iniquus campus seems secure. They could bring me here to hunker down." She turned to Harper. "Is that what they say, 'hunker'?"

Harper shrugged. She wasn't the one to ask about tactical vocabulary.

"It's possible you'd be brought here," Lynx said. "It depends on the situation." She waved toward the laptops that were set up. "These intake forms will help give us a clearer picture of our role. Understanding your needs and the people around you are important planning components. From your chat this morning—"

Berlin sent a scowl to Harper. "I ended up having to talk to them, Harper. You weren't answering your phone."

"Yeah. Sorry about that. I was involved in the kidnapping thing this morning. I needed to—" Harper turned to Lynx. "Did something change since this morning?"

"Our new contract lists Berlin and CiCi Cummings as our principals," Lynx said. "Supporting staff group includes DeWayne, Carlos, and you, Harper."

"Yes, but those three are employees. They're not important." Uncharacteristically self-aware enough to hear how that sounded, Berlin quickly added, "*Of course* they're important. I mean, they're not the—what did you call CiCi and me, the principals? Security only covers the principals."

"We need to do an intake on everyone in your group," Lynx explained.

"Why's that?" Harper asked. She wanted to be left out of it.

Lynx addressed her answer to Berlin. "If there were an event where protection was needed, our job is, of course, to focus on you and CiCi. We have found that often the principal insists on the group being saved. Understandably so. No one wants to leave their staff behind when there's danger."

Berlin would certainly allow that. If there was any danger, she'd be out for herself. That isn't me being petty,

Harper told herself. To each their own personality and life, right? "You shouldn't be worried about the bigger picture. Berlin won't be latching on to anyone to save them," Harper agreed with her boss. "Save her. DeWayne, Carlos, and I can take care of ourselves."

Berlin nodded. "That's right. As I was saying, they're not important. The obsessed fan wouldn't hurt them. They'd be focused on me. And maybe CiCi."

If Lynx was surprised by Berlin's assertions, she didn't show it. "DeWayne is a photographer. Carlos is?"

"Berlin's stylist," Harper said. "He does hair, makeup, and dresses Berlin. And now, CiCi."

Lynx gestured toward the computers. "Shall we get started? All of your answers are secure and used in house only. They will never be shared, so please answer to the best of your ability. We need to plan with personalities in mind. Yours, Berlin, is more in-depth and will take a little longer than Harper's."

Berlin nodded as she sat primly, scooting forward on the roller chair, and putting her fingers on the mouse as she read the first screen prompts.

Harper leaned back in her chair at the other end of the table, stalling. "You've been through some difficult things, Lynx. And yet you still do this job. How do you do that?"

Lynx dragged out a chair and sat down next to her. "I acknowledge the emotions and consciously set them aside so I can focus on the task. Same with pain. If I'm injured, and the event is still in progress, I can't tap out and say, 'oh well, that's it.' I have to consciously set the pain into a compartment in my brain."

"Sort of like, 'Yeah, it's there, but I can't focus on it and still get the job done?'"

"In my line of work, the job usually has a life or death component to it."

Harper looked at the screen, asking for her basic information—name, address, insurance. Harper didn't want to put any of this down. Secure or not. In house or not. She needed to figure a way out of this. She typed Harper Katz into the namespace. "The psych eval. Explain why you're doing that for Berlin? I mean, if something bad were happening, you don't have to worry about her trying to play the hero. She'll do what she's told." Harper looked down the table at Berlin, biting her lip and filling out the fields.

"Not just Berlin. We'll need that from all five of you. It paints a good picture of the personality types we're protecting. If a bad situation comes up, we've pre-planned for how players might react."

"What are you looking for? How does that work?" Applied psychology always sparked Harper's interest. She studied it quite a bit as she used it to inform her paintings—human emotions as well as human perceptions.

"The biggest thing we need to understand is a person's locus of control."

Harper shook her head, flipping through the screens, trying to remember where she'd heard that before, until she landed on the page that said, "Tell Us About You."

"Locus of control, I'm not remembering what it means."

"There's internal locus of control and external locus. People with an internal locus of control tend to show a higher interest in learning. People who believe they have some elements of control over a situation believe they have options about their destinies—to them, things aren't predestined."

Harper looked up to the ceiling, thinking that idea

through. She'd proven to herself she had some control. She was still alive, wasn't she? But then again, what but providence could have put her in place this morning, and that time before? "'It is not in the stars to hold our destiny but in ourselves. William Shakespeare.'"

"Maybe if Julius Caesar had picked better friends or been a better person."

"The girls this morning weren't destined to be kidnapped," Harper said. "Berlin, on the other hand, is predestined to greatness." Harper raised her voice for that last bit, making her words loud enough to carry to Berlin, so Lynx could see her reaction.

Berlin stuck a fist in the air. "Whoop! Damned straight I am!" Then Berlin focused back on the screen.

"I'm guessing that's a sign of external locus with a positive spin. I guess the others are kind of doomsdayers. Huh?"

"And you?" Lynx asked.

"I'm doing my best to get by. Maybe I'm hoping that I have some control over how my life unfolds. I often think of it as a trip—I'm heading down a street. I turn left. I turn right. I have no idea how I ended up where I am, but for sure, it was based on little decisions until I make a big one."

"Do you have a big one planned?"

"Yeah. I do, actually. The road less traveled, but I'm sure it will make all the difference. What else is there about someone who thinks they have power over their destinies?"

"People with an internal locus of control will try to anticipate circumstances and what they would do."

"I can give you a good example. You know about the airplane pilot, Sully Sullenberger, who landed his plane in the Hudson River and saved everyone on board."

She tipped her head. "Go on."

"If I were a passenger, I would be dependent on the pilot. That's external locus, right? They're the passenger, so their fate is in the pilot's hands? When I get on a plane, I'm hoping we'll have a Sully Sullenberger and not someone who was drunk. Or new. Or I guess there was that pilot that wanted to commit suicide and took everyone with him. The Germanwings copilot that crashed in the Alps. Over a hundred people died on that flight. What was that guy's name?"

"I remember that happening, but I don't think they mentioned his name. In Europe, they try not to make martyrs or rock-stars out of their mass murderers. It takes away one of the incentives for committing atrocities."

Harper nodded. She hadn't thought about that.

"Let's think about Sully Sullenberger coming over the loudspeaker and saying, 'Brace for impact.' If you thought nothing would save you from your fate, you might jump up and scream, knowing you were going to die."

Harper's brows shot up. "That would spark panic. Distract the pilot."

"Each person—and Sully Sullenberger says the same thing—every person on that plane.

was part of a winning team. And like Sullenberger, our team plots possible scenarios and prepares plans for them." She swept her hand toward the 3D model at the center of the table. "Before the crash that no one could have predicted, Sully Sullenberger had studied past air events. What went wrong. What went right. He tried to compensate for the things that led to bad outcomes and increase the things that led to good outcomes. That forethought is part of our model for success." Lynx smiled.

"Yeah. Cerberus Team prepares like that. I've watched

them talk scenarios through. They throw out ideas."
Harper's computer was prompting her to go back and fill
out the first page. She winced and focused back on Lynx.
"They pick at things to find the weak spots in the plan."

"Most people assume that personal protection happens
when we're standing next to the person. But it's like art.
When you're working on a canvas, someone could walk
in and say, 'oh, you have such a natural talent.' What
they don't see is the training. The years of experimenta-
tion, trial and error, honing skills—it looks so easy but
moving toward proficiency is not an easy road. It doesn't
have a lot of shortcuts. When we stand behind Berlin, we
bring a combined-decades of study—physical, mental,
emotional—to that moment. We also bring the professionalism to prepare in advance. Our tools, K9 or weapons, are all prepared. Standing there looks easy. Getting
there is not."

Lynx had raised her voice just a tad, and this seemed
to be information that Lynx wanted Berlin to overhear.
The security wasn't there to carry her packages and flex
for her photos. They were professionals—Berlin should
understand that already.

But she didn't.

And that was fine.

They'd be flying out tomorrow night, sleeping on the
plane as they headed back to California. Iniquus wouldn't
have to worry about Berlin for very long.

Harper leaned over and typed her cell phone number
and Berlin's address into the next two lines of computer
prompts. Under apartment number, she entered 'pool
house.' She skipped the part about her health insurance
carrier. And tried to press ENTER, but it wouldn't let her
advance. She went back and put NONE in the insurance
carrier line, then it let her proceed. Harper could feel

Lynx's eyes on her. And because Harper wasn't doing a great job moderating her emotions, she flashed her eyes up. "What?"

Lynx smiled. "It's unusual for someone like you with a strong *inner* locus of control to be a loner. Usually, they're the people building human capital, pulling folks into their inner circle. I've heard that you do that for Berlin. I don't see you doing it for you."

Harper looked down at her lap. She took what Lynx said as a warning. They were paying attention to her. Had she sparked their concern somehow? Tripped some alarm bell?

If only Berlin had hired Acme Protection—some guy who was a bar bouncer—for the job. Berlin had purposefully chosen to go this more expensive route. She hired the best of the best, associating her name with Iniquus's to borrow some of their glow.

While Iniquus was thorough and professional, Harper would try to slip under their radar. She wasn't sure if her alias was up to the job. What could she do, refuse?

That would look suspicious and put a magnifying glass on her.

Quit?

She needed the money, and she needed a few more months. January. She just had to get to January.

Here was the real question: Was Harper's being back here in D.C. putting Berlin in danger?

Only if someone figured out who she was.

Chapter 14

Harper

Berlin had been off in Bob's office discussing who would be on her security team now that CiCi was joining her, and there was a change in their plans.

Poor Bob. Berlin usually found a way to finagle the outcome she wanted. She could be very creative; Harper would give her that.

Surely, Berlin could make the argument for Ryder over Didit. Harper just didn't want to be involved. Instead, she took advantage of some time to sit there under a tree and watch as the dogs came and went. Ridge had let Zeus stay with her while he went in to take a phone call that she wasn't supposed to overhear.

A moment to herself. A warm breeze. The smell of

pine. Zeus lying belly up with Harper's hand resting on his chest while he slept. Peace.

She thought about the painting she'd work on next, something with the theme of renewal. Hidden treasures camouflaged in a landscape. Yeah, that might be interesting.

The side door swung open. There was Ridge, holding the screen wide for Berlin.

She danced out onto the deck, put her hand to her mouth, and called out, "Harper!"

Zeus rolled over fully awake, attention focused on Ridge.

Ridge signaled him, and Zeus turned to check Harper, then trotted over to Ridge.

Scrambling to her feet, Harper brushed the dirt off her bottom. She'd better go find out what was happening. As she clambered up the steps to the deck, Harper promised herself, "You get cake tonight. Macaroni and cheese and cake."

"This, Berlin—" Ridge leaned into the railing across the back deck "—is why I want you to have Didit with you instead of insisting on Ryder." He pointed toward the German shepherd juggling to bite a Kong that he'd failed to catch. Once he got hold, he performed a strange sideways galumph across the field. "The dog you saw jogging with Ryder is a rescue German shepherd that he's working with for his cousin."

"She named him Chewie Barka!" Berlin held her hands in front of her heart and performed what Harper had designated her "butterfly clap," palms sealed together, flapping her hands as quickly as she could against each other. "How cute is that?"

"Do you want 'cute' on a protection assignment?"

Harper thought that DeWayne would have a time of it, trying to get Chewie to look like a trained protection K9. "Ryder's cousin agreed to this?"

"I do! And she did!" Bounce. Bounce. Then she stopped and sent Ridge a pouty face. "You said I couldn't have Tripwire and Valor the way I wanted because Valor won't bite."

"They're teaching a class tomorrow," Harper reminded Berlin. She sent a skeptical gaze toward the dog, who was once again trying to retrieve the Kong he'd dropped. "Will Chewie bite?"

"Not unless you wrap yourself in bacon," Ridge said. "Even then, I have my doubts."

They watched as Ryder got Chewie to sit next to him. Ryder held up a hand signal for "stay," took a step, and— nope. Back Ryder went to set up again. He got Chewie into a sit, and then the big old pooch lay down and rolled over, sending Ryder an expectant smile, exposing his belly for a rub.

Ryder was extremely patient with him.

"Do you know how I got around the rules?" Berlin grinned.

"How?" Harper kept looking at the door, thinking that at any moment, someone would burst through, waving papers over their head. "Harper Katz is an alias! Harper Katz doesn't exist!"

Berlin plucked her sunglasses from her dress and slid them into place. "I proposed that I hire Ryder to handle Chewie Barka and not as my close protection guy. Well, not when he has the dog. But tonight, I wouldn't mind the close part of the close protection." She bobbled her brows in case Harper had missed the double entendre.

"Berlin," Harper leaned in and whispered in Berlin's

ear, "I'm going to remind you here—this isn't meant to embarrass you—but you're not allowed to fool around with your security force. It's in the paperwork. You know that they keep the lines clear. They can't get physically or emotionally involved with you."

"I've seen it in the movies." She giggled then affected a movie announcer's voice. "They're machines of war, cold and distant." She leaned in with a stage whisper: "Like Ridge there. Who is and always will be a stick in the mud with his 'rules are rules' stuff." She wrinkled her nose and stood back up to smile over at Ridge.

If he heard that, he gave no sign.

"What were you saying about tonight?" Harper asked.

"I was talking about security tonight when I go dancing with CiCi at the Cash Cow. Anyway." She flipped her hair out of her face. "Ryder isn't on duty. It's the other two, Gator and Blaze. *Such* a shame there's the no-touch policy."

"Keep going with Ryder…you were saying that you hired him to handle Chewie."

"Yes!" Bounce. Bounce. "Genius! I hired Chewie Barka as my emotional support animal for tomorrow, and Ryder will be there to handle him until it's time for my speech. When we get there, DeWayne can take some pictures of Ryder and Ridge and the dogs. Then Ryder and Ridge will have the afternoon off. But Gator and Blaze will guard my body." She slid her hands down her sides and gave a little wiggle. "Have you seen them?"

"Gator and Blaze?" Harper shook her head.

"They. Are. Gorgeous!" She bent her knees and pulled her fists to her chest like she was going to spring up in a cheerleader whoop. Luckily, she reined herself in saying, "Mmm, yummy!" Then straightened herself back out, laying a hand on Harper's arm. "Now, Blaze is a redhead, which I normally don't like. But it works on him. And Gator, cute, cute, cute! And he has a Cajun accent that is just delish. If only I could get them on video talking, I could turn them into stars. But Command said no. But!" Bounce. Bounce. "They did agree to Chewie and Ryder, so I get what I wanted." She hugged herself. "They're so sweet in Command."

Harper had been the one who had negotiated with Iniquus Command during the storm and at the beginning for Berlin's security detail. They were far from sweet. They were hard-edged professionals. Though it was true, there was wiggle room in what they did. When Harper booked Iniquus for Berlin's Washington stay, they said they dealt with celebrities a lot and understood that their team needed to be flexible and accommodating. "*However*—" long pause for extra emphasis "—the no video, no photos, and no audio recording rule is stringently in place." That Berlin said Command had okayed an emotional support dog showed Harper that Iniquus was serious about keeping their clients happy, even if it meant a bit of absurdity.

Harper adjusted her cap to shield her eyes from the bright sunlight.

Ryder had Chew Barka in what Ridge had taught Harper was called a "sit-stay." The handler was supposed to put a K9 on a spot and go away for twenty minutes. During this time, the K9 shouldn't budge even when the handler was out of sight. It looked like Ryder had given up on that and was attempting to do a call out.

Chewie sat, sat, sat. *Good boy.* Harper sent her congratulations in a picture like she imagined Lynx did for Zeus.

Ryder got a good distance out, turned, then signaled. "Come!" He was using English like Tripwire did with

Valor. Only the dual-trained dogs—the dogs who were a nose and a bite—received commands in other languages. With the signal, Chewie took off at a gallop like a new colt, testing its legs. Head leaning off to the right, tongue dangling out, eyes wide and unblinking, he focused on Ryder. Galumph.

Ryder stood statue-like, focusing straight ahead.

When Chewie reached Ryder's side, he could not contain his joy at being such a good boy. He leaped in circles. Around and around. Around some more. Around one more time.

Ryder faced stoically forward so as not to reward Chewie's behavior.

Berlin was laughing so hard, tears streamed down her face. Butterfly clapping.

Harper was sure Chew Barka could hear and was egged on. She wanted to slam her hip into Berlin's side, give her a stink face to make her stop. But Berlin was her boss.

Around and around three more times, then he moved right out in front of Ryder, instead of to his side, where he was supposed to be, plopping his butt down and sticking his nose straight up to the sky, so he could see Ryder's expression.

"Well," Ridge said. "That's a huge improvement."

"Yay, Chewie!" Berlin lifted a fist in the air. "Yay! Good boy!" She cupped her hands around her mouth as she called out.

Bob startled Harper when he said, "You're sure about wanting them, Berlin? Ridge can go on his own."

Harper hadn't heard Bob come out on the deck to join them.

He stood with his back to the wall, arms akimbo.

"I want matching bookends," Berlin said. "Besides, Chewie is there as my comfort animal to help soothe me after this morning's trauma. My Instagram followers will *love* him. And I'll be doing a public service by role-modeling, for people who are having a difficult time after a harrowing event, that getting support is important."

Harper's eyelids stretched wide. *Was she serious right now?*

"See? Here I am, able to laugh again," Berlin said. "He's good medicine." She grinned at Bob. "Now, don't worry. I'll make sure everyone knows I have one dog who's a biter and another who's a licker."

Chapter 15

Harper

Berlin swiped her phone to check the time. "O.M.G.!" She gripped Harper's arm. "I have to go. I only have a few hours for Carlos to style me." She adjusted to post a hand on each of Harper's shoulders. "Listen, CiCi is coming to my suite, and we're practicing our speeches for tomorrow. She said her stylist picked out a forest-green dress because it's like Mother Earth. I told her you were insisting I wear red. I think if CiCi is wearing green, I should wear blue."

"No," Harper said.

Bob lifted a hand to signal Ryder in.

Ryder jogged over. Chew Barka was doing his goober best, trotting at Ryder's side the way Ryder was training Chewie to do.

Harper hadn't greeted Bob yet, and she felt remiss. She'd go give him a hug as soon as she could get Berlin on her way.

"Why no?" Berlin scowled and dropped her hands. "Why not blue?" She stomped her foot in its little, strappy Grecian sandal. "I *want* to wear blue. I'm talking about Guam and corals and water. It should be blue to match the water theme."

Ryder called from the steps. "G'day."

"Kiwi!" Bounce. Bounce. Bounce.

"He's from Australia, not New Zealand," Harper said under her breath.

Berlin heard. "But I like kiwis. I had them at breakfast just this morning. Sweet with a bit of tart. And Kiwi doesn't mind if I call him that. Do you?" She batted her eyelashes at Ryder.

"Kiwi the bird, not the fruit," Harper mouthed, too low for Berlin to pick it up.

"Whatever makes you happiest," Ryder said. "G'day, Harper. I hear you're today's hero. Good on you."

"Thank you," Harper muttered.

"Do you know what would make me happy?" Berlin asked Ryder. "Wearing a blue dress tomorrow. But Harpy Harper here says no, I have to wear red." She paused to make a face at Harper. "Look at you, blushing. It must mean the color choice has something to do with sex."

Nope, Harper thought, you just called me a harpy in front of everyone. Berlin probably didn't know what a harpy was, but the men didn't know that Berlin sometimes just liked the sound of things, and they got stuck in her repertoire.

Like "Kiwi" had.

"Then she'll say that me being sexually attractive is

inappropriate for my speech. As if I could dim my natural sexuality. You know she made me change my clothes before I came over here, don't you? And blue isn't even a sex—" Berlin looked at her feet. "Oh, yes, it is. Little blue pills give men erections." Her smile slid from man to man. "Harper must not want the men to be thinking about hard-ons while I'm talking about climate change." She held up a hand to hide her mouth as if telling a secret, but she used a normal tone of voice. "She's a bit of a prude." She made a face and gave her head a sarcastic dip to the side.

"Berlin, you're welcome to wear a blue dress. You asked me what the best color for this occasion would be, and it's not blue. Green might be what CiCi needs to wear for the speech because green reduces anxiety. You're not an anxious person. You don't need green."

"How is it that she should wear red, not blue?" Ryder asked, dragging chairs over for Harper and Berlin.

Harper accepted the seat gratefully, settling onto the thick padding. "Berlin mentioned little blue pills, which has become a synonym for Viagra." She leaned forward to rub a hand over Chewie's back as he settled in front of her. "Interestingly, though, researchers color code pills when they're used for placebos. They've found that when they give someone a pill—whether the placebo or the drug they're testing—they're more effective if they're certain colors. Blue is best for putting someone to sleep."

Berlin moved over and sat next to her. "That seems weird. Are you sure? Why would the little blue pill be blue then?"

Harper shrugged. "I read one hypothesis that linked it back to Italy."

"A country of stud muffins." Berlin arched a single brow.

"Well, soccer players, anyway. They have a soccer team called the Italian word for blue. Men—and women, too, I guess—started associating heightened stimulation with the color blue."

Bob leaned his hips into the handrail. "They purposefully choose the colors for our prescriptions?"

"And over-the-counter drugs." Harper nodded. "Blue is for sleep. Red for waking up. Red." She focused pointedly on Berlin. "You don't want anyone snoozing while you speak, Berlin. Those would make for bad pictures."

Berlin frowned.

"Yellow is for depression. Green works for anxiety," Harper finished.

"White?" Ryder asked.

"Uhm, ulcers if I'm remembering correctly. The brain is pretty crazy. I'll tell you another placebo story. This is a story about 'red,' Berlin. The researcher takes some plain gelatin, no color, no taste, they put it in four bowls, all exactly the same. The researchers add food coloring. Red, yellow, blue, and green."

Ridge looked around when he heard Zeus get up and move to the shade.

"They blindfolded the participants who tasted a bite from each bowl before the colorant and after. Nobody tasted anything. 'Nope—no taste,' they said. 'Nope—they aren't different. They're all the same,' they said. From that, we know there is no smell difference and no taste difference. Off come the blindfolds. Ta-da! There sit four bowls of colored gelatin. The same thing as they just identified as having no smell and no taste, mind you."

The men nodded.

"Each person—across age ranges, gender spectrums,

nationalities, and geographical locations—is given bites from each bowl."

"And they tasted different?" Ryder took up a place next to Bob, on the rail, ankles crossed, arms crossed over his chest, relaxed.

"Very much so. The red was sweet." She looked over at Berlin. "Red is sweet while green is bitter. You don't want to be seen as bitter."

"Exactly. I'm sweet." She batted her lashes and looked around to make sure everyone agreed with her.

"The yellow sour, and the blue unpleasant."

"Unpleasant?" Ridge asked.

"They couldn't place why it was unpleasant, though."

"I can get the associations sweet like a strawberry, sour like a lemon. When you said green, I got a tart taste in my mouth," Ryder said. "I guess I conjured green apples. I don't get the blue."

"The researchers think that 'unpleasant' was the overall take because blue might look overripe, bruised, or decaying. Which we don't want. Do we, Berlin?"

"No, we do *not*."

"We don't have Jell-O-blue in our natural world, so there might not be a connotation. They speculate that's why the people came up with 'unpleasant.'"

"Interesting," Ridge said.

"Even more interesting to me was that following the experiment, they told the subjects that none of the colored bowls of gelatin had any taste at all, and no one would believe them. Just wouldn't. They thought the researchers were trying to trick them and that that trick was the actual experiment."

"Do you use color associations in your paintings?" Bob asked.

"I do. I can't account for an individual's experience or culture. If you're an Italian soccer fan, you might not get the same soothing experience from my blue painting as I had aimed to develop. I use color psychology to stimulate the brain with universal experiences. And since I'm out of the art world, for now, I use it to tell Berlin what color she should wear to stimulate the right part of the other person's brain, so she can have her desired impact."

"Really cool," Ryder said.

"But red is sweet, and while I don't mind being seen as sweet, don't you think I should have something on that makes me look smart?"

"And you will be. Red will help your listeners focus on risk avoidance."

"Red is a stop sign. Like that?" Ridge asked.

"Yes, and well…like toothpaste."

"Here we go," Berlin said. "Okay, toothpaste, what has *that* got to do with anything?"

"When a toothpaste brand is trying to convince you that it'll stop cavities, stop gingivitis, stop the *bad things*, they'll package it in red. If, on the other hand, you want to have a positive message like whiten your teeth, fluoride protects tooth enamel. Then blue."

"So I'm the 'stop bad things' person, and CiCi will be the 'things will be better if' no-anxiety person?"

"Which is smart if that's the message CiCi is delivering. It's not the message you're presenting. You want people to stop acidifying the oceans."

"*You* want people to stop acidifying the oceans. You wrote the speech."

"That's best delivered in a red dress. Red is more primal. It's an ancient color of recognition. Blood. Fire." She held up her palm. "Men see it as a color of health, and therefore fertility. If you're on a first date, black and red are always the best colors. Given the age of the congress-people, this might well be the first time they're meeting you. You could think of it as a first date."

"You said stop sign and avoidance," Berlin said.

"In mating and courtship, red increases attraction to mates. Men think of women as more fertile when they wear red. They're also more likely to spend money on women wearing red. You want the lawmakers, mostly men, to put money into your concerns."

"Red on women makes men spend money?" Berlin grinned as if she'd just unwrapped an unexpected gift.

Harper dearly wanted to steer the conversation away from that trajectory. "As it turns out, women will natu-rally choose to wear the color red on their most fertile days of their cycle."

"So what day of the cycle is pumpkin orange?" Berlin cocked an eyebrow. "I'd guess bloating day." She laughed.

Harper licked her lips. Ridge saw her dressed in or-ange this morning, *yay*.

Berlin wasn't wrong, though. This was the end of her cycle, and she'd lose a good three pounds off the scale by tomorrow. She'd also be in a far better mood, she told herself.

This thread of conversation, though, was too famil-iar of a topic amongst the security operators. Harper no-ticed that their faces had all gone blank. And she thought, *Hear no evil; see no evil…* "Anthropologists know an-cient Egyptians used red lipstick to increase fertility cues. And in paintings, where I want to evoke those kinds of thoughts, I always paint my subjects' lips red. It's like an aphrodisiac. In a competitive head to head, red gives you the advantage. Now, I know CiCi is a friend. And

I know this isn't a competition between the two of you. You're in competition with industries who want to put the mighty dollar ahead of a healthy Earth."

"Wear red to save the planet!" Berlin raised a fist in the air.

"The planet will be fine. It will self-heal once humans are gone. We're trying to make a sustainable planet for our children."

"Grandchildren," she said.

"No, Berlin, did you read the speech? The world's stocks of seafood will have collapsed by 2050 at present rates of destruction by fishing. If you had a baby this year—"

Berlin reached out and grabbed Harper's arm. "God forbid."

"Yes," Harper agreed. "God forbid. You're going to tell people in the speech that a four-year study of our world's ecosystems concludes that the long-term trend is both clear and predictable. By the time a child who is born *this* year is about your age now, there won't be seafood."

Berlin rolled her eyes with a wave of her hand, erasing Harper's words. "Then they can eat hamburgers or something."

Chapter 16

Ridge

Walking side by side, Ridge and Harper traced along the fence line.

Zeus trotted at Ridge's heels.

Harper had changed moods. She didn't seem nearly as delicate as she had this morning when Zeus had summoned Lynx. After interacting with her professional hat on when Berlin had been here, Harper seemed to be back in the practical, thoughtful part of her mind.

Berlin heading back to The Lily seemed to ease the strain around Harper's eyes.

He hoped Harper wasn't swallowing things down. Better out than in when it came to distressing emotions. Face them. Experience them. Add them to your baggage.

Baggage...

When Harper told him she was heading back to the

East Coast for a couple of days, he'd been excited. It was going to be his opportunity to test the waters. Did Harper want to move them from friendship to relationship, even if it meant their relationship was long-distance?

There was his baggage hurdle to leap over.

It was a sizable leap.

It meant that he couldn't leave his job or location to make their relationship easier. He'd never ask her to change for him. Still—he slid his hands into his pockets and rolled his lips in, trying to push down the sudden nervous buzzing in his stomach—if she'd consider *more*, he was confident they could come up with some way to work it out.

"This is the K9 conditioning area." He pointed to his left, where there was an obstacle course set up. "Windows to jump through, walls to go over, ramps, tubes, textures, most things that the doggos might encounter on a mission. We run the dogs through here in all different times of day and weather conditions. Sometimes we'll lay scent trails. That way, we can assess the dogs' ability to follow the scent and not be deterred by obstacles. Sometimes, we have them run it with silent hand gestures or following voice command over their radio collars."

"That's so cool." She smiled up at him. Even with sad eyes, her smile was beautiful. Sweet. Kind. "What an amazing job you have."

"I can't argue with you there." He pointed at the K9s as they passed the kennel. "Scorpion. Rocket. Money Bags."

"Oh, wow, that one's huge." She slid her hand into the crook of his arm, and he smiled down at her.

"He's Moose. This one here is Grief, as in good grief! Ginger because she likes to snap."

Harper slid back a step.

"Only bad guys. And this last one is named Classified, Classy for short."

When Ridge came to a stop, Zeus sat like a sentinel. Eyes scanning.

"See that?" Ridge asked. "Zeus is always left of bang." He picked up a ball and a ball launcher that would give Zeus a farther distance to run. Ridge sent the ball out, waiting for it to stop bouncing to release Zeus.

Zeus hadn't moved his eyes from the trajectory.

"*Bring.*" Ridge used the German command for fetch, and Zeus tore off to retrieve the toy.

"What does that mean, 'left of bang?'" Harper asked.

"Left of bang is situational awareness. Bang is the impact of an event. Right of bang is the aftermath. I want you to work on reacting left of bang."

"This morning, I reacted…well, the gun didn't bang, but I reacted at bang, I guess. Did I do it wrong?"

"You were out running?"

"Yes."

"Do you run a lot?"

"Yes." She looked away when she said it. So a topic she didn't want to tell him about.

"Have you ever thought of getting a dog to run with?" Zeus arrived to drop the slobber ball in his hand. Ridge whipped the launcher to toss it out again. "*Bring.*"

"With my job? No. It's impractical."

"There are some things I could teach you about situational awareness."

"I've read articles about that. But it would be antithetical to why I run."

Zeus was back with the ball. This time Ridge threw it into the training ring. Zeus tore after it, scrambling up the first ramp.

Ridge had discovered over time that Harper was more comfortable talking about personal things when she was distracted. That's why he'd started playing chess with her over video chat. And that's why he'd walked her out here to watch Zeus exercise. "Okay, tell me about why you run."

"It's my creative time. The time I purposefully use to get my art juices flowing."

"Since a dog is impractical, maybe a running partner?"

"Too distracting. And who am I going to run with, Carlos?"

"That wouldn't work."

"No." She chuckled. "Carlos is anti-exercise." She slid her hand down his arm, but instead of holding his hand, she tipped it over and painted her fingertip over the permanent callous in the wedge between his thumb and trigger finger. She looked up at him with troubled eyes. "These are from shooting?"

"Thousands of rounds. Day in day out, I trained my body from mind to nervous system, to hands and fingers until 'bad guy to bang' was a single motion."

"Maybe the solution is for me to get a concealed carry license and carry a gun."

"I was trained to shoot the tiny piece of head sticking out from behind the hostage. Most people don't need that level of training. But if you're going to put a gun in your hand, you have to train consistently. Mind and body. The mind is the biggest thing."

"Why do you say that?"

Zeus was back, and Ridge took a moment to send the ball out again, this time into the maze. "Because TV isn't reality." He was thinking of Berlin. Berlin would trust that if Harper had a gun that Berlin was safe to act even more outlandishly than usual. "If you're pulling a gun, you've decided the other person is going to die."

"Die?" she squeaked. "No, that's not necessarily so."

"Because?"

"You can pull out a gun and scare them off." She dropped his hand.

"That's a good way to get yourself killed, Harper. Is that your goal when you have a gun?"

"To die? No, quite the opposite."

"If you pull a gun as a warning, they're warned. They can pull out their own gun and shoot you because they don't have the mindset that they have it for warning purposes and won't use it. If you hesitate, they can use your response as the go-ahead to disarm you and turn the gun on you. You've just armed the bad guy."

She stood there silently.

"Have you ever been to a gun shop?" He canted his head, trying to see her expression beneath the tip of her cap's brim.

"Yes," she whispered. Her shoulders caved, and she seemed…not embarrassed. Guilty?

"I bet I can tell you exactly what happened. You said you were interested in buying a gun for protection. It was a guy standing there behind the counter. He asked you if you've ever used a gun before. You said no. He said, 'Fo' you, little lady, I'd suggest a revolver. It's point and shoot. It can't jam. You just put the bullets in the little holes, and if a bad guy comes around, you point and shoot.'"

She pressed her lips together in a frown.

"And then he said that the other type of gun he'd suggest—and I'm right, aren't I? It was a guy, wasn't it? Older guy, pot belly, whiskers."

"Yes." She hadn't lifted her eyes since she'd admitted to going to buy the gun.

"He told you to get a shotgun. He said that you just rack the shotgun, and that noise would scare anyone away, and you wouldn't even need to shoot it."

"Yes." Her eyes flashed up momentarily. "That's exactly what happened."

Ridge put his finger under her chin and tipped her head back. "Did you buy the gun?"

She swallowed.

"Harper?"

"No. I didn't like the guy. I didn't feel safe around him, so I didn't trust his advice."

"I have a question for you."

"Okay."

He was going to ask the why of her trip to the gun shop. It had to be something big. Bigger than today? If it were, that precipitate wasn't something she'd talked about. He didn't want her to shut down. He'd hold those questions for later. Instead, he decided to focus on today. "A couple of questions, actually. You said that this morning the car came up the street. You focused on it and watched it make a three-point turn."

"Yes."

"Did your senses pick up anything there? Did you have any body responses?"

"Yes, relief."

"Relief?"

"Yes."

"Relieved for what reason?"

She frowned. "Oddly, I felt angry when he was slowing down near me, then I saw him turning, and I felt relief."

"When did you know there was danger?"

"When the door opened, and I saw a gun. Well, not the gun. I think I was still too far away to be sure it was a gun—the posture. If I were doing a quick sketch of a guy with a gun, those are the shapes and forms I would use. I was considerably closer when I could affirm it was a gun." She faltered. "Ridge, he had a gun. And tape. Zip ties. And condoms." She was shaking and spun into his arms, ducking her head and hugging him tightly.

It hadn't been his intention to light her nervous system up.

Zeus scrambled to the top of the walkway and glared at him. Ridge raised a hand to let Zeus know Harper wasn't in danger. "You're safe," he whispered. "You made it through. You did great."

She leaned her head back and blinked at him, then her gaze moved to the side.

Ridge looked that way. "That's Gage. He's on Panther Force. It looks like he's trying to catch Lynx's attention. Do you see her there in the field with her Dobermans?" Ridge put his hand over Harper's ear, pressed her head to his chest, and then gave a high-pitched whistle.

Lynx turned her attention their way, lifting her hand to shield her eyes.

Ridge pointed toward Gage.

Lynx jogged her way over, her Dobermans, Beetle and Bella, at her heels.

"Take a breath." He kissed the top of Harper's head. "We're going to keep talking about this. We need to get it out of your body. Okay? The more you talk about it, the better for you in the long run."

She gulped and nodded.

"Ready?"

Chapter 17

Harper

Harper shook Gage's hand. "Nice to have met you, Gage." She gave Lynx a little hug. "Thank you for introducing Beetle and Bella. They're beautiful."

"We'll catch up with you later?" Gage asked. She didn't like how he was staring at her face. Like he was taking mental pictures.

"Doubtful." Harper angled her head so the brim of her hat would obscure her features. She didn't want to be recognizable. "I'm here until tomorrow night, then it's back to California. Are you on Lynx's team? Do you have anything to do with Berlin's security tonight?"

"He's on Panther Force," Lynx said with one of her butter smiles—a smile that seemed to soothe and placate.

Why did Harper need to be placated? Harper's nerves fired up.

Ridge held up his cell phone. "Bob wants to talk to us."
Bob knew.

He had to know. Why else was Bob calling them to his office, like a wayward kid to the principal? Was that the reason for Lynx's butter smile?

Harper had lied on her intake information, and now, Bob was going to call her on it in front of Ridge.

She dragged her feet as they moved toward Cerberus Headquarters.

When she got to his office, Bob pulled her into his arms for a fatherly hug. "I was waiting for Berlin to leave before I gave you a hug and made sure you were okay. I know you always act professionally when you're on the job. But I wanted to check in with you on a personal basis."

"I'm..." She could hardly catch her breath. She plopped into a chair and smoothed her hands down her pants.

Part of her wanted to come clean. Just wanted to say, "Hey, you guys, I'm scared for my life. I've done what I can figure out to hide from the killers. Can you help me?"

And while she trusted Bob and Ridge completely, the people she didn't trust were the chain of authorities they would contact. Better to shut her mouth, get back to California, and refuse to come back to the East Coast even if it meant quitting her job earlier than she wanted to.

"I have the reports in from Ridge and Tripwire. I saw your art. You always impress me, Kiddo." He put his hand on top of her cap and wiggled it like a coach, talking to his Little League player.

She focused on her fingers, how they gripped the ends of her knees. How that grip made the knuckles more pronounced. The strain made the bone structure more prominent beneath her skin. In paintings, Harper tried to catch the emotion, not just in the eyes and face. She'd found the hands to be just as telling. She'd replicate the way her hands looked at some point. Yes, she needed to remember how the grip made her flesh turn white and how the strain ran up her forearms to her elbows.

"Looking at the pictures, it's interesting to think you have situational amnesia." Bob took a seat behind his desk, and Ridge sidled behind her to get to the other office chair. "It's common to get a blank space. Usually, it fills in quick enough once your body agrees it's out of danger. Those drawings tell the story, though, don't they? The emotions. Whoosh. They got to me right here." He pounded a fist into his chest.

"It's really odd—kind of frightening, to be honest." Maybe this was just a check-in. Maybe she'd slid under their radar. After all, she was a bit player. Why would they look? "I didn't like that feeling at all—not being able to get my brain into gear." She peeked up at Bob and thought her ball cap was disrespectful, so she dragged it off and draped it over her knee, sliding her hand over her hair to tamp down the fly-aways. "It's kind of interesting, though, that I could recall the images, and I could translate those images into information for someone else to know what happened without having to swim through that weird blank space in my brain. If I were to describe my art—before I was a commercial artist, which means I was doing art that was for a wider audience—you know, when I did art for myself…" She looked off through the window behind Bob.

Both men sat patiently quiet.

"Okay. Sorry, I was trying to get my thoughts to line up." She shifted back to face Bob. "I think I've found the best way to describe this." She licked her lips. "My graduate show for my MFA was called *A Breath Before*. It was oil, some mixed media." She waggled a hand in the air. "And they were scenes. Pleasant, ordinary, everyday scenes of people's lives with a change element in the picture but not acting on the participants yet. They didn't know it was there."

"Interesting." Bob leaned back in his seat, lacing his fingers and resting them on his chest.

"I got ideas from reading newspaper articles about ordinary people thrust into extraordinary circumstances. Take Beirut, recently. People were going about their day with no idea that events nearby would kill, maim, render them homeless, or jobless…changed." She paused and sniffed. She wished Zeus was here with her, but Ridge had put him in the kennel for the night.

He'd explained that Zeus stayed there a night or two each week. Sometimes they deployed to forward operating bases when their principals were visiting conflict zones, and their K9s had to follow the rules. In some places, the K9s have to be in the kennel when not actively on duty. Cerberus wanted their dogs to be used to the noise and atmosphere, so they weren't stressed by the requirements. Since Ridge planned to take Harper to the club that night and then see her home later, it was a good time for Zeus to put in his kennel time.

Harper wished Ridge had waited until the last possible moment. But, too, she didn't know what the requirements were. Still, picturing Zeus had a calming effect. "Did either of you see the viral video of the bride in Beirut who was in the middle of having her wedding pictures taken, then her skirt was blown up around her ears by the blast concussion?" She flicked her gaze toward Ridge to see him nod.

"Hiroshima in a past generation. Just a day, everything was fine, and then devastation. The tsunami in Sri Lanka. Some of my works depicted vast population-wide effects like those I just mentioned. Some are more intimate."

Bob tipped his head. "Can you give me an example of that?"

"I watched a horrifying security camera video of two men who had targeted a woman. They waited for her to come out of the grocery store. She was unaware as she loaded her packages into the back seat, just a girl out getting her milk and bread for breakfast. She shut the back door of her car, and timed to perfection through obvious repetition, a man opened her passenger-side back door and climbed in, paced exactly with this young woman's movements as she opened the driver's door and slid behind the wheel. You couldn't see on the video how he gained control of her once they were in the car. But the second man came to the driver's side door. Waited, opened it, and then climbed in behind the wheel. Obviously, the woman was following directives and moved to the front passenger seat." She turned toward Ridge. "They drove off."

Ridge's face hardened.

"I was horrified. I'm still horrified." She put her hands on either side of her eyes like she was wearing blinders. "I watched the video, and it gave me nightmares for weeks." She petted a hand up her arm. "A crawling horror that—every time I think of it." A tremor moved through her body.

Ridge reached for her hand, and she took hold of it, gladly. Holding Ridge's hand was like a tether. A safety line. She felt connected and cared for. She was lucky to have Ridge as her friend. And she felt horrible that everything about her was a lie. "I have no idea what happened to that woman," she said. "Nothing good comes from being taken to a secondary location."

"Which is what you said to the police this morning," Ridge said.

"I did, didn't I?" Her brows pulled together. "Yes, I always wondered why that woman didn't dive back out of the car. Why she didn't get herself out in public. Something. I thought maybe no one had ever said to her, you have to do whatever is necessary even if it's against the norms."

"Who said that to you?" Bob asked.

"My mom. We'd be in the house, and she'd say things like, 'There's a fire, and you can't get to a door. What do you do?' I was expected to say, 'Pick up a chair and break the window, make your own exit.' Or there was a time we were in the grocery store, and a weird woman was following us. Mom said, 'Norms are bullshit if there's an emergency. You do what you have to do.' She'd then remind us that if someone is trying to harm me in a store, I can always start throwing glass jars on the ground or topple over display cases. The breaking sound would pull everyone over to see what was happening. Think outside of the box, Kit-Katz." She cleared her throat.

Harper had to be more careful when she told stories. Giving away clues, or possibly her name in recounting stories, was one of the reasons why she trained herself to never talk past-tense. Tried to. Ridge kept asking questions, though. It was getting harder to deflect.

Maybe it was time to distance herself from him.

Yes, it was probably time to distance herself.

When she got home. She'd do it then.

Harper felt her heart pick up its beat. A cold sweat shimmered over her skin. Yeah, the thought of not hav-

ing Ridge in her life would be a terrible sacrifice. Still…
there were worse things, weren't there?

Her safety had to come first, she reminded herself.

Ridge was looking at her like he was trying to translate a foreign language. Like he was trying to read her
innermost secrets. She needed to play it cool. "If I used
that scene for my show, I would have painted the woman
at the car, the groceries, the men in the parking lot with
carts, looking like they were going about their business.
It was 'the breath before' her life changed. And while I
painted that, I'd think, what would have made the difference? Nothing good was heading her way once they
left the parking lot. I would argue that it was worth the
risk to do something else rather than comply. That if he'd
grabbed her hair or pointed a gun or a knife at her, throwing herself sideways out the door and screaming at the
top of her lungs to gain attention might have gotten her
shot or stabbed, but help was nearby."

"It sounds like an amazing art show." Bob tapped beneath his chin with steepled fingers. "Thought-provoking
for those who understood what you were painting. How
did it change your perspective?"

"Since I worked on that show, it became a habit to
assess. When people posted things on social media or
what have you, I'd pick a point that I might have painted
for the show. At what point was that person 'a breath
before?' How many lives changed based on decisions
made in the unfolding events? I'm not victim bashing—
I wasn't there."

"You were today," Bob pointed out.

"And people could look at what I did and assign blame.
It is what it is." She stopped to heave a sigh. "I didn't
have much control over my brain or my body. I have to

assume that's true for others in extreme circumstances. Again, not judging, just imagining possibilities as elements that I could paint into a picture—choice of colors, energy of motion…"

"I think it's very interesting," Ridge said. "I'm wondering if we can't arrange for you to give a talk here at Iniquus with a slide show of your paintings. We like to have different points of view."

Come back here? No. Never again. This had been a mistake. She'd only come because it was such a quick trip; what could go wrong?

"Others' perspectives help us to keep from enclosing ourselves in our own bubble."

And she'd decided to come because she'd get to see Ridge.

He paused, scrutinizing her. "What was that thought?"

"Nothing… I've done some knee-jerk things that changed my life's trajectory and other people's too. I'm not a great person to teach you all anything. You would probably know better than me why a human acts the way they do under extreme circumstances. Did they train you about the psychology of all that?"

"Iniquus has excellent support for our clients who were part of any critical incident," Bob said. "Would you like to talk to someone?"

"I wasn't the victim." She glanced over to Ridge, wondering why he was so silent. Harper didn't like this spotlight. "I was a witness. And I'm not a client. Berlin is. Honestly, you all are very sweet to me. I appreciate you. But I'm fine. I promise. I'm just going to put my head down, do my job, get back on the plane, and leave that story behind me."

Bob's phone rang. He looked at the caller ID. "I need to take this. I'll be right back." And he left his office.

"Okay, I'm going to ask," Ridge said as soon as the door shut. "Tell me if I'm out of bounds."

She nodded. *Gah!*

"I don't want you staying by yourself tonight. I'd like to stay with you at your hotel."

Was that why Zeus was in the kennel? "I…have one bed."

"This isn't a play for you, Harper. You've had one hell of a day. This is me wanting you to feel safe enough to get some sleep. You sleep under the covers, and I'll sleep dressed on top."

She blinked. "You'd do that?"

He sat still.

Of course, he'd do that. He was Ridge. "Yes," she exhaled. "Thank you."

No one knew she was here. No one knew who she was. Twenty-four hours, and she'd be headed back to California. She could give herself this one night as a birthday gift.

Chapter 18

Ridge

When Bob came back into his office, his energy had shifted. This was no longer a "checking in on you" kind of chat.

Harper must have sensed it too. She'd stopped blinking, and the muscles in her face hardened as if she was waiting for an impact.

"Harper, that was Sy."

Her head bobbed in a nod.

"One of the things that we do at Iniquus is to protect our clients' public posture."

Her brows climbed toward her hairline.

"As we do with all such incidents, your picture and the event from this morning were sent to our AI system. Sy said that a video was pinging."

Her lips tugged down into a frown.

"I'm going to show it to you, so you're aware that it exists. It was put up by Shawna's mother as a warning for other parents that their kids weren't safe standing at the bus stops by themselves."

She nodded.

"Sy already contacted her and asked her to take down the video, which she did. Because Berlin had mentioned the incident, this video got shared a number of times before we could get the original video down. I want to assure you that our AI system is excellent at finding and removing content. This will be gone soon. But we understand how Berlin is with social networking, and we wanted you to have seen it if you want to discuss it with her."

Harper was motionless. Ridge didn't think she was breathing. He wiggled her hand, and she sniffed air loudly into her nostrils.

Bob tapped his computer and spun it around.

"Holy smokes, look at that!" It was a young girl's voice. An arm, a leg, a swish of hair. He could tell that several girls were standing around the person who was videotaping. In the picture, Harper, in her safety-orange, was running down the road, using perfect form, except for the phone in her hand.

The car that Harper would end up taking was to the side of the video. The girl turned the phone, and for a brief flash, there was the target's face.

Ridge's fist balled.

The camera was pointed back at Harper. "I didn't realize it was the season for the Great Pumpkin. Big yikes. I've never seen anyone that porky run so fast."

"Shawna, stop, no reason to be salty. Who is this guy? Do you know him?"

"Look at her. Rattle, rattle, here come the cattle. Stampede! It's like there's a cowboy with a lasso chasing her."

When the car stopped, Shawna turned toward the vehicle. There was the gun, pointing right at her.

Straining, he could just hear Harper yelling, "Hey!" The phone dropped to the ground. Ridge had seen that image, the tumbling cellphone, in one of Harper's drawings.

Then the video was pointing at the sky.

A moment later, there was a shriek of tires.

The video was over. Bob closed the computer and rounded the desk, settling his hips back onto the top.

"Harper." Ridge reached a hand over to her shoulder and shook her. "Harper?"

She turned her face to him. She was white as a sheet.

"You're okay. It's over."

She seemed to flounder around for some words. She licked her lips and said, "I'm dead." She shook her head as blood rose to her face. "I mean… I… I… I… I'm going to be fired."

"Your face isn't in the video, Harper," Bob said. "You were wearing the ball cap. We enhanced it to make sure, even with our advanced software, we couldn't get it to anything that wasn't highly pixelated."

"No? Okay, that's the good part," she exhaled, crumpling over until her forearm balanced on her knee.

"And Sy said the police don't have your full name or contact information. This isn't going to come back on you. Like I said, the AI is scrubbing it. In the next hour or so, it should be down. I'm just telling you because one, Berlin. And two." Bob grinned. "I wanted to ask how fast you were running? You had to be doing like eight miles an hour before it was even a crime scene. Like Usain Bolt."

"I… Uhm, I. Yes, well, no. Today, I was taking it easy. Jet lag."

Bob seemed to be trying to jostle Harper's stuttering brain away from the crime scene.

Harper gulped in some air. "I… I'm training for my next marathon. I was giving myself an easy day. Seven miles per hour was my pace." She coughed. "This morning."

Bob nodded encouragement. "Excellent."

Ridge and she talked daily. Sometimes for hours a day. She'd never mentioned marathoning or even exercising. He wondered if it was because she got flak about her size.

Ridge loved Harper's curves. She was *precisely* Ridge's type.

But her experience with people's feedback might have been like Shawna's on the video. If that were the case, kudos to her for persisting. He could see why Harper might keep her talent hidden, not wanting to chance dealing with someone's disrespect.

He wondered what Shawna thought now after saying such cruel things about a woman who would end up saving Shawna's life.

Those pictures Harper drew for the police more than told the story; they expressed the horror the kids experienced. She'd been there as the only adult. Harper had to have felt the heavy weight of responsibility.

One night at the lodge, Berlin chided Harper, "You know, Harper, I can never understand why you aren't a suburban housewife with four kids, three dogs, and a herd of cats. You really do need that many beings around you to spread out the nagging."

Red-faced, Harper had quickly left the room.

Ridge kind of felt the same as Berlin's ill-phrased assessment. He could see what an amazing, creative, loving mother Harper would make. He wondered why she'd chosen not to go that route. Surely, men were lined up.

He'd seen it himself. Men, outside of the Cerberus Team, who were at the lodge, had flirted with her. They were monied and powerful in their various careers. She could have had her pick. Harper didn't seem to notice.

And Ridge had stayed close, staking his claim. Well, his aspiration.

Ridge had tried a different route. It was a gamble. But instead of presenting himself as a suitor, which Harper seemed to shut down quickly in others, he was going to inch his way in by building their friendship. Nothing to lose there. Spending time with Harper was always good.

Even today.

He'd hoped that her trip to the East Coast would give him the space to change gears.

Then *this* happened. Ridge put his planned walk under the moonlight and long talk about the things he hadn't explained to Harper on pause. Asking her to be his would have to wait.

"Are you okay?" Ridge asked.

"Yes." She cleared her throat. "It was just startling to see that. His face. The car."

"Take a breath."

She smiled and shook her head. "I'm fine. It's all good. I'm not going to upstage Berlin, so I get to keep my job. And everyone is where they're supposed to be. Shawna, home safe and sound with her family. The bad guy is in jail."

"Yeah?" Bob asked.

"Yeah," she said.

"Okay then, I'm going to put that in the rearview for a minute. You didn't complete your intake form. We need an emergency contact other than Berlin and a copy of your insurance card."

"Can I use Ridge?" she asked.

"If that's what you want. I could get the paperwork together so that Ridge could confer with the doctors if there were an emergency. You two have been friends for a while now. I'm sure he knows how to get in touch with your family."

"No family, just me."

They hadn't talked about family. That had been Ridge's conscious decision. And she'd never asked. Was that a conscious decision, too?

Bob scratched his head. "Mom? Dad?"

"There was a boating accident while I was in my last year of undergrad." She rubbed her hand up and down her thigh. "So Mom, Dad, my sister Vicky, my dog Clayborn. Yup. Blink of an eye. I supposed they were having a great day on Lake Lanier. The locals say it has a reputation for bad things happening. My parents weren't superstitious, though. If someone told them, they wouldn't have paid them any attention." She flipped her hands up. "Obviously."

"I'm so sorry," Bob said.

"Yeah. My art project I was telling you about. It was my catharsis. I took the art psychology classes. I painted the paintings, then I got rid of the paintings—sold, donated, out of my space with all the bad juju in each brushstroke. Those paintings are probably hanging on people's walls, stinking up their rooms with my grief." She was rocking, ever so slightly.

Bob noticed.

Both of them sat quietly, listening.

"I didn't know the philosophy about emotional energy." She brushed her hands through the air. "Energy in motion tends to stay in motion." She focused on Ridge. "Getting emotional energy out of my space didn't necessarily mean that it disappeared." She turned to Bob. "There's a school of thought that says emotions can be embedded into art. It sticks there in the oil paints. If I think about it too much, it makes me feel guilty. Maybe folks realized what they had and threw them out, or burned some sage, or something." She looked from Bob to Ridge and back again. "California." She laughed. "Babbling."

"It's allowed." Bob nodded toward Ridge. "He can be your emergency contact. On your medical insurance, you listed none. None?"

"It's cool, see? I wear an emergency bracelet." She held up her wrist, where a slim gold band had a blank medallion. "It has a website engraved on the back where I store my medical information. My directives and all. I just tell them the code."

"What if you're not awake for the code?" Ridge asked.

She said nothing.

"I don't want to pry into your medical history," Bob said, "but we choose the medical equipment that we carry with us when we're on assignment based on possible emergencies. Is there a specific condition that calls for you to wear that bracelet?"

"Nope."

Bob lifted a brow. He was back to looking at Harper like she was his niece. And his lifted brow said "spill."

"I've been a nomadic single woman for a long time. This suits my needs for medical safety."

Bob nodded. "Good plan. It would still be nice to have it on our forms."

She leaned forward and looked into Bob's cup. "That smells really good. Is it chai?"

"Would you like some?"

"I would. Thank you."

Neither he nor Bob fell for the ploy.

Ridge thought back to what Lynx had said that morning at the boulder. Zeus had sent her pictures about Harper needing protection since they were at the lodge. If he didn't have the history he did with Lynx and Zeus, he'd brush that off as nothing.

Too many red flags were waving.

Something was up.

Chapter 19

Harper

Leaning forward, peering into the visor mirror, Harper adjusted her black ball cap with the nighttime rhinestone bling.

Ridge was rounding the front of the SUV. He'd opened the door and helped her in. He'd complimented her on how she looked, though she looked her usual, black jeans and this time a silky black blouse. But still, her typical under-the-radar uniform.

This isn't a date, she reminded herself as he opened the door and climbed in.

Man, that smile.

Tonight, he wore a pair of black dress trousers and a smoky plum silk shirt. The fabric draped over his shoulders and chest in a way that would make every woman at the club imagine how those muscles would feel under their palms.

Harper knew.

She'd "lost" a bet at the lodge and had to give Ridge a back massage. It had required exquisite restraint to keep herself from licking her tongue over him. She'd had fantasies ever since about pulling off her top and bra, slathering oil over her torso, and massaging him with her boobs.

Ridge had brought an overnight bag in. They were going to sleep together tonight.

He thought she could *sleep* with him next to her?

Maybe if she took a long cold shower before she climbed under the covers.

They clipped their safety belts in place. The route to the club was on his navigation screen.

This was crazy. She felt *crazy*. Tingly. Happy. *Horny.* In love.

Her eyes sprang wide. What had she just admitted to herself? She stared out the side window, trying to rein in her galloping heartbeat. Love was *not* allowed, she reprimanded herself in the sternest inner voice she could muster.

Think about what that would mean to her. To *him*.

Think about the men, powerful and deadly.

Imagine your funeral, Harper. Your embalmed body in a casket.

Yeah, that chilled her blood.

Doused the fire of her lust.

Ridge reached over and put his hand on her knee.

Her leg jerked reflexively at his touch, and he moved his hand back to the steering wheel.

"What are you thinking?" he asked, clicking on his blinker and waiting while a pair of headlights whizzed past.

"Huckleberry Finn."

The lights of the oncoming car lit his face enough that Harper could see the laugh lines crinkling the corners of Ridge's eyes. "Okay, I'll bite."

"I see what you did there, fishing allusion."

He winked, then spun the wheel, pressing the gas, and moving them into traffic. "Catfish allusion, to be exact."

"Tom Sawyer and Huckleberry Finn got to attend their own funerals and hear what folks thought about them—see the grief that their passing caused." She tipped her head to the side. "This is morbid, sorry."

He glanced her way. Then kept driving in silence.

"Your funeral," Harper said after a while, "will be filled with an outpouring of gratitude, grief, pain, and exalting words."

"Yeah, this is morbid."

She leaned forward and adjusted the vent so it wouldn't blow the tiny hairs around the edges of her face, annoying her.

"There was another side of that thought," Ridge said.

"My funeral pews would be empty."

"Surely not."

"Today's my birthday."

"I had no idea, Harper." He turned her way, his brows crowding together.

"Did you know, according to the BBC's Quite Interesting, that one is likelier to die on their birthday than any other day of the year?" She wrinkled her nose and sighed out. "Yay me! A few more hours, and I will have beat that statistic for another year."

"I wish you'd told me."

She laid her hands flat on her thighs, fingers wide.

"A hell of a birthday."

"Yeah." She swallowed and looked out her window.

Ridge didn't say anything for the rest of the twenty-minute drive.

At the club, a valet opened her door.

She stood amongst a throng of glittery, satiny, highly perfumed club-goers, waiting for their turn to go in.

The keys were handed off. The valet drove away.

Walking past the line, straight up to the doorman, Ridge lowered his head to the much smaller man and told him their names. A scan down his VIP list, a nod of his head.

The door swung open.

Harper needed a stiff drink to drown the butterflies in her stomach.

Ridge went through the door, somehow reconfiguring her, so she was behind him, her arms wrapping his waist. He pressed one hand down to hold her in place; the other held up to steer them through the throng of heaving humanity.

She hated the claustrophobia of too many bodies shoved into too little space.

He reached around, and now she was tucked under his arm. Standing on her toes, she could see what Ridge was pointing out.

There was Berlin, CiCi, and DeWayne perched on a Victorian velvet couch in a cordoned off VIP area. Behind them stood two men in the Iniquus operators' uniforms, arms crossed over their chests, looking every bit like they could kill with their pinkie fingers.

They, like Ridge, stood head and shoulders above the rest of the club goers. When Ridge raised his hand in a salute, the men's heads turned their way.

Berlin was right; they were good looking men. The

blond was more college football, and the one with rusty red hair had more of a cowboy vibe about him.

Ridge turned sideways and was muscling them over. "Almost there," he said with that slow smile of his.

He was sexy as hell.

Harper needed to focus on her work and getting back to the left coast without getting her heart shredded.

Twenty-four hours and she'd be away from the chemistry.

Harper had much better control over video chat. Physical distance meant she could keep her emotional distance.

Not true.

She felt the stir of affection when they talked, when they laughed, especially in the comfortable silences that could lie long and amicable between them. One night he called when she'd just cracked open a new book. Ridge said that he'd been reading, too, but wanted some company. With almost three-thousand miles between their computer screens, they'd lain out on their respective sofas, reading.

Glancing up, Harper watched as he'd turn the page, catch her eye, and smile as he focused back down again. It was sweet. He was so sweet.

Harper supposed that he was getting something out of their friendship. She couldn't fathom what.

"Ryder's here," Ridge said.

Maybe the thing that Ridge got from her was that she wasn't after him; she had no agendas.

Ryder made his way through the crush toward them. Ridge stood and waited for him to catch up.

As Ryder wended closer, Harper could see the sly way women's heads turned, assessing. Their gazes caught on Harper, and she was dismissed as not a threat to their hunt. The ladies then licked their high gloss red lips, their panties getting we—

"It's nuts in here," Ryder called out as he reached them.

It must be exhausting for men like them to keep the harems away.

And then she imagined a painting of the guys, lying back against richly colored pillows, surrounded by a bevy of scantily clad women. Why would these guys *want* to keep that away?

Ridiculous.

Harper was just glad that Ridge had never mentioned the women he was bedding to her.

They started for the VIP section again. She was sandwiched between the two.

Maybe she was the "easy to be around fat girl." No pressure there. She wasn't putting out the "Pick me! Pick me!" vibes that needed to be turned down.

God, she hoped she wasn't.

She felt them and suppressed them.

She was just a girl whose job was to be a shadow.

The shadow was safe.

Seven months, thirteen days, and she'd have enough money to move on with her life. Onto a plane, over the ocean, and safe.

Chapter 20

Harper

Harper gave Gator and Blaze a little wave as she stepped over the cordon. She was glad Ryder and Ridge were right there, so the men didn't mistake her for a crazed fan. They dipped their heads in acknowledgment, then their focus came right back up. Their gazes were sharp as they scanned the room. With them standing sentinel like that, the crowd didn't even think of encroaching on the space to push against the velvet ropes.

She noticed that just to the right of the VIP section, before the massive speaker, was an emergency exit. It made it easy for security to scoop up their people and shove them out the door before anyone else could get there first, should something come up.

When Harper's friend Trish was pregnant, she'd located the nearest bathroom upon entering any room. For Harper, it was the emergency exit.

Making her way over to CiCi, Harper bent to give her the three cheek kisses—right, left, right—that she liked to use as her greeting. CiCi felt it gave her an international flair.

Berlin was perched on the edge of the sofa. Bounce. Bounce. Bounce. "Yay! Kiwi's here." She grabbed at CiCi's arm. "He's the one I was telling you about." She turned Ryder's way. Bounce. "Kiwi, can you do the Haka for us? CiCi saw them doing it on the TV when Matteo was watching rugby."

Ryder stood stoic. Maybe he didn't hear. Maybe he was *pretending* not to hear.

Harper bent between the two women. "Ryder is from Australia, not New Zealand. They do the Haka in New Zealand as a ritual dance on specially prescribed occasions."

"This is a special occasion," CiCi said.

"I don't disagree." Harper smiled. "But Ryder still isn't from the culture that does it. That's from a different country than the one where he was raised."

"Oh." CiCi dragged out the syllable. "Bummer."

"I know. Sorry." Harper nodded. "Have you gotten some good photos?"

"We have. DeWayne got some delicious shots of us on the couch. He cut the picture off at the guys' necks." She waggled her hand toward Gator and Blaze. "At least we got those pecs and biceps! DeWayne said you read him the riot act."

"It's important." Harper smiled. "Do you have your drinks? Is there anything I can do to make you more comfortable?"

"Yes! We want to take some dancing pictures!" Bounce. "Go and talk to the DJ. Make him play one of our songs." She pointed between Ridge, Ryder, and herself.

"Which?" Harper glanced toward the DJ's setup.

"You know." Berlin's eyebrows stretched high for emphasis. "One of the songs we did at the lodge."

All right, Harper was going to pick her battles. She knew exactly what Berlin was up to. Ridge and Ryder could decide how they wanted to handle her. Handle this.

Holding up a finger to signal she'd be back, Harper made her way behind the speaker toward the DJ.

There, he was making a show of how busy and important he was. Harper stood to the side. She could wait all night. And might even prefer it. At least there was a nice cool breeze coming off the guy's fan.

Harper scanned back through her memory to the lodge and which songs Berlin had preferred.

Belgian Malinois and German Shepherds could get rambunctious and destructive if they didn't get enough exercise. The handlers took turns putting the dogs on the handful of treadmills the lodge maintained in their pocket-sized gym. Harper had had to go do her runs in the middle of the night to make sure she was there alone.

To get their own exercise, Cerberus cleared out the ballroom.

Ridge said that from their inception back about forty years ago, the Delta Force had had a volleyball game at the end of their day. It was part fun, part teamwork, part endurance, and it had a lot to do with what Ridge called "Getting off the X." The ability to move and move quickly in any direction necessary in a nanosecond.

He said that it didn't build all the muscles necessary to quickly and safely change direction if you run in a straight line. She'd proven that true this morning. She was running in a straight line, completely unable to swerve from her trajectory.

While Cerberus kept the Delta Force volleyball tradition alive, sometimes their accommodations made that impossible. In that case, the team's second go-to was group dance routines. They pumped up the music. Off they went—hip hop, street moves, Latin, Caribbean, some jazz. What about a country line dance? No, Berlin would hate that...

Harper pinched the bridge of her nose, thinking back. Which routine did Berlin like best?

The Cerberus team had invited Harper, or anyone else who wanted, to join in.

Berlin had been in her element. She had a cheer-dancing background. She could stand at the side of the room and watch, making hand gestures to replicate the steps, counting under her breath. One, and two, and three, and elbow, elbow, hop, twist, fade...

The next day, she could line up with them and replicate their moves with a couple of stutters.

The third day she had it down pat.

Harper had to admit it, watching the team dance was one of her favorite times of the day. They were tight. Athletic. Graceful. Yeah, stunning.

When Berlin was back in California, she'd taught the dances to CiCi—of course, that's what they wanted for pictures. Ryder and Ridge, CiCi and Berlin being badass on the dance floor, everyone gawking in adoration.

The DJ looked her way, sighing heavily. "Yeah?"

"Request from Berlin Tracy."

He sat up straighter.

"Could you play a little K-Pop?"

"Yeah, sure. Name your poison."

"Broken Wide."

"You've got it. This song has four and a half minutes left. Does that give her enough time to get placed?"

Harper gave him a thumbs-up. *Accommodating.*

She spun back around the speaker to the VIP section. "Hey, four minutes, and then '*Broken Wide*' by Battery *Drain*."

"Oooooh! I love that one!" Butterfly clap. "Ryder!" Big grin. "Ridge! Ready for some K-Pop? Let's do this thing!"

CiCi was on her feet, dragging at Ryder's hand.

Ridge focused on Harper. If he didn't go dance, the repercussions would come back on her. She smiled at him and made little shooing motions. Then gestured to Blaze and Gator. She was fine.

"Oooh, child, this is going to be good," DeWayne was saying. "I'm gonna lay down on the ground to get the lights just so." He stepped over the velvet rope. "Don't you step on me."

Harper snagged his shirt and pulled him in. "Zero face pictures of the men. Zero."

"Psh, girl." He shimmied while making a duck face. "That is not at all what I'm gonna focus on. Thighs like those, and you think I want their faces? Where's the fantasy in that?"

Harper plopped on the sofa, wishing she had a drink.

The club went dark. The lights came back up. In the center of an overflowing dance floor, Harper could see Ridge and Ryder. Six feet three each. Looming large.

With the first chords, the first twitches of bodies, as usual, the other dancers pushed back to make a ring.

The whispered "Berlin Tracy… CiCi Cummings" rippled across the room.

And there they were, stars all.

Harper scratched at her chest with a sour-grapes look on her face. Where's the fantasy in that, indeed.

What was she thinking, putting herself in danger coming here to see Ridge?

Ridge was not for her.

And this was stupid. A body in motion tends to stay in motion. They were friends. There was no other path. It was a straight line. There was never a point where she'd be getting off the X and into something more. And now that she realized what she was doing and how stupid it all was, she could stop.

Just stop.

"Harper!"

Shit. She's back. That song had flown by.

"Harper, listen, it's a Latin beat! You and Ridge would dance to this at the lodge. Ridge! You should dance with Harper. You'd do that, wouldn't you?"

My god, could it sound any more like she was asking the cute guy to dance a pity dance with the wallflower? Her mind went to Jane Austen's *Emma*, the scene where Knightley danced with Harriet Smith. How had she allowed herself to become a Harriet?

Miserable. Miserable. Miserable day.

The smile faded from Ridge's face. He didn't turn her way. "Berlin, Harper's had a—"

"Sad day. It should be festive because you said it was her birthday! She deserves a dance."

Huh. Worse and worse.

Berlin stroked a hand down Harper's arm while she made a face at Ridge like she knew it was onerous, but

Ridge should go along with it as a kindness. When Berlin's hand reached Harper's wrist, she lifted it and thrust Harper's hand out to Ridge.

"Harper." Ridge held out his hand. "Would you honor me with a dance?"

Harper thought her face would catch flame; she was so embarrassed.

Sure, Knightley. She sent him a tight-lipped smile, letting him lead her out to the dance floor. As she walked away, Berlin grabbed the brim of Harper's hat and pulled it from her head.

Buried in the middle of the pack, away from laughing eyes, Ridge tugged her in tight. A hand on her lower back held her flush to him. They swayed. "I had wanted to ask you to dance myself. Berlin beat me to it."

"That's nice of you to say."

Harper had put her forehead on Ridge's chest and wished she could just erase this day. She had the photoshoot tomorrow mid-morning. The congressional speech was at one, then they'd be on the jet home to California.

Reaching for her hand, Ridge rubbed his thumb into her palm, then rested her palm over his heart, holding her hand in place.

Harper couldn't tell if the beat she was feeling was from his heart pounding or the music throbbing around them. Luckily, in this crush of people, they could stand still and sway.

And luckily, Ridge had stopped talking.

With eyes closed, she relished this moment.

She wasn't going to get her truffle oil macaroni and cheese or send herself into a birthday cake icing coma, but could anything be as good as this?

There they stayed, locked in each other's arms until the DJ decided that it was time to pick up the pace.

The mid-song switch was to a fast-paced rumba.

In college, Harper's first roommate had been an exchange student from Belize. They went to Salsa Club every Thursday evening. There, Harper learned more than salsa, of course. She had practiced most of the dances with a South American beat. It had been one of Harper's favorite things to do. It seemed to be the way her body liked to move. The rhythm that spoke to her inner dancing-goddess.

As the music chose its new chords, Ridge took a tentative step, testing the waters. He probably wasn't sure if Harper would follow him or not. But Ridge was an incredible, fluid dancer. No ego. No hesitation.

He had been so fun to dance with at the lodge.

The lodge had been a moment in her life when she could finally take a full breath. It had been like a time-out that had been absolutely one of the happiest periods she could remember. Harper wanted to be back there, even if it was just in her memory, so she closed her eyes and stepped left with Ridge. Moved her hips with his. Let him guide her under his arm for a slow, luxurious twirl out and a hot as sin tug that coiled her back to him. Down into a dip, brushing her hair along the floor, her leg bending up, with a pointed toe.

The air between them heated.

She started to admonish herself, and then she thought, you know what? It's my birthday. This is my cake. I *don't* care. I'm going to bathe in this feeling. Dive deep and be a mermaid in the waters. That image made her laugh.

And when she did, the smile on Ridge's face was a reward.

He gave her a nod that said "let's do this right."

One thing Harper had learned in her Salsa Club was that half the dance was the attitude. The seduction. Do you want it? You can't have it. Maybe you can have it. No, I changed my mind.

The dance was a tease.

It was the feel of her body as graceful as the lick of a flame and just as hot.

Too close?

Spin and cool the temperatures.

Too cold?

Slide up and blanket yourself in the man's arms. Ridge's arms.

He was smooth as silk. Graceful and bold. Exactly as her dance instructors had always coached them, the man is the frame for the woman's glorious colors. And that was exactly how this felt as they swayed their hips and traced their feet in synchronicity.

Just as he had at the lodge, Ridge knew that attitude was the dance.

And like at the lodge, he looked at her with heat in his eyes that made her feel beautiful, made her body want to show off languid lines.

Her voluptuous curves felt sensuous, luxurious, decadent.

His hand slid over her thigh to the back of her knee. He jerked her into his hip.

My god. If ever a man could get a girl's panties in a bu—

And the music came to a sudden stop. There she was, her leg draped over his hip, bending back with his hand, easily supporting her in a dip.

In the silence, he pulled her up, took her hand, and

spun her wide. And when he did, she saw that they were alone on the dance floor, and the others had gathered in a circle around her and were clapping.

"Yes, a big hand for the birthday girl," the DJ said.

Berlin had set that up. *Shit.*

Harper found her way through the crowd back to Berlin and CiCi. Thank goodness, they were sitting on their couch, their heads down, posting their dance videos to Instagram. They hadn't seen that.

Harper stood just inside of the velvet rope, dazed. Out of her body.

Ridge tapped Berlin on the shoulder. "Berlin," he called over the cacophony, "I'm taking Harper back to the hotel. She's hit a wall."

"I can see that. Looks more like she hit the side of the Grand Canyon. Yeah, you do that." She patted his arm. "Tuck her in tight." Then the sarcastic wink.

Harper just stood there in shock.

It was undeniable now. She couldn't hide it from herself anymore. She was gobsmacked, over the moon, crazy, crazy, crazy in love with Ridge.

Wow. Did that suck.

Chapter 21

Ridge

She hadn't said anything to him since their dance.

Man alive, *that* dance.

Had he stomped on things? Pushed? *I mean, we were dancing, and I was putting it out there same as she was.*

Maybe she'd just been dancing, blowing off steam on the dance floor, and now she wished she hadn't.

Her eyes had been fiery.

It sure had looked like lust. Felt like lust.

For him, it was. But this was cold.

She hadn't waited for him to come around and open her door.

Maybe that was too date-like, and she wanted to make sure she set her boundaries.

He couldn't read this mood. "Okay?" he asked, putting his hand on her lower back as they moved through the sliding doors of the hotel.

She nodded as she dug her phone from her back pocket. They arrived at the elevator bank. She stabbed her finger on the up button.

"Are you upset about something to do with Berlin?"

"No."

"Your job?"

"No."

"Me?"

She turned to face him. Her eyes wide, she rolled her lips in, rubbing them against each other. The elevator pinged. The door slid open. She flashed the key code at the monitor. The doors slid closed.

"No," she said.

"Okay."

They rode up in silence.

When the door slid open, she got off first and turned right toward her room.

"Harper, tell me how you'd like things to go here." He wasn't about to sleep in her room if she didn't want him there.

"I'd like to get cleaned up for bed. Let you get cleaned up for bed. Then I'd like for us to go to sleep."

"That sounds like a plan."

This was it. It had been a rollercoaster of a day. But he was going to do this anyway. She was leaving tomorrow. If she left them like this, it was friendship-zone from here on. He wasn't even sure about that. Even that felt fragile.

Okay. He was going to do it, tonight, *now*, he was going to tell her about Brandy.

She opened the door, walked in, and turned at the

bathroom. She left that door open, though. It wasn't slammed in his face. That was good, right?

Ridge shut the room door, twisted the lock, threw the safety latch. He went to stand just outside of the bathroom, his shoulder to the wall.

"How had you planned to spend your birthday, Harper?"

She turned, her toothbrush in hand, toothpaste bubbles around her mouth. She spat into the sink then talked to the mirror. "If you really want to know, I planned to sit on my bed cross-legged and naked as I ate macaroni and cheese, then went into a sugar coma eating chocolate icing off a piece or three of birthday cake."

That image came full-blown into his psyche, and his dick sprang to attention. He stepped back out of her view, reached down the front of his pants, and adjusted himself so the zipper could restrain his cock. It wasn't enough. He untucked his shirt.

"Not every girl, though, can say that they successfully stole a car on their birthday. It's memorable." She sounded like she was straining to be light and funny. The joke fell flat.

He moved back to a place where he could see her again. She had a cloth in her hand and was removing her makeup. He liked how she looked when she wasn't wearing any.

Or, maybe it was that when she wasn't wearing any makeup, he felt like she was trusting him to like her for her.

Something like that.

"I'm going to try to offer a way to reframe this. It was a hard day. A frightening, adrenaline-filled day. But someday, you'll look back at this with pride, and you'll remember that your actions saved a young girl from horror."

She shook her head. "That was you and Zeus."

"Nope." Ridge crossed his arms over his chest. "That guy's car was his escape. If he'd had the car, he would have been long gone before we were on the scene. Even if the guy had the girl in the car, we wouldn't have chased him down—no lights and sirens. A high-speed chase would have put innocent people in danger. We'd have called it into P.D. and stuck with him to the extent that we legally could. Those are our rules."

"You break the rules."

"We improvise where necessary. We don't break the rules."

She stopped and caught his eye in the mirror. She was starting to look a little more like herself. Whatever mood had grabbed hold of her on the way home was easing.

"After you took the car, he was plowing ahead without thinking. Once his adrenaline settled into his gut, he would reevaluate the situation, leave the girl in the thorns, tell her he was scoping things out, and if she moved, he'd shoot her. He would just walk out of the woods and get himself out of the area. A free man. Having learned from his experience, he'd come up with a better, more successful plan, and he'd act on it soon. A different victim. A string of victims. That's how predators work."

She hugged the towel to her. "You don't know that."

"I can guess that, given my experiences with bad guys. By the time Shawna figured out she wasn't being watched and got herself out of the bushes, she'd have to figure out where she was and how to get home. He'd have an hour minimum. You thwarted his plan. Today will someday be a source of pride, I promise you. '*Things that are hard to bear are sweet to remember.*'"

"Who said that?"

"Seneca."

"Ah, okay, Roman philosopher—" She picked up a tube of lotion and squirted it on her fingers. "Seneca's image came up in my art history classes. We had to apply some of his sayings to various pieces of art, as I remember it. He's used a lot on corporate motivational posters. Not the quote you said. Others." She spread the lotion over her face. "'*Luck is what happens when preparation meets opportunity.*' Which could easily be hung in the Cerberus hallway."

"'*Fate leads the willing and drags along the reluctant.*'"

She laughed, and he was so relieved.

She put on a Mae West accent and said, "'*There are more things, Lucilius, that frighten us than injure us, and we suffer more in imagination than in reality.*' That last one, I explored as a theme. I did a series of paintings of people being afraid of things that couldn't hurt them. Ha ha. One of my paintings was of me flying."

"On a plane? You don't like to fly?"

"I was fine until I went to Norway over Christmas break junior year. And now I fight a mild phobia." She closed the door to within an inch. He could see her arms moving over her body and her jostling around as she took off her clothes.

He cleared his throat and gave himself a good shake. Man, he wanted to push that door wide. "Are you going to tell me the story?"

"Imagine if you will a very bumpy flight. Imagine that there is no alcohol being served. Center seat between two people who were even bigger than I am. We weren't allowed to stand or visit the restrooms."

"All the way back from Norway?"

"The second leg of the flight. Amsterdam–Washington, D.C. Now, imagine the pilot coming over the loudspeaker every once in a while to mention that the turbulence is bad. Every time he did, he ended the announcement with, 'May God bless your souls.'"

"No."

"Worse."

"Sully Sullenberger worse?"

"Fortunately, no. But it was getting more turbulent. People were vomiting into their little white bags. The smell was getting to me, along with, you know, the lifts and drops. I was watching *Friends* on the inflight entertainment, thinking, whelp, if I'm gonna die, I might as well end with nostalgia. I wasn't watching it, though, just listening." There was a bump in the bathroom, a clatter, and then a burst of water from the faucet. "I had my tray down and was using it to prop my arms and head. It was the least nauseating setup I could configure. We were bumping around. I could hear people crying. Gasps as we went over rollercoaster-like air flows. And then, the pilot comes on and says we're approaching the airport."

"Home, safe."

She affected a man's voice as it would come over a radio. "'If everyone would please take your emergency instructions from the back of your seat pockets and review the procedures. May God rest your souls.' Rest, Ridge. Not bless this time. May God *rest* your souls. We were all going to die."

"Wow."

"That about sums it up."

"Why were you in Norway?"

"I wanted to see the aurora borealis."

"Did you?"

"Sort of."

"Okay…"

"Have you ever been to Mosquito Bay?" she asked.

"To see the bioluminescence?" Yeah, he'd gone there on his honeymoon.

He had to tell Harper. Tonight. After that dance, he had to act. He needed her in his arms, not as a friend, as *his*.

But he wouldn't make a move. He wouldn't even kiss her… Touch her. Until she knew, and then she could decide if she could deal with his crap.

"Yeah. I went there after seeing the pictures of the bright blue," Harper said. "It isn't that way at all. It's creamy mint green. You'd have to be trained to see the color to notice any. Not to say it wasn't one of the most spectacular opportunities of my life. I sat there in the bowl of the universe, watching the fish shooting through the water—the luminescent droplets dripping from my paddle. Anyway, the color for the bioluminescence only shows up on film. And that was my experience in Norway. The Northern Lights were the same color as the bioluminescence in Mosquito Bay to me." She opened the door, and she stood there in a long night T-shirt, a little see-through against the bathroom light, and nothing underneath. "A hint of purple. A delicate green. They swirled, and it was nice." She shrugged, then scooped her clothes off the counter. Frowned. "I have to use the…"

"Okay."

She pushed her clothes into his arms. He looked down at the top of the bundle. There rested the little lace panties he'd seen her collect this morning when she was changing from her running clothes.

She grabbed her clothes back and threw them into the closet, shut the bathroom door, put the faucet on full strength, and he stood there, grinning like an idiot. *Charming.* It was the only word that came to him. She charmed him.

He moved into the bedroom, so he didn't seem to be looming.

The toilet flushed.

The water at the sink turned off.

He grabbed up his bag from where he'd left it earlier today, opening it to find his Dopp kit. When she came back out, pulling at her T-shirt, he plowed on like nothing had interrupted them. "But, you'd expected the aurora to be intensely green?"

"The green showed up like that in my photographs."

He decided that things had smoothed out enough that he could change into a pair of shorts and a t-shirt instead of sleeping in his dress pants.

She bent down. When she came back up, she was holding the envelope, unopened, that must have fallen out without him noticing.

"Is this yours?" She flipped it over. "CaleBooboo Hansen." She blinked at it. "CaleBooboo..." She handed it back to him. "A handwritten letter in cursive. That's—" She swallowed. "Old fashioned." She moved to the bed and slid all the way over, up next to the wall, hugging a pillow to her. "Sweet." She forced a smile of sorts.

"Not really. It's from my ex-wife." And this was the entry point he'd been looking for.

"Oh." She blinked mechanically for a long moment.

"You were married. And she writes to you. And calls you CaleBooboo."

"When she wants something from me, she does. We knew each other before I joined the services, and we were married before anyone called me Ridge." He put his hand to his chest, and like a dork, he reminded her his name was Caleb.

She licked her lips and looked distressed, and even though this sucked—everything he was about to tell her sucked—her reaction told him they weren't just friends. If they were friends-only, this would be a non-thing. She cared that he was attached to someone else.

They were possible.

Chapter 22

Ridge

He picked up a chair from beside the table. Carrying it over, spinning it around, Ridge sat on it backward. He'd found that having the back as a barrier between him and someone in a tense conversation gave the other person a reprieve. He was big. And some people might even call him intimidating.

He crossed his arms over the back.

One hurdle down. Harper had feelings for him.

This next step, though, might be right off the high rise, into the air, and then splat.

Here we go. "Yeah, I married Brandy—" he pointed toward the envelope where Harper had left it on the corner of the bed "—right after boot camp. She was pretty and fun. The antithesis of the military. The yin and yang of my life. I loved both of them."

"How long were you married?"

"Fourteen years. From the time I was twenty until I was thirty-four."

"That's…a long time. Do you have children?"

"None of my own." That was another conversation. Ridge wanted to see if this one scared her off first.

"How long have you been divorced?"

"It's going on two years now."

"You've dated since then?"

"I have."

"Is there anyone in your life right now?"

A slow smile spread across his face. She was kneading the pillow. She was anxious about his answer. He dropped the smile. The person in his life right now was her. "I haven't been in a dating relationship since Christmas."

"Ah." She focused on the envelope. "You were a Delta Force when it ended. But she's still writing you letters? CaleBooboo. Are they love letters? Forgive me and take me back letters?" She sent him a wide-eyed face full of contrition. "I'm sorry. I'm poking my nose where it doesn't belong."

"I'm going to tell you the story, okay?"

She nodded.

Where to start?

"Brandy saw an opportunity, took it. Saw red and blue lights flashing in her rearview mirror. And then she found a new home in the federal pen. She'll be there for thirty years with good behavior."

"What? Oh my goodness!"

He took a deep breath and plunged in. "Back about ten years ago, now, I was deployed to Africa. Brandy had to have minor surgery, an ovarian cyst that was giving her issues. She was given oxycodone, and she got hooked right off. The docs cut her off pretty quick, the way they should have. Later, I found out she started spending money on going to clinics outside of the military health system—doctors who were known to take cash payments to write prescriptions. I had no idea this all was going on. Our communications were short and infrequent, given my job."

Harper nodded. A frown of concentration pulled at her brows.

"We mostly wrote to each other. I didn't see anything in Brandy's letters that made me worried. She was good at hiding her addiction. This went on for years. She kept a job. She kept up her friendships. There was tension in our relationship. Brandy always seemed glad when I was gone. I thought that would need some work along the way."

He paused to look up at the ceiling. How far should he take this?

Ridge decided he'd explain how things unraveled and leave it up to Harper to ask for details. He needed to make sure she got what she needed out of this conversation. Enough to make a decision.

"You asked about kids. I asked about them, too. Brandy told me that when she had the operation, the doctor said having kids would put her at substantial risk. And I'd never have allowed that. Ever. I brought up the possibility of adopting or being foster parents. That made her cry. I hoped that time would change her mind. But a kid needs to feel loved. I wasn't going to bring a child into a home full of resentment." He put his hand to his chest. "But I'd really like to be a dad someday."

Harper bit her upper lip and nodded.

"So the drugs. That was the reason Brandy didn't want

to get pregnant. It turns out that when her resources for oxycodone dried up, she turned to heroin. Since she couldn't afford her habit, she started prostituting. And as it turns out, her not wanting kids had nothing to do with her medical history. She thought that pregnancy would cut down on her clientele. I am always grateful that we didn't have any children. I was gone—I just can't imagine."

Yeah, in the end, that was the only bright spot in this mess. At least no kids were hurt.

Harper put her hand over her mouth. Her eyes stretched wide.

He flicked a finger through the air. "When I found that out, I had, of course, been sleeping with her. She was still my wife. I went to the clinic and had every test known to man performed. The condoms did their job. I didn't walk away with any cooties."

Harper blinked.

"Say something, please."

"Thirty years seems like a long time to go to prison for drug addiction or—" she held her hand out to the side "—prostitution."

"While Brandy was a prostitute, one of her regular johns hired her to go to a party with him as his date. She went. Big old mansion. Fancy cars."

"She must be pretty."

Ridge stopped.

"I mean. I don't know anything about prostitutes, but if she looked like she was strung out, the guy wouldn't have invited her to a party at a mansion."

"She was pretty, yes. And she was a high-functioning addict. At this party, she was looking around the rooms. She was carrying a big hobo bag like the one Berlin had this morning. I'm sure she was looking for things she could steal and pawn. What she came across was a table with money on it." He shook his head. "She didn't think it through. She simply wasn't thinking. She was around a pile of money. She had a bag. What she didn't realize was that it was a sting, set up for another set of bad guys, and she tripped that up. The bills were wrapped in bands with GPS capability."

"I…" Harper's hand came up around her throat. "I guess sometimes things happen. Things happen when we don't expect them to. I guess sometimes our bodies just act, and even we're surprised by it. Would never have imagined that we'd act that way, and then, there we are…"

"Maybe." Ridge's gaze was on her. He wasn't sure how to interpret Harper's expression or what she was saying.

"You don't think it was a freak thing that happened?"

"No, I don't. I think Brandy has some serious mental health issues. Looking back, they were always there. But we were young, and I thought she was edgy and fun. Wild." He glanced her way with a plastic grin and jazz hands.

"You were married when she was arrested?"

He scraped his teeth over his upper lip.

"What did you do?" She still had shock and horror written across her face. But also…empathy.

"My plan was to get her the best law representation I could and then the best mental health help. I was ready to re-up my contract with Uncle Sam. Instead, I signed on with Iniquus. The pay is considerably better. I couldn't have afforded much on my military salary."

"And the lawyer, he-she couldn't get Brandy off the charges?"

He rubbed his palms together. "The FBI was kind of

pissed that she messed up their work. It was bad. What she did had long-reaching ramifications."

"Self-medicating those mental health issues." She took a breath in and sighed it out. "Does she have a diagnosis now?"

"Bipolar disorder."

"I…" She shook her head. "I never studied that. But surely you realize that you can't love someone hard enough that they are healed from a mental health disorder." She crisscrossed her legs.

Ridge thought she'd forgotten what she was wearing. And he was grateful for that little corner of the pillow that covered her. Because his mind was telling him this was the worst moment to be a perv. And his body was still revved from their dance.

"That is something that needs trained professionals— doctors and psychologists. Families can't love them into better health any more than they could love someone enough to stop lupus or arthritis. All a family can do is be loving and supportive."

"And *there*," Ridge said. "I wasn't there. I was halfway around the world."

Silence lay thick between them. He gave her time to process, waiting for another question. She didn't offer one up, but her eyes did find his again.

"I hired a psychiatrist to work with Brandy," he said. "Part of the doctor's treatment requirements included me. I did therapy for six months. Eye-opening, I learned a lot about addiction. I don't take responsibility anymore."

"You divorced. Was that Brandy's choice or yours?"

"Mutual. She married the guy she was seeing on the side—her dealer. Pimp."

"Oh, wow."

"See? I'm sharing all my dirty laundry with you tonight. Sorry about this."

"No sorry needed." She brushed the hair from her face. "We're friends. I'm glad to learn about your struggles. And I'm going to admit that I'm curious why she's still writing to you from prison." Harper gestured toward the envelope.

The pillow shifted.

He bent forward and picked up the letter because he needed to look somewhere else. He ripped it open and scanned down it. Then lay it on the lowboy. "You're welcome to read it. And Harper, you're flashing me. Which I don't mind. I just thought…you know."

She pulled another pillow across her legs, her face turned pink.

Man, he loved her blushes. They told him that she was genuine. And kind. And so damned intelligent. When he made obscure references, she was right there meeting him. Quoting Seneca. Getting his plays on words. Being with Harper was just easy.

"I still pay for her psychiatrist to go work with her." Ridge jerked his thumb toward the letter. "Her psychiatrist encouraged her to write to me this time. Usually, she's just asking me to put money in her account so she can buy things at the canteen."

"How…sorry."

"What?"

"And if she has a medical reason for her bad behavior, couldn't, maybe, the judge let her out earlier?"

"Brandy has been picking fights. No one's going to go lenient on her."

"Her meds are off?"

"My theory is that she wants to get injured, so they

give her painkillers. I'm not sure she's going to survive the environment. They've moved her from housing with non-violent criminals to violent criminals."

"How are you doing with all that?"

"Conflicted. I worked through a lot of this in that mandatory six months with the psychiatrist. Though I'm not responsible, she was part of my family. I won't abandon her. But I also won't see her or respond to her letters. I skim down to the ask—money, reload her account, and pay her doctor's bill. That's the extent of it for me." He frowned at Harper. "I guess few of us get to our thirties without—hmm, I was going to say baggage. I was thinking about some friends with ex-wives who have custody of the children. That's not baggage. Children can be a complicating factor, yes. But Brandy doesn't complicate my life. But she is, in a small way, part of my life and always will be. I feel an obligation to vows that I took in earnest."

"You still love her."

"I do not. I loved who she was. I loved who we were when we were dating and a newly married couple. She isn't that person. I don't recognize her anymore. And so we've both moved on."

"Thanks for trusting me with your story, Ridge."

There was a funny little quiver to her voice. A different look in her eyes. He wanted to interpret it as… shame. Maybe discomfort. Whatever it was, it seemed to be inwardly directed.

"She's remarried?" Harper asked. "Does he know you're paying her bills? He's okay with that?"

Ridge dipped his head. "I met the guy. It was a hard meeting because I knew he was part of getting Brandy her heroin. Of course, if it wasn't him, it would have been somebody else."

"Still…"

"Yeah. Still. Being in that room with him took a lot of self-control. I wanted to make sure that Brandy had what she needed. He's not going to do that for her. My theory is that they married so they couldn't be compelled to be called as witnesses against each other. I'll admit, though, there's a piece of me that wants to pay the bills to satisfy any guilt I might have."

"*Guilt?*"

"Marriage, to me, is sacrosanct. I took vows, and I meant them. But when Brandy divorced me, all I felt was relief. I have a chance to find love again." He paused. Swallowed. Observed how she received that.

Their gazes met. Harper's lips parted.

Too much. Back the hell off. "Companionship. If Brandy hadn't divorced me and remarried, I'd miss that opportunity."

"Seriously?"

"I don't know how to interpret that tone. You sound… shocked."

"I am. I guess I've never felt that level of conviction about anything. And yeah, I have to say that I anticipate good days and bad days when it comes to marriage. Mundane, boring days… I don't expect it to be something out of a fairy tale, but if I were to fall out of love with the man I married, I wouldn't tie myself to them in misery." With each word, her voice rose and tightened down hard until she was squeaking out. "That's not one of the vows. It's not a vow that you should have to stay in a relationship that's toxic and abusive." She stopped suddenly. Froze.

"Do you want to tell me what that was about?"

Harper drew a breath in and sighed it out. "The idea of being trapped makes me anxious. Claustrophobic."

"That's not anti-marriage claustrophobia. It's caught in a dangerous relationship claustrophobia?"

She swallowed. "I don't know where that came from. That emotion kind of took me by surprise. I don't have an abusive past if that's the seed I planted. Average kid upbringing. No abusive romantic relationships are hidden in my dark psyche."

Ridge nodded, but his eyes showed a churning mind. He didn't know where else to take the conversation right now. He scratched by the side of his lip. Harper looked wrung out. "You need to sleep. Tuck in, Harper. I'll be here beside you. I won't let anything bad happen. You're safe tonight."

While he turned to click off the lights, she wrestled herself under the covers and rolled herself onto her belly.

He moved onto the bed beside her. On top of the covers, the way he'd promised. "Is it okay if I rubbed your back 'til you fall asleep?" He'd get himself changed once she was out.

"That would be nice. Thanks." She closed her eyes and turned her head toward the wall.

Okay, Brandy was hurdle number one. Now, he had to tell Harper about Rachel.

Chapter 23

Ridge

Ridge had slept surprisingly well. He'd anticipated a night staring at the ceiling. But Harper had gone unconscious almost immediately and had rolled into his arms.

It had felt right. Good. But as soon as he woke up, he'd untangled himself from her. He didn't want there to be anything awkward between them. He had this morning with her as a civilian, then he'd be putting on his Iniquus uniform, and their relationship would necessarily shift.

Tomorrow, bright and early, he'd put her on Matteo's jet, and she'd be heading back to California.

But they'd opened a new chapter in their story.

He felt good about things. About *them*.

Rolling from the bed, Ridge slipped into the bathroom to clean up, checking his phone for any messages that would have come in overnight.

Lynx: Text me when you have a second.

Ridge: I'm up. Are you?

Lynx: Alone for a private conversation?

Ridge: Two seconds. I'll call.

It wasn't about Zeus, or she would have called immediately. He changed into his running clothes, shorts, and a T-shirt. He took a moment to slip on his socks and tie his shoes. Making sure to click off the light before exiting the bathroom so he didn't wake Harper, he carefully moved to the hall door.

When he walked out, he flipped the safety bar between the door and the frame to keep it propped open. Ridge walked across the hall to a little alcove, lined in carpeting, seemingly made for the purpose of a private phone conversation. He hoped Harper didn't wake up and find him missing. That would start the day off in the wrong way. He'd promised to stay with her.

Ridge tapped the phone icon on his text screen to call Lynx on video chat.

She answered on the first ring. "Good morning. Zeus is fine." Lynx tipped the phone down, and Ridge could see Zeus was walking beside her. "I knew that would be your first concern. We're getting back from our morning run, just like I promised you."

"Thanks. Were Beetle and Bella jealous?"

"They went out with Striker and Jack. There shouldn't be any sibling rivalry in the K9 world."

"Okay." He shot a glance toward Harper's door. "I need you to get right to it."

"Harper."

"Shit."

"Yeah."

"Okay, what's going on."

"She doesn't exist. Well, obviously, she exists. She just doesn't exist. I'm going to tell you my red flags are waving."

It was the same wording Ridge had used in his own mind yesterday on their walk to the water's edge.

"I told you I'd look into things when we went for the walk yesterday."

"I remember."

"Harper Katz is not a person who has a birth certificate, visa, or any other government-sanctioned identification."

"I'm not Ridge either. You're not Lynx."

"Has she ever given you any other name?"

Ridge looked down the corridor, trying to remember. "She was telling a story to Bob yesterday and said her mom called her Kit-Kats."

"Plural?"

"As I remember it."

"I don't think that's going to help. Now, while Harper Katz is not an individual, Harper Katz *is* an LLC. This LLC was created in January of last year. I want you to hold on to that date."

"Okay." He did a sweep of the hallway. He didn't like having Lynx on speakerphone, but he wanted to see her face as she spoke. He'd left his earbuds in the room.

"An LLC requires a street address and not a P.O. box number. Harper Katz, LLC, is a box at a mailing store. It's allowed. No storefront or office supports Harper Katz, LLC."

"What kind of business?"

"Communications."

"In California?"

"New Jersey. Since California is three hours behind us timewise, I contacted Berlin's accountant last night."

Ridge scowled into the phone. "You put a bull's-eye on Harper's back."

"I didn't. I wouldn't do that. Berlin, DeWayne, and Carlos all have the same insurer on their intake. I called to check that Berlin's three staff members traveling with her were covered by the same medical insurance agency and see if they had travel insurance. If yes, could I have the policy number as part of our records?"

"Okay."

"Berlin, DeWayne, and Carlos are covered. Harper Katz, he said, has her own LLC and prefers to be an independent contractor. She buys her own insurance. They just increase her pay to cover it."

"It's probably nothing," he said. "It's just we don't understand."

"Okay. Here's something else I was able to turn up. Harper Katz LLC has been associated with Berlin Tracy since June of last year."

"January the LLC was formed. June, the LLC was attached to Berlin."

"Right. So what was happening with the LLC from January to June, I wondered. I think I caught the accountant a couple of martinis into his cocktail hour. I was able to get him chatting. And I posed the question to him, 'How did Berlin hook up with Harper Katz?'"

Ridge stared into the phone. Was this due diligence to keep Berlin safe, or was this prying into something that was none of their business?

"He said that Berlin had been drinking one night and had hit Harper's van. Since they were in Canada, that posed some legal problems without a lot of leverage. Harper and Berlin came to a resolution. That resolution included their contract with her LLC."

"Huh."

"And I have more. The reason that Harper is contractually living in Berlin's pool house is that Berlin totaled Harper's van, which was under a different LLC called Van Go Arts. Van Go Arts posted on Instagram from February until June of last year. Van Go Arts was a never named artist who lived out of her converted van, traveling around doing art commissions and mailing them off. There's a converging point. Van Go Arts, LLC, had the same street address, the mailing store, as Harper Katz, LLC. And Van Go Arts had one contractor it paid every month according to the accountant, Harper Katz LLC. He said that she'd layered the LLCs to keep her communications and her art business separate. But that he thought that since Van Go Arts contracted Harper Katz LLC and paid it monthly, that Harper was doing it so no one could pierce the corporate veil and figure out who owns the LLCs."

"Chatty."

"I'd like to claim I had superpowers to get folks to spill. I think I lucked out that the accountant was three sheets to the wind."

"It seems excessive, don't you think?" he asked.

"The amount of alcohol he imbibed? Yes. The layers of LLCs? I don't know. There could be a pragmatic accounting reason. It could be it's required if one business was communications and the other was arts. I called the store that had the mailbox for Van Go Arts. They said that the Van Go Arts box had been a six-month contract and had ended July of last year."

"January Harper Katz started. February Van Go Arts started. And the accountant is saying both these LLCs were run by one person. The person we know as Harper Katz. On Instagram, were there any pictures of the artist or just the art?"

"The pictures on her Instagram are of her van, which was totally cute, by the way, her art, the scenery, sometimes her feet."

"Her feet?"

"She has lovely feet. Also, it allows her to be in the picture without anything truly identifying her. While lovely, her feet don't stand out as unique." Lynx paused.

Ridge didn't know what to say about this.

"Van Go looks like it was popular, and she was making good money. You know her art. She's incredibly talented. We have to assume that she's making at least what she made before, working for Berlin. What we don't know is why she seems to have led this ghost lifestyle."

"*If* it is a ghost lifestyle."

"Ridge, come on. We're responsible for Berlin's safety. And this is odd, but does it rise to the degree where we need to intervene? Surely, Berlin has a clue about the setup. She'd have to."

"She wouldn't have to," Ridge countered. "She might have asked her lawyer and accountant to figure out how to get her out of difficulties with the accident."

"Do we ask Harper what this is all about?" Lynx asked.

"I don't know." He rubbed a hand across the back of his neck. "She said she's been living a nomadic life. Van Go Arts could be what she was talking about. I could try to work it into a conversation. On the surface, it looks like she could be on the run. But it's Harper…"

"We *could* ask her," Lynx said.

"She could lie."

"Would she lie to you?"

"Depends on the reason for all this, doesn't it? Would our

knowing make her feel endangered, and she disappears? Does she give us a simple explanation, and that's that?"

"Can you imagine a simple explanation?"

He stuck his hand on his hip, tipping his head back to stare up at the ceiling. "Not really."

"I'm going to add another piece to this puzzle."

"Wait." Ridge nodded at the guy in his exercise kit headed past him. When he got around the corner, Ridge said, "All clear."

"Gage went out to the K9 exercise field to talk to me last night."

What had Gage to do with this? "Must have been something not to have called."

"He had seen Harper in the cafeteria and wanted to take another look at her. He asked if I had her photo, which I don't. Do you?"

"No. She's not our principal. We don't collect those on people not included in the contract."

"But you're friends."

"She's camera shy."

"Huh. Okay. Well, when Gage texted me, and I told him Harper was still at Cerberus…"

Ridge rubbed a hand over his face.

"Do you know the circumstances under which Gage joined Iniquus?" Lynx asked.

"No."

"You said you're on a tight time frame, so here it is in a nutshell. Gage is engaged to Dr. Zoe Kealoha, a DARPA scientist. December a year and a half ago, note the month."

"A month before Harper Katz, LLC. I'm with you."

"Two men broke into Zoe's apartment and tried to kidnap her."

"Tried."

"Gage killed them. He was still a Marine at the time."

"Shit."

"Gage, with the help of Panther Force, tried to save her."

"Again with the tried."

"Yeah, it all boils down to Gage saw Harper, thought of her as associated with the crimes surrounding Zoe. He can't figure out why. It's one of those tingles in the hairs on the back of the neck feelings with nothing to back it. And it's making him, and I quote here, 'skittery.'"

"Shit."

"Have you got anything else for me to look into to figure out what her legal name is?"

"Yesterday was her birthday." He saw Lynx scribble that down. "Her mother, father, sister, Vicky, and their dog were killed in a boating accident on Lake Lanier in her junior year of college. I don't know where she did her undergraduate. Her MFA was from VCU in Richmond, and she did a show called *The Breath Before*, as, I guess, whatever the equivalent of a thesis is in the art world."

"Those are all good. I should be able to find her legal name through that."

"What do you want to do here?"

"Assume that Berlin knows what's going on and is fine with it. She had a lawyer involved, and the accountant said everything is legal. This search is an abundance of caution. I'd suggest that Harper has a doppelganger."

Ridge shook his head.

"I'm going to add this." She tipped the phone, so he could see Zeus. "Zeus sent me pictures of Harper from back when you were at the lodge. Zeus can smell a bad guy. And Zeus wants the two of you to protect Harper. Remember that he was mad that she's not sleeping in your bed and not in your apartment at the barracks?"

"Yeah."

"Zeus sent me pictures asking me to go to your car in the parking lot this morning, told me to feed her. He wanted me to give her a hug. Zeus wouldn't want her cared for and protected if she didn't need protection. If Harper's hiding her identity because of the attacks on Zoe, that's Montrim Industries—we're talking both military and political clout and billions of dollars. That's a formidable power. Harper would understand that. If that turns out to be what this is, Harper would have zero chance going up against them by herself. Unlike Zoe, she didn't have a Gage."

"Didn't."

Lynx nodded slowly. "I get that things have changed from a year and a half ago. But if Gage is right, Harper would trust no one because power can't be trusted. If I were in a situation where, for example, I knew something about those crimes, I could see myself becoming a nomadic woman, living in a van, with no name."

Ridge felt his muscles harden, his chest swell. If anyone was going after Harper—no matter who she really was—they'd have to come through him first. "What's your gut telling you, Lynx?"

"That not enough bad guys were rounded up in Zoe's case because of what happened to the D.A. Nobody wants crazy aimed their way. Also, Harper seems to have a knee-jerk, save-the-day reaction when bad things unfold." Lynx tipped her head. "What does your gut tell you?"

"That I'm walking a tightrope over a canyon."

Chapter 24

Ridge

He closed the door softly, slid the locks back into place, and paced further into the room.

Harper was still asleep.

He lowered quietly into a chair. It was uncomfortable; she was right. And he couldn't just sit here and stare at her like a goon. That would be creepy as hell.

Resting his forearms on his thighs, he dimmed the light on his phone and stared at an online newspaper, blind to the words.

Here's what he knew: For a year and a half, this woman had seemingly been living a shadow life. She'd done an outstanding job of it. She didn't exist. He'd searched her before to see if more of her art was posted. There was nothing on the Internet.

She wore black and a hat or oversized sunglasses when she was outside, ritually.

In her heart, she protected others. He'd never heard her say a word that put anyone down, never complained about her boss, though, he was sure that Harper and Berlin held very different views of the world.

He'd seen her personality up close while they were at the lodge. Day in and day out since the day she'd flown back to California, they'd been in touch.

And he always trusted his dog.

Montrim Industries was part of the military-industrial complex that Eisenhower had long ago warned America about. There would, indeed, be super spies swarming around Montrim, but Harper? No, there wasn't a fleck of anything that felt truthful in Harper's involvement in that mess.

And how would artist Harper have anything to do with DARPA scientists? That thought rang hollow, too. Those scientists had to go through tight scrutiny to get their high-ranking security clearances.

No, if Gage was right, and Harper had some involvement, it would have been by happenstance. Ridge couldn't come up with a single scenario where that might be true. Where power players would have contact with her unless it was possibly through buying her art.

Lynx would have Harper's legal name for him by the time he got back from his morning run. She'd have run that name through their A.I. systems.

Ridge didn't like that. He just wanted Harper to tell him the truth.

And then he had to consider his own truth. How long did it take Ridge to tell Harper about his ex-wife? The ongoing situation with Brandy had been a deal-breaker in the relationships where he'd told his dates. He'd learned to hang on to that information and make sure that the relationship was going somewhere before he'd brought it up. Since he made that decision, none of the relationships got far enough that he felt the need to broach the topic of Brandy. Ridge grew bored quickly and moved on.

Not with Harper, though.

Harper always had something interesting to say. And she didn't need to say anything at all. They spent hours over the video chat companionably and comfortably moving about their evenings. It was soothing to him.

When he told her about Brandy, she met the story with compassion for Brandy. And for him.

Harper stretched out and blinked her eyes open. "Hey."

Her hair was a mess, and her face had a red line across her cheek from her pillow. She was beautiful. "Good morning."

"Have you been up long?" She glanced at the clock.

"Nope. Just long enough to get cleaned up. I was going for a run and wasn't sure where you were in your training schedule."

"Everyday."

"Do you eat first or after?"

"Uhm. Protein shake mixed in my coffee. Do you want one? Or order what you want from room service." She pointed to the phone. "The bill goes to Berlin."

"Coffee and protein shake sounds like the breakfast of champions." He stood. "Do you just make coffee in the pot and mix?"

"Gross, I know. It does the job."

Ridge took the pot into the bathroom, filled it with water, returned it, and set it up to percolate. Their first morning waking up together. He wished the circumstances were different. Opening the fridge, he found the shakes.

She scratched the back of her head. "I have tall cups there next to the television. If you're doing that, I'm going to go get dressed."

She climbed from the bed, gathered her clothes from her suitcase, then headed into the bathroom. After the toilet flushed, she opened the door, so they could talk.

"You know, I was thinking last night at the club that Ridge Ryder sounds like a 1950's movie star or maybe a rock and roll band."

"You think? I'll have to tell Ryder that. It'll give him a laugh. Neither one of us can carry a tune in a bucket."

"Tripwire can. He's quite good, isn't he?" It sounded like she was talking with a toothbrush in her mouth.

"I was thinking about your name, too. Harper, it's quite unusual, isn't it?" He unscrewed the top on the first protein shake, not quite sure how she did this. "Pour the whole shake in?"

"Yeah, then top it off with the caffeine."

"Is Harper a nickname?"

There was a long pause. She could just be spitting the toothpaste out.

"Middle name that I use as a first name. My mother was a musician. A harpist."

"You're pulling my leg."

"Nope. She majored in strings. New England Conservatory of Music in Boston. She was playing in the symphony when she met my dad, fell in love."

"And…"

"He had a job that moved him frequently. You can't work in music moving around like that, especially with two kids in tow. She became a stay at home mom. Mostly unpacking us, finding a new place to live, and packing us up again."

"Military?"

"Middle management. Hardware."

"Oh."

"Yeah, I get that a lot. Anyway. She got to name me after the Harp. My sister Vicky was really Viola."

"Twelfth Night?"

"String instrument, but yes, they pronounced it like Shakespeare."

Her tone had turned cautious, so Ridge took the pressure off. "I had a friend in college whose dad had been on the Junior Olympic Team for archery. He named his son Fletcher."

"I like Fletcher. It's kind of romantic. I told you I was in school in Richmond. The tennis player Arthur Ashe was a big deal there. He has the Arthur Ashe Center, and near the museums on Monument Avenue, he has a statue of him. His wife had been a photographer. They named their daughter Camera, which is kind of poetic." She emerged from the bathroom. "Is it ready?"

Ridge held up the drinks.

"Down the hatch." She took hers and chugged it.

He followed suit, then wiped his mouth with the towel lying on the table. "What next?"

"Now, we run." She put her phone in her thigh pocket and walked out the door.

"I saw you on the tape yesterday." He shut the door carefully, and they headed down the hall. "You've been holding out on me. I'm kind of intimidated."

She pushed the button on the elevator and rolled her eyes at him.

"You think I'm kidding?" The elevator *dinged*, the

door opened, they climbed on. "What does your training schedule look like?"

"My short days are eight miles. I do that in an hour. My medium days are ten miles. Once a week, I do thirteen or more."

"How many marathons have you done now?"

"Four." The elevator thunked, and they exited in the lobby. "The first one was pitiful. It took me eight hours to run and three days of crying in bed. My goal has been to get my time down by one hour each year." Outside, she stuck her nose in the air and sniffed. "Oh, it's a beautiful day. This is going to be lovely for Berlin and CiCi's photos, not much humidity at all." She started her warmup stretches. "Anyway, this year, I want to be under four hours. And that's as fast as I aim to run."

"And once you hit that goal, do you set a new one?"

"Once I hit this one, I'd like to try triathlons. I'm not trying to set the world on fire. I just want to experience a new set of challenges. I'm not competitive by nature. But I am goal-oriented." She started off at a slow jog, warming up.

"You have a rigorous workout routine."

"For a fat chick."

"Why would you say that?"

She brushed her hand down to encompass her body.

"People come in different sizes. Sometimes it depends on their activity levels, and sometimes it doesn't."

"Sometimes it depends on the amount of Ben and Jerry's one shovels into their mouth at three in the morning."

"You eat healthfully."

"Maybe. Maybe it's just a show I put on when folks are judging me."

"Do you do that, Harper?"

"No. I eat healthfully. Except for three times a year. Thanksgiving, Christmas, and my birthday. And since yesterday got messed up—"

"And you didn't get to eat naked macaroni and cheese."

"God, you remember me saying that."

He popped his brow. "It painted quite the picture in my mind."

She snorted and took off at a slow jog.

"All right then. So tell me what the plan is for this morning. Am I going to be able to keep up?"

"You're a freaking Delta Force, best of the best."

"Thanks for the sarcasm of the jazz hands."

She sent him a grin. "Okay. I'm just going to run the short day. Eight miles in an hour. That'll give us time to shower before we're on duty."

"Can you talk and run?"

"Yup. I sometimes end up having to slide some of my work in while I'm running, depending on Berlin's schedule. I'd rather do that than skip."

"How did you get into long-distance running?"

"I read a psychological study when I was working on a paper. I was writing on perspective and the brain's ability to decipher distance."

He had to shorten his gait to match hers. But they fell into a rhythm. He could tell how she was slowly bringing up the pace as they warmed their muscles. "I knew it was going to be something besides 'I made a drunken bet at a bar one night.' What about that study inspired you?"

"I caught on the 'illusion of proximity.' There was an interview with an Olympic gold medalist, Joan Benoit Samuelson, right? So she was a women's marathoner who won the 1984 Olympics in Los Angeles. She came from a running background. She ran in college. She was only five foot two, which meant she didn't depend on long legs to give her the edge." She thrust out an elbow.

It was true, Harper was about five foot six, and he stood a good nine inches taller than she did. His leg length gave him the advantage in sports and in his jobs.

"Samuelson was setting records left and right, short distances, long distances. When she was in the Olympics, she ran so fast that she was the only person in the stadium doing the last lap to the winner's tape." Harper spun her finger in the air. "She is a phenom. So they studied her. You know, they wanted to discover what about her made that possible." Harper put her hand on her chest. "I'm not personally interested in the mechanics of her running. I was interested in the studies they did on her perspective."

"Mind over matter?"

"In a way. She said that her trick is to narrow her focus. She chooses a point up ahead. Like, I've already chosen that bench up there, do you see it?"

"Yes." Ridge had noticed they were running in the opposite direction, away from where Harper had been running yesterday, and he was glad.

"That bench is my visual beacon. Then I put on blinders to anything else around me. And you would hate this because it means I only have an awareness of what's between me and my beacon."

"You're right. I hate this idea."

"I home in on my beacon. When I pass it, I set my next goal and focus on that one. There is no sense that I'm taking on the task of twenty-six miles. I'd be exhausted and demoralized by that concept. Nope." They passed the bench. They were now up to her eight-mile an hour speed. "I'm running to the stop sign there, see it?"

"Got it."

"There's no way in heck I can get my fat ass down the road at eight miles an hour for an entire hour, but see that? I'm almost to my stop sign." She smiled. Her breath was coming a little heavier. "Scientists found that using this technique takes seventeen percent less effort."

"But you can't have situational awareness."

"True. You can either have a focused beacon and save yourself seventeen percent effort, or you can be aware. Seventeen percent less effort is significant to me, especially at the beginning. I spent a lot of time in front of my easel. My body was a slug."

"You worked through it. Not many people can run marathons. What are you focusing on now?"

"That person there in the pink shorts."

"Got her."

"Yeah, sometimes it's a geographical feature. Sometimes it's a person. Once there was a hummingbird just ahead of me. It was spectacularly beautiful, and I followed it…" Her voice trailed off. A deep frown melted her mouth down her jaw. She seemed to collapse as the memory washed over her. A sandcastle obliterated by a rising wave.

Ridge reached out and grabbed her shoulder, afraid she was going to faint. "What was that?" Ridge asked as she regained some color.

She had her hands on her knees panting, just like she had yesterday morning with the attempted attack. After a moment, she stood up, her eyes roaming the space a little wildly. She focused on the gas station the next block over.

"Did something happen to the hummingbird?"

"No," she whispered, starting up her run again. "It fluttered into a garden to its nest hidden amongst some honeysuckle vines." She focused so hard on the gas station that she'd stopped blinking.

"Harper." His voice was a command. "Tell me what happened."

Her breath hitched. She rubbed her thighs, then pointed. "I need to use the restroom, is all."

That might be true about needing a restroom. But she didn't tell him the truth about what happened when she had had her running blinders on and had set that hummingbird as her beacon.

A prickle raced over his scalp.

Something the hell happened. And it was bad.

Chapter 25

Ridge

Lynx: Katherine Harper Zelensky

Lynx: She called herself Kat. You said her mom called her Kit-Kats? Maybe it was Kit-Kat Z.?
   Harper Katz.

Lynx: AI search came up clean. Not even a parking ticket.
   Salutatorian of her high school in Memphis, Tennessee. Summa Cum Laude BA from Rutgers. New Brunswick, N.J.—same city as Harper Katz, LLC's mailing address. And you know about her MFA. She graduated

with honors from VCU—a top 4 school. Talented. Creative. Smart cookie. Def. not a rule breaker.

"Is everything okay?" Harper asked. She was done with her turn in the shower. Dressed in all black, her baseball cap pulled over wet hair, Harper closed the bathroom door behind her.

Ridge swiped his phone, disappearing the texts from view. "Text from Strike Force. The vehicles should be here momentarily."

"'Momentarily' is such a close protection kind of word." They walked out of her room.

Ridge was glad to see Harper turn and test the door to make sure it locked behind them.

"I thought that it's interesting you can run and text at the same time. You know our brains work on what we call 'system one programs' and 'system two programs.'"

She tipped her head up to watch his face as they walked to the elevator.

"A system one program is when we are doing something, and your brain is on autopilot. It's also when our brains say, 'Get out of the way, I'm doing what I want here.'"

She shook her head.

"I'll give you an example, snakes and spiders. By default, humans—though sure there are some outliers where this doesn't apply—are afraid of snakes and spiders. Until we learn better, it's our fight or flight reactions to get away from them. No thought at all. System two is learning that this is a garden snake and of no threat. It's back to system one again, when you know not to be afraid, and you can ignore it."

"Okay?" She pressed the down button.

"Here's another system two thing, learning to ride a bike. At first, it took attention. After a lot of practice, it becomes a system one thing; you can ride without thought. That you can text and keep your pace steady tells me you've done it long enough and accurately enough that it's become a system one, a sign of proficiency."

"I don't know how to ride a bike."

"What?"

"I've always had a fat butt. I'm not very comfortable on a bike seat."

"Did anyone ever teach you how?"

"Nope."

"You sat on a bike, though?" He put his hand on her lower back to escort her onto the elevator car.

"Nope." She pressed L.

"I'm putting that on my list of things we could try together—teach you to ride a bike. Your butt is perfect, and butt size has nothing to do with riding."

"List? Perfect," he heard Harper say under her breath.

He turned his head so she didn't catch and possibly misinterpret the smile that spread across his face.

Her round ass was a major turn-on.

They exited in silence and made their way toward the seating section of the lobby. The rest of their group waited in a knot for the vehicles to pull up.

DeWayne plowed through his camera bags, muttering under his breath.

CiCi perched on the sofa next to Berlin.

Carlos was aflutter, seeming to do everything and nothing at the same time, with an abundance of graceful arm and hand gestures, clucking and cooing. An exotic bird doing his mating dance was the overall impression that always struck Ridge when he was around Carlos.

While Harper wore head-to-toe black, including her baseball cap, Carlos and DeWayne wore some pretty wild colors for Washington, D.C. Ridge felt he could safely remove the idea of black as a uniform from his understanding of Harper's attire.

He looked out the plate glass window when he saw an Iniquus SUV motoring into the parking lot. Ridge lifted his chin toward the door. "The SUVs are here."

Gator rounded the first vehicle, opening the back door, standing ready to assist.

Blaze rounded the second.

Ryder stayed with the third. He had Zeus in his crate in the back. With Chew Barka. *This is going to be interesting.*

CiCi and Berlin affected regal airs as they strutted out to Blaze's car. The one in the protected middle, Ridge guessed.

Gator helped Carlos and DeWayne load their gear into the back of the first car.

"Is it okay if I ride in the K9 car?" Harper asked.

Dressed in the same charcoal gray Iniquus uniform as his fellow operators, Ridge opened the back door for Harper and helped her climb in. He wanted to sit in back with her, but protocol put him in the front.

"Hey, Ryder." She gave him a finger wave.

"G'day."

"How are the puppies today?" She turned around and wriggled her fingers through the crate holes to scratch Zeus.

"Zeus is fine. Chewie is… Chewie." He put the car into gear and followed behind the convoy. "I get his responsibilities today. Let's say that good ol' Chewie might not be up to the task."

"Yeah, well, having people around isn't always helpful. I'm sure it's the same with dogs."

"True," Ryder said. He pressed a finger to the middle of his chest and said, "Affirmative."

"I don't see earbuds," Harper said. "Who are you answering?"

"That was Gator in the lead vehicle. Our buds are down in our ear canals."

"Fancy."

Ryder peeked into his rearview mirror. "It's a bit of a drive. I'm up for a tale. Can you give me an example of unreliable humanity?"

He was glad that it was Ryder who asked the very question that was on the tip of Ridge's tongue.

"Okay, let me think. The last guy I dated. I was lighting a candle on the dinner table. A sudden gust of wind came through the window and blew my hair—I had longer hair then. It blew my hair into the flame. A bright light of the flame flashed. Realizing I was on fire, I yelled, 'Help! Help!' Boyfriend was right around the corner, mind you. And I heard back: 'Give me ten minutes, and I'll be right there.'"

Ridge shifted so he could see her. "You'd think he'd be able to pick out the difference in tone between 'I can't get the lid off the jar,' and 'I'm on fire.'"

"Go figure. Luckily, my body was doing its own thing. What is that? System one?"

"Yeah."

"Without thinking about it, I picked up the hose on the sink and squirted myself down. The ex came into the room." She pulled her head back and puffed her chest out, affecting a man's voice. "'What is that horrible smell. It smells like burned chicken feathers.' 'It's me. I was on fire.' So I learned not to yell 'help' around him. He didn't understand even, as you pointed out, with my tone, that I was in instant need. Fast forward. We were at a friend of mine's house. She has epilepsy. She started to fall down in a seizure in a dangerous space against an exercise mirror. There were all of these hand weights around her. If her head banged against any of the surfaces, she could kill herself. So I threw myself down. Wrapping her head with my body, to protect her, and then I yelled for him, 'Craig!' His name was Craig."

Ridge nodded.

"'Here. Now!' I was getting beaten to hell, and I knew 'help' wasn't going to work. My friend was obviously getting hurt. He came roaring into the room." She acted like an angry guy. "'How dare you order me around!'"

"Did he see what was going on and snap to?" Ryder asked.

She waved a hand over her face. "He stood there with a vacant expression. After a string of cuss words, I explained the situation. That we needed to get her over on the carpet, away from the dangerous edges, and he helped. But after twice being in dangerous circumstances and not being able to depend on him, I decided I was better off without that kind of person in my life."

"Probably," Ryder said.

"As an introvert, I like small circles of interactions. If I have only a few people around me, I need to be extra selective. Reliability and ability are important components in my friends." She smiled toward Ridge.

Friends.

Ryder sent him a shit-eating grin. Then focused on the road. "You're not dating now?"

"Nope. I've had enough bad relationships. As a matter of fact, I decided to take a year off dating altogether."

"What makes it a bad relationship?" Ryder asked.

Harper was quiet for the length of the red light. As they took off again, she said, "Me wanting the relationship too much. Not the guy's fault. The guy is the guy. I need to learn how the guy is the guy, and I'm me."

"What does that look like?" Ryder asked.

Ridge didn't usually need a wingman of sorts. But he owed Ryder a beer for this conversation.

"You know, one in which I don't have to change to smooth the relationship. I mean, part of the fun of dating someone new is that you get exposed to things that might not be part of your repertoire. And I'm not in junior high. I recognize that the guy I'm dating and I don't have to like the same things—music and movies, what have you. But we do need to have things that we mutually enjoy talking about and doing together. I dislike the abrasions of relationships. I hate fighting. The family I was raised in—it was a childhood with all the moves— could be stressful. There was some eggshell walking, trying not to upset my parents. It's a knee-jerk reaction to go along to get along." She looked at Ridge. "System one?"

"Yeah."

"And I saw that in my relationships. I suggest something, the guy doesn't want to, he suggests something, I go along."

"Then everything is about him," Ridge said, searching back in his memory to see if that applied to him.

"Bingo," she said.

Did she go along to get along? Ridge didn't think so because he liked that Harper's mind took him to new places, new ideas. They were pretty balanced, it seemed to him. He'd have to think that through. Pay attention. Ridge thought about the list of things he wanted to do with her; he'd told her he had one. Maybe that sounded like her own set of red flags.

"So you took a year off from dating. What were your goals?" Ridge asked.

"To find me again. To remember the things I like doing."

"Like...?" Ryder asked.

"Mmmm eating healthfully, not meat and potatoes. Fruits and vegetables. Not beer. Not champagne." She wrinkled her nose. "Not to yuck anyone's yum, but I dated this high-power advertising executive who always ordered champagne for me. I really dislike it. It gives me a headache."

"You didn't tell him?" Ridge asked.

"He looked so pleased with himself when he ordered it...meh." She shrugged.

"Yeah, I can see how that would be a problem," Ryder said. "What I'm taking away from this is that I need to check in with my date before I tell her my preference. Where are you in this year of remembering who you are? Near done?"

"Two and a half years in. Apparently, I'm a slow learner."

Chapter 26

Harper

CiCi crawled onto the blanket that Harper spread. "What should we do first? Tell me again what the goal is in these pictures?"

"CiCi and Berlin are here in Washington, D.C." Harper did air quotes. They were near the gift shop across from the Lincoln Memorial. Harper had been successful in dissuading them from doing a photo shoot at the Vietnam Veterans Memorial. "These are transition shots for the narrative that Berlin started yesterday from the hotel. And her mentioning that she had an emotional support K9 today. Topics for posts might be, uhm, patriotism. American heritage. The importance of the upcoming environmental speeches. The importance of taking care of your mental health." She focused on Berlin, who was getting her hair swept into what would look like a haphazard messy bun, but which was, in fact, done by Carlos's professional hand.

"Where are the puppies?" Berlin asked.

Blaze and Gator, with sunglasses this time, scanned the area and gave folks who looked like they might approach a staredown. Their task, Berlin said, was to try to keep folks from walking into their shots.

"This is a public space. There's only so much they can legally do, Berlin," she said under her breath. She was picking her battles. The men could handle Berlin on this topic.

Harper thought the Iniquus guys were getting more attention than Berlin was. If they didn't watch it, she'd get pissed. "I asked Ridge and Ryder to keep the K9s in their crates until we had things set up. The dogs are more comfortable in the air conditioning."

"They should have more control over the dogs than to need to keep them in crates."

"Zeus, yes, no problem. But then there's Chewie."

"Yay!" Butterfly clap. "He's the cutest!"

"I'm ready." DeWayne put his hand up by his mouth and called, "Doggies! I'm ready!"

Berlin saw Gator tap his chest, and he mouthed something. The doors of the SUV opened, Ryder and Ridge circled to the back of their vehicle.

They looked grim.

Harper could understand that. They were outside of their usual professional constraints with Chewie in tow. As Harper had discovered during her tenure with Berlin, everyone just needed to hunker down and power through this.

Carlos sidled over, extending a pink plastic bottle out

to CiCi. "CiCi is going to have a bubble bottle and wand. But I have a bubble machine, so no strain, CiCi."

"Thank you!"

"Berlin, you sit on the blanket. Let's get Chewie to lie next to you." Carlos tipped his head down with pursed lips and fluttering eyelashes.

Ridge and Zeus stood sentinel. They looked… *Whew!* Magnificent. Erm. Professional.

Ryder looked…bemused.

Chewie dragged at his lead, his tongue lolling out, trying to get to the blanket.

"Let him go!" Berlin called.

The bubble machine turned on and—Mayhem.

CiCi and Berlin collapsed on each other, laughing as Chewie leaped about, trying to eat the bubbles. He'd chomp down, then look up in surprise that it disappeared in his mouth.

Harper made a yikes face as she caught Ryder's eye.

He posted his hands to his hips, closed his eyes, and shook his head.

Jump. Pounce. Confused face. Head tilt. Head tilt. Leap! Chewie was such a goofy, sweet boy. Harper was laughing along with the women while Carlos and DeWayne egged it on. The Iniquus men stood stoic.

CiCi held the wand in front of Chewie.

Chewie lifted one eyebrow, then the other, then he tried to eat it.

CiCi yanked it behind her back, and Chewie chased after it.

Round and round and round.

"Good! You'll like these." DeWayne made a slashing motion across his neck, and Carlos cut the bubble machine.

Chewie stopped on a dime, not understanding where his toy had gone.

Ryder strode forward and grabbed up his lead.

"Nice. Okay, let's walk over to the Lincoln Memorial." DeWayne picked up his camera bag and slung it over his shoulder. "We can get that in the background. Maybe some of the Reflecting Pool."

Harper gathered up the blanket, and Carlos held up another one. He had a different blouse over each of his shoulders. Berlin moved between them and changed her shirt in the makeshift dressing room, then CiCi changed hers. Carlos reached up and plucked a pin from Berlin's hair. Now she had a high ponytail and looked completely different.

They started in the direction that Ridge pointed them.

"CiCi!" Bounce. Bounce. "I have the best idea!" Bounce.

CiCi caught her hands and turned to her friend, eyes alight, ready for the new adventure, bouncing with her. Bounce. Bounce.

Chewie pulled at his lead, wanting to go over and bounce, too.

Ryder held tight.

"I'm giving a talk about Guam," Berlin said. "You have water in your talk, too. What. If. We. Went there?!"

"Where? Guam?" CiCi held her eyes wide with excitement. "I have Matteo's jet. How far away is it?" CiCi turned to Ridge.

"About twenty-four hours from D.C., give or take, based on fueling and pilot changes."

"We could do that!" CiCi said. "We leave tonight. We were heading home to California anyway. We pick up a fresh pilot out there. Fly to Guam, spend two or three days, and fly back to California. We can put the boys on a commercial flight home to D.C." She flapped her hand at the Iniquus operators.

Harper became a statue. *Guam? Tonight?* She started moving pieces around in her head, everything she would need to get arranged and thought through. It sounded like Berlin meant to extend the Iniquus contract. She'd said "boys."

"Let me do a little research while you do this next setup."

A siren went by, and Chewie, while walking lazily beside Ryder, stuck his nose in the air and started howling in tune. His paws still a bit too big for his body as he padded along like a goob, singing a song. As Berlin would say, "Adorbs!"

Berlin reached for his lead.

DeWayne and Carlos jogged ahead, then DeWayne turned to walk backward to video the event while Carlos navigated for him.

CiCi and Berlin were arm in arm, bumping into each other, looking adoringly at Chewie. They tried on their own dog howls, and then the siren stopped. Chewie stopped. And Berlin handed the lead back to Ryder.

They rounded the corner, and Harper took up a spot under the tree, pulled out her phone, and started to research. "Right away, I can tell you, no dogs can come with us to Guam." *Did that mean no Ridge?*

"Yes! I want them there," Berlin called over as she sat on the bench and patted her knees.

Chewie climbed into her lap like a seventy-five-pound baby.

CiCi sat beside her with her feet up.

Carlos dashed in and rearranged their hair and shirts.

Stepped back to assess. Stepped back again to allow De-Wayne in with his camera.

"Yeah, well, we'd need more lead time. The dogs require a process. Paperwork. It looks complex and time-consuming. I can't get it done by tonight."

"Look for things we can do while we're there, Harper. Think, I don't know, surfing, watery things." She turned to Gator. "You surf, right?"

"Yes, ma'am."

Berlin snap-snapped her fingers. "How about you, Blaze?"

"Surf? Yes, ma'am."

"That's good. Let's try something else," DeWayne said.

Berlin pushed Chewie off her lap and stood, brushing her clothes and spitting dog hair from her mouth.

"Uhm, I see here that there's a place you can scuba dive with some sharks." Harper had her phone out doing a quick Internet search. "It's inside a tank. That could work from a photographic point of view. You know you'd get good pictures, and there would be no danger."

"Yes!" CiCi yelled. "I love that idea! Let's do that. And corals. Can we do corals with tropical fish? I can wear my little orange bikini. I'll look so cute. And you, Berlin. You would look amazing in scuba gear."

"I would, wouldn't I?"

"We'll need clothes that have an island-y flair. Carlos packed my things for Washington with only conservative-urban vibe, since I'm here doing serious things. Carlos can style you, too, CiCi. We don't need to stop by our houses and repack."

"This is going to be so excellent and such a great

follow-up! Carlos," CiCi said. "We need to look kind of tough. Like that Lara Croft chick."

"Angelina Jolie? I can do that," Carlos said.

"Yes!" Berlin said while Harper was making lists on her phone. "Angelina had great looks. Think tough chick wearing shorts and a belt and form-fitting tank, all of that. That's what I want. Harper, look up things that we can do so we can create a sporty, you know, badass, danger…" She held up jazz hands. "But nothing where I'll get scratched or bruised or anything."

"If one of us were to get hurt, though, that could be a thing," CiCi said.

"It could." Berlin nodded.

Harper followed Berlin's gaze as she turned to Ridge.

Zeus sat stoically. Ridge's eyebrows moved up his forehead toward his hairline.

"Nothing bad," Berlin said with a twist of her shoulders. "I know you boys wouldn't let anything bad happen. Not like a poisonous snake bite." She looked at Harper. "Are there poisonous snakes?" She looked back at Ridge. "I don't want any, you know, permanent thing. No scars. But if a little something were to happen that we could juice up by selective photography, that could be good."

Harper needed to cut this line off. "I think, Berlin, that you want to show that you can be successful on location. If you run publicity off an illness or injury, then you lose the reputation you're trying to build."

Berlin pointed at her. "Right. Good thinking."

CiCi made a pout face. "We need to add on to our time in Guam. Twenty-four hours in the air will be horrible for our skin. Dry. Awful. Red eyes. Even sleeping in the jet bed will be difficult."

"I could see if I can schedule a spa day for the first day we get there," Harper suggested.

"Oh, passports!" Berlin said. "I guess we need to make a stopover in California anyway. We can get our passports then."

Harper shook her head. "Guam is a US territory."

They blinked at her.

"People who live on the island are US citizens."

They blinked again.

"It's like flying from California to Hawaii. You don't need a passport."

"Oh!" CiCi grinned. "Then, it's easy!"

Berlin snapped her fingers and pointed at Harper. "Okay, Harper, you plan. Carlos! While we're giving our speech, DeWayne needs to stay and photograph us. But I want you to get a Lyft or something and go get us clothes. Some Angelina like, but I'm also remembering that my agent said there was a script floating around out there, kind of like a Bond film. Yes to the Angelina jungle cat but also some Pussy Galore."

"Berlin, I hate to be the one to remind you of March when we tried the action shots…" DeWayne said.

"Do it like the sharks in the tank. It doesn't have to be real. People just need to believe that's what we're doing. Gator and Blaze say they know how to surf. CiCi and I can just show them how to do a couple of cheerleader lifts, and we don't have to surf at all. Gator and Blaze can just hold us up over their heads while *they* do the surfing!"

"Yay! Fun!" CiCi grinned.

Harper held her head very still so as not to look around and see the men's reactions.

"Action! Action! And sexy!" CiCi struck a pose where

she spiked her butt up in the air and looked over her shoulder.

DeWayne snapped the picture.

"There's not much that's sexy about bleached corals and a dying ocean," Harper said under her breath. Louder, she said, "There are two major military bases on Guam. You could go pay your respects to the troops who are so far from home."

CiCi pointed. "Clever girl. I look good next to a man in uniform. Those pictures from the club last night got a shit ton of likes."

"You're mentioning in your speech, Berlin, that Guam is beginning to have reduced freshwater during the dry season. There's increasing damage from flooding and typhoons and an increased average air temperature, which means days when the heat index is dangerously high, will become more common and impede military operations. So you can show them images that support your speech."

"I said sexy," Berlin pouted, "and the speech *you* wrote isn't sexy at all."

"Okay. I'm going to remind you that sexy, here, isn't your goal. You're interested in the role of Giselle Newcomb in Heatwave. She's an advocate that was taken seriously by the legislature in real life. That's why I got you booked for this event and styled your speech to catch the people's attention on the various committees so Hollywood can see you in that environment and can picture hiring you for the film. And that's why Carlos is styling you in red. Not only is it correct color psychology for your task, but the dress is very similar to the one Giselle wore in her presentation to the same committee."

"But not too obvious, right?" Berlin raised her brows.

"You and Giselle have very different figure types.

Giselle is more like me, so no, it won't be too obvious to anyone."

"No, no one would ever think of me while looking at you."

The women moved closer to the water, and Berlin grabbed at Chewie's lead.

"Uhm, the water…" Ryder started.

Berlin batted a go-away hand at him. "Sexy environmentalists!" she said to Carlos, bending to hug Chewie. "Get on that."

DeWayne snapped the picture.

Berlin turned, and CiCi grabbed her hands and screamed while doing a little dance. "We're going to Guam!"

Chewie had been lumbering along the edge of the Reflecting Pool, but when CiCi grabbed Berlin, Berlin yanked Chewie's lead, and he lost his balance.

Huge splash.

Shrieks went up as Berlin and CiCi covered their heads to protect themselves from the shower.

Ryder hauled Chewie out, sopping wet.

With his free arm, Ryder tried to push CiCi and Berlin out of the way, but they wouldn't budge.

Chewie jingled his collar and sent up a spray as he shook the water from his coat.

DeWayne snapped pictures, yelling, "Yum! These are delicious! Keep going!"

Chapter 27

Harper

Harper stood at her hotel room window, watching a couple by the water fountain. They looked blissfully in love.

Her phone sounded with Ridge's dedicated ringtone. Of course, it did. It happened almost without fail. It was the etheric joke. "Hello?"

Ridge smiled at her via video call. "What are you doing?"

"Feeling overwhelmed." She put her hand to her forehead. "Berlin expected me to figure out Guam, and Guam isn't happening. There was a lot of reconfiguring to do, but I think it's handled now."

"Yeah, Lynx called and said there was a change of plans. We're going to Camden, New Jersey? That's a major shift."

"You're telling me. It's the best I can do, short notice."

"Lynx said you're keeping Gator and Blaze, and Bob said you requested Ryder and me."

"Is that okay? I know Voodoo is convalescing. Does Ryder need to be with him? What about Zeus? This would be a no K9—I don't know, what do you call it? Deployment?"

"Assignment. Ryder and I do close protection without the K9s fairly frequently. It's not a problem. In this case, Lynx's dogs, Beetle and Bella, went to the training farm to help out with something. Lynx said she'd keep Zeus until I got back. Tripwire has Voodoo covered."

Harper moved her hand from her head to her heart. "It's for the day. We leave out in the morning and fly back by nine tomorrow night. Staying at The Lily solves all kinds of logistical problems."

"Two flights in one day."

"Stop. Please. I don't need the hives. Inevitable, but I'd like to delay them."

"Why was Guam nixed? And why Camden?" His phone jostled as he repositioned. "Strike Force has your schedule. They're developing the close protection plans. I haven't seen them yet."

"Are you in the SUV?"

"Yeah, Ryder's filling the tank."

"About Guam." She paused to take a sip of water. "It's the rainy season there. The weather says it's going to be pouring rain for the next week. Even if CiCi and Berlin were inside seeing the military and swimming in the shark tank, Carlos would be freaking out. High humidity. Frizzy hair to battle."

"Ah."

"So we're going to Camden. They have an aquarium

where they have a dive tank with air hoses, so scuba equipment isn't needed. They brought in specialized equipment for another group to use. Neither Berlin nor CiCi knows how to scuba dive."

A smile twitched the corners of his mouth, and Harper wondered what he was thinking.

"We leave in the morning," she said. "We come back tomorrow night. I just didn't want to deal with all of CiCi and Berlin's luggage and other hassles. Plane. Lunch. Shark dive. Home. Well, The Lily."

"I think they have tourist diving at the National Aquarium in Baltimore. You could skip the plane ride."

"I checked. They're booked solid. Same with Caribbean Coral Reef down at Disney. I lucked out with the one in New Jersey. I mean, *really* lucky. I called the booking office just as the lady was getting off the phone with a private dive cancellation. Apparently, the guy was going to propose underwater, but they broke up last night. They have an underwater photographer scheduled and everything. Carlos and DeWayne can be there and do their thing. They just don't have to do their thing in the tank. Which, knowing both of them, is good."

"Bummer about the couple, though."

"You never know," she said. "It might be for the best. And I don't have to say no to Berlin, just tweaking the plans a bit."

"Are the women back?"

"No, and I'm not expecting them. Here's what's happening as of three minutes ago—Berlin and CiCi hooked up with a couple of Washington high rollers at their lunch table. They are taking the cars with Gator and Blaze around D.C. for a tour. At five, Iniquus will drop Berlin and her friends off at some private club. I'm told it's high security. As such, no outside cameras, stylists, or close protection are allowed. Iniquus will drop Carlos and DeWayne off here. Then they're off for the night."

"That's a new development. What's the plan for transporting CiCi and Berlin back to The Lily?"

"I hired a limo. Iniquus doesn't have to worry about it. You all are dismissed at five this evening and are back on schedule tomorrow at ten to head to the airport."

"Your job is like a juggling act."

"Feels that way." She offered up a wry smile.

"Okay, what about you?"

Harper moved further into her room. "What about me?"

"What are you doing for dinner?"

She pulled her sketchbook from the drawer. "Belated birthday." Harper focused on Ridge's face. Even sitting in the car, she could see his eyes darken. Harper hadn't been off the dating field so long that she didn't recognize lust when she saw it. "You just pictured me naked with macaroni and cheese, didn't you?"

"Would that be a bad thing?"

Harper's own dose of desire flooded her system. "Uhm, no. Actually. That wouldn't be bad at all." Was she going to do this? "If I ordered for two, would you come? I mean," she floundered, realizing the double entendre. "It's not dinnertime yet. But we could find something fun to do if you'd like." Yeah, apparently, she was going to do this.

"I would like. Very much so."

His wolfish smile told Harper she hadn't misinterpreted this conversation.

"Forty minutes, okay? I'll have Ryder drop me."

"Yup." Shit. Shit. Shit. This was *not* friend-zone behavior.

"Shall I bring in my overnight bag?"

"Yup." And, apparently, she didn't care.

"Forty minutes then."

She tapped the button, bringing the phone to her lips. If Harper looked up inner conflict in the dictionary, she bet she'd find this scenario as an example.

Okay—she talked herself down—not much was changing. She was still heading back to California in the next twenty-four hours. She'd deal with the fallout. She could very consciously put the existential crisis on hold until then. Right?

When the tap finally sounded at her door, Harper was ready. She'd changed into a wrap dress that would come apart with the tug of her belt. Underneath, she wore a lingerie set that made her feel the most beautiful, voluptuous, and luxuriant.

Sure the women's magazines were always telling her she wasn't worthy. But in Harper's experience, men liked what they liked. Some might say in public that they wanted what was on the shiny covers, but she knew that her body was desirable in private. That she was sexy. She could find a sex partner anytime she wanted one.

It's just that she hadn't wanted one in quite a while.

And certainly, she'd never wanted anyone as much as she wanted Ridge.

"Coming." Harper peeked into the mirror as she passed and took a second to fuss at one of the natural waves in her auburn hair, encouraging it to go in the most flattering direction.

She must be Ridge's type. He said her butt was perfect.

Harper twisted to look over her shoulder. Yeah, her butt was pretty good. Perfect? A smile slid across her face with laughter wiggling the corners of her lips.

Skipping over to the door, a quick check through the security viewer, and she tugged the knob.

Ridge was still in his Iniquus uniform. He held a vase of exotic flowers with happy birthday picks, both festive and elegant.

His smile warmed his eyes. And then, Harper saw his gaze heat.

Her outfit was sending off the right signals.

"Thank you." She accepted the vase and moved into the room, a lilting sway to her hips. As she set the flowers in the middle of the table, she could hear him throw the latch. Harper lifted her cell. "I'm putting my phone on airplane mode."

"Same," he said.

She turned, and there he was, hard muscles displayed under a compression shirt. "I like your uniform."

Ridge said nothing.

She licked her lips. "Take it off."

On demand, off came the shirt. His arms opened wide. Harper slid forward and laid her cheek against his chest, letting herself breathe. Letting herself switch gears. Work to play—friends to lovers.

It took only two breaths.

She tipped her head up. His lips found hers. Soft.

Another kiss then he lifted to hover, barely touching, she could feel his smile.

"I thought so" was what he said. He pressed another kiss against her mouth.

"Thought what?"

"That it would feel like this." He pulled her flush against him.

His lips tickling her neck made her wriggle, her nerves bright with expectation.

His hard-on pressed against her belly, and her body responded, making her warm and wet. Needy.

Desire spun her head, danced over her nerves, left her panting.

"This feels perfect."

Perfect. She didn't mind that was the adjective he seemed to pick for her.

Ridge stepped back and tugged her belt, watching as the cloth draped open. "Like it has always been." He petted his hand, warm and calloused, down her side, making her skin feel silken and womanly.

He pulled her close again, his lips resting in her hair. Scooping his thumbs under her dress's shoulders, Ridge drew the satin slowly down her arms, letting it fall in a pool at her feet.

He stopped and breathed deeply. His exhale told her that this right here, not even moving further, was something he'd wanted. That her in his arms this way was satisfying. Just here. Just the two of them. He was right; it felt like they had always been.

His words hummed over her system as he stepped them closer to the bed.

"I want the lights on. I want to look at you," Ridge said.

She swung a foot back onto the bed and lowered herself to the mattress. She moved back to the center, giving Ridge room to join her.

He stood back, his eyes intensely focused on her. It

was as if he were drinking her in. Giving her space in his inner world. A place of importance.

The way he looked at her made her feel like a queen on the throne. Yes, if she was painting a canvas to capture the way Ridge was looking at her now, she would try to capture the essence of chivalry and strength.

Harper stroked her hands over the satin of her bra. She traced the lace with her fingers, circling around the areolas, her nipples hardening with the attention.

With a luxuriant stretch, Harper allowed herself to become soft.

Sex was a dance. And while Ridge gracefully undressed, she used the time to relax into her femininity.

She dipped her head to hide her smirk as he moved naked and lithe to the bed.

"What was that?" he asked.

"Oh, you know—" she looked up, coyly slipping one strap of her bra down her shoulder "—one of the first things I noticed about you was the size of your feet." Then came the other strap. She lifted her breasts, holding the satin in place while her other hand sought around the back to unclasp the hooks. "You don't disappoint, Mr. Hansen." She tossed the bra to the side.

"At your service, Ms. Katz."

His hands on her thighs, his mouth on her breasts, felt as satisfying and right as a well-composed canvas—one where she'd worked patiently to build the layers of pigment. And, now that she was adding the last layer, the painting could sing.

A symphony, really.

A sensory masterpiece.

He dipped her back, his lips to her neck, trailing kisses down to her belly.

Just like at the club, he reached under her knee and pulled her leg over his hip, rasping her clit on his thigh.

But while their rumbas on the dance floor had been fun and heady, sex with Ridge satisfied a deep hunger in her and conversely made her realize how starved she had been.

The perfection of Ridge inside her, stretching her, filling her, moving with her.

The salt of their sweat on her tongue.

The low sweep of their moans of pleasure.

Their bodies already knew how to move together from their dancing.

Voraciously. Gluttonously. Insatiably.

Ridge and Harper made love all afternoon, all night, and in the morning, after her last orgasm, she exhaustedly admitted, "I do believe I've crossed the finish line on a marathon." She laced her fingers with Ridge's, stretching her arm up where she could see their entwined hands in the tiny bit of sunlight that peeked past her closed curtains.

"Thank god." Ridge chuckled. "If you bounced out of bed this morning for an eight-mile run, I'd be in trouble."

Trouble. That was exactly what Harper was thinking. What had she done?

Chapter 28

Ridge

"I can't believe I'm going to New Jersey instead of Guam," Berlin grumped, sliding into the seat just inside of the jet's door.

When she settled, Harper handed Berlin a travel mug of coffee: Triple, Venti, Half Sweet, Non-Fat Caramel Macchiato, with a "kiss" of whipped cream.

The pilot climbed on board. "Is everyone set? The weather created some early morning delays. Enjoy your coffees, relax. We'll have a runway in about twenty minutes or so. We're in queue, and I can make up the time once we're in the air." He stepped forward to his seat.

CiCi came up the steps, hand on her head, looking thoroughly hungover.

"Have you heard from Matteo this morning?" Berlin

asked. "Did you tell him about our great success giving the speeches?"

CiCi batted a hand at Berlin. "I'm going to lay down." She wended her way to the back of the plane to the tiny bedroom.

The plane's setup consisted of three sections, four seats on the right-facing, three seats on the left, in the front. One less because of the door.

Carlos and DeWayne sat in the mid-section. Two sets of side by side rows, facing forward next to the galley. The men had their phones out and were busy scrolling.

There was a bathroom behind the back seats.

And in the very back of the jet was the bedroom, where CiCi disappeared. It was basically a room filled with a king-sized mattress and a space to stand while you shut the mirrored door.

Ridge sat on the right alongside Gator, Blaze, and Ryder.

Berlin pulled the handle to recline and prop up her feet. Her coffee in the holder, top off to cool.

Harper sat next to the galley, leaving a space between her and Berlin.

"Have you been working for Berlin long?" Ryder asked Harper. "How did you two meet?"

"A year in June," Harper said as if that was the only thing he needed to know.

"We met up in Canada." Berlin floundered around, trying to get comfortable. "I was skiing. Harper and I crossed paths while she was heading south."

"What was your trip about, just exploring?" Ridge was looking at Harper.

"Oh, I'd gone up north to swim in the Arctic Ocean. It's my goal to swim in every ocean and every sea. So far, I've done Pacific, Atlantic, Indian, and the Arctic. Just one more of those to go."

"The Arctic Ocean, I've done some winter training up there," Blaze said. "It's a harsh landscape."

"It was. And a challenge to capture in my art."

"Was that your idea of a vacation?" Ridge asked. "Did your job send you up there?"

"Job?"

Her gaze scanned over the plane's interior. She seemed uncomfortable—would she mention Van Go Arts, or was she keeping that a secret?

"No. My family died when I was in college. I inherited their estate. Not huge. But some. It was enough, if I lived frugally, to let me just do my art. I mean, I mostly supported myself on tourist art at that time. But I had a home studio, and I could do canvases that were just for me. That trip was to feed my imagination. Art leaving my imagination to go on canvas means I need new doses of ideas going in to fill the empty spaces. What time of the year were you up there, Blaze?" She turned the conversation away from herself.

It was another piece of information. He stored that away.

"Winter," Blaze said with a wry smile. "Snag, Yukon. It got down to negative eighty-three one night."

"That's like a twenty-dog night?" Ryder asked.

"It was a night when you just wrapped your body around the potbelly stove and prayed. Actually, I was in an igloo, and it wasn't all that bad with the right parka and the right sleeping bag. An interesting experience."

"I was there in June, and it was in the low seventies. I was comfortable in my little van home."

A point for Lynx. She'd figured that out.

"A nomad," Gator said with a grin.

Harper nodded.

"You said this had to do with your art. What were you working on?" Blaze asked.

"Oh, let's see, I was developing my ability to be conservative with my strokes and, at the same time, create a dynamic and evocative line. The north was a challenge for sure. The culture was very different. Looking back at it, it was a terrible trip. Things just kept going wrong. But that's the interesting thing about memories, isn't it?" She turned to Ridge. "You and I were talking about the Seneca quote, weren't we? *Things that are hard to bear are sweet to remember.*"

"Right." Ridge hoped she'd keep talking. This was information. The money from her family. He still didn't get the why of her working for Berlin. It wasn't the why behind the mystery of her shadow life. But the more he knew, the better he could support Harper. The most important thing, though, was for her to feel safe with him. Know that she could trust and lean on him if something were happening, and she needed help.

If he pushed, and Harper ran because of it, he would lose all ability to intervene should she need him.

Harper focused on Blaze when she said, "When you look back at things you know were flat-out miserable—even negative eighty-degree nights—there's kind of a glow around it. Those things become the stories that you hold on to and can tell about. They make your life experience unique and interesting. I hope that extrapolates to my art."

"You always have the longest epilogues. Just get to the meat of the story. He was asking about how we hooked up. I wasn't up at the Yukon, that's for sure. No desire.

Zero. I was in Whistler. Tons to do in June. I was skiing on the Horstman Glacier and went to the beach at—" Berlin turned to Harper. Snap. Snap. "Where were we?"

"Lost Lake Park."

"Yeah. There. I hit Harper's van and totaled it. Since she was living in that van, and I destroyed almost everything she owned, I gave her a job and a place to live."

Harper looked over at Ridge. "I wasn't hurt. Just the van."

He nodded. Good, another secret cleared. He didn't like knowing things about Harper that she wasn't willing to share.

"Harper signed an NDA. They say any publicity is good publicity, but I had been drinking that night, and I didn't need to get arrested on foreign soil. I'm down for a little dirt here and there. But I'm more of a 'proximities' kind of girl. It's an illusion rather than actual experiences. Like in the movies. I don't need to get handcuffed for real. Now in the bedroom—" She batted her eyelashes at Gator. "I don't mind a little role play. But nope." She stretched and yawned, then swigged some coffee. "I'm not sleeping on a cell shelf to grab a headline."

"Aren't you breaking the NDA by telling us about it?" Blaze asked.

"Harper's not allowed to talk about me. I'm allowed to talk about her, but there really isn't much to say. Except—" she turned to Harper "—you should tell them about kissing the dead man's toe." She laughed.

Gator rubbed the length of his lower lip between his thumb and index finger as if he were trying to figure out if he was about to fall for a stunt. "You kissed a dead man?"

"Just his dismembered toe, not the whole guy. And

not randomly," Harper added. "It was part of a cocktail experience."

All four guys were looking at her with revulsion vaguely hidden behind stoicism.

"It's called the Sourtoe Cocktail."

"Get out of here," Gator said.

"In Dawson City, there's a place on Queen and Second Avenue, a couple of blocks off the Yukon River. See? The details are unforgettable when kissing a dead man's dismembered toe."

"Are you going to keep saying that over and over?" Ridge's mouth pulled up with disgust.

"Dismembered toe," Harper said. "It's been a thing since the mid-seventies, and it's exactly what you might conjure."

"She always gets that weird twang in her voice when she tells this story," Berlin said.

Harper glanced Berlin's way then continued. "A human toe is dehydrated and preserved in salt and used as a garnish for your drink."

"No," Blaze said, "just no."

"The legend says that the first toe belonged to a guy who was a rum runner named Louie Linken. Now old Louie got frostbite and had to have his toe amputated back in the 1920s. For whatever reason, Louie preserved it in a jar of alcohol. Fast forward fifty years."

"Please, don't," Blaze said.

Ryder laughed.

"A Yukon guy, Dick Stevenson."

"Of course, there was a dick in this story," Berlin said.

"Found the jar. Captain Dick—"

"Oh, he was a captain? Captain of what?" Berlin asked.

"No clue. This is the story as I remember it being told.

Captain Dick brought the toe to the saloon to show everyone. And because I guess he was a bit of—"

"A dick," Berlin said.

Harper held out an open palm and nodded her agreement. "Captain Dick, living up to his name, dropped the toe in folks' drinks to see if they were brave enough to drink it. And that's how the Sourtoe Club formed."

"A whole club?" Blaze asked.

"Yes, and you have to join the club if you want to drink a Sourtoe Cocktail."

"Which no one does," Blaze said.

"Which everyone does," Harper responded. "Sadly, Louie's toe is not the toe in present-day use."

"What?" Blaze was shaking his head, with both hands wrapping his stomach.

"A miner was trying for the Sourtoe record. He was drinking his thirteenth glass when his chair tipped over, and he swallowed the toe."

"No!" The men all shouted like they just watched a lousy football play.

"They use a rubber one now?" Ridge asked.

"There has been a succession of dehydrated toes. A guy had an inoperable corn. Then another frostbite toe, again accidentally swallowed. There was an anonymous toe that they got, but a hunter stole it. Some guy put it in his will that he wanted to donate two toes when he died, but it came with the stipulation that his nurses got free drinks."

"A fair exchange," Ryder said. "Surely, that's all."

"One from a diabetic." She ticked off on her fingers. "One came in a jar of alcohol with the note saying one shouldn't mow the lawn in sandals."

"Noted," Ridge said. "It's the garnish? It floats in your drink, they fish it out, and put it in someone else's drink?"

"The rhyme is, 'You can drink it fast or drink it slow, but the lips have got to touch the toe." Harper sent him an air kiss.

Ridge shook his head. And mouthed, "No."

"To answer your question, when you do a shot, you press the toe to your lips. It's fairly unpleasant."

"Are you making this up?" Gator asked.

"Absolutely not."

"You put a dead person's toe to your mouth?" Ryder asked.

She grimaced. "When in Rome…"

"Okay." Berlin waved her hand in the air. "Why aren't we flying yet?"

"Another ten minutes," Harper said.

"I'm bored. Let's have some fun." Butterfly clap. "Tell me something I would never guess about you. Want to play?"

Chapter 29

Nobody looked like they had any interest at all in playing games with Berlin. The men's faces all went passive.

"I have an incentive. A hundred dollars to the charity of your choice to the winner. Kiwi! You go first."

Ryder tipped his head back, jutting his jaw out. His gaze rested on the line of up-lights hidden behind the molding to add a sense of expansive height to the jet's ceiling. He brought his gaze down to meet Berlin's and flicked his hand over to point at her. "I boxed a trained kangaroo."

"Ten points for that. Who won?"

"The kangaroo, though he cheated, right? He leaned back on that tail of his and did me a push kick straight out of the ring." He rubbed his chest. "Right here, left me bruised for weeks."

"Why did you do it?"

"There was a girl involved." Carlos leaned out of his seat with a snicker.

"Charity event for a kiddie hospital."

"Good-hearted man." Harper sent him a smile.

"Though there was a very nice medic who took excellent care of me." He sent Harper a wink.

"Have you got a picture?" Berlin asked.

Ryder tugged at the Velcroed thigh pocket where he kept his phone, scrolled, and handed it to Berlin.

Harper leaned in to see it, too.

It was an image of him in boxing kit in a corral-like enclosure. A kangaroo with boxing gloves was smashing Ryder across the jaw. An amazing action shot. Hysterical.

"I'm sending this to my phone," Berlin said, not asking permission.

"Yeah, that's alright. With my face smashed in like that, you can't tell who I am. Call me Kiwi, though, if you're posting it."

"I always do." She looked up and handed the phone back to him. "Ryder's a good name, but I want the women to fantasize about your accent."

A slow smile slid across Ryder's face. "Ha!" He shoved the phone into the pocket of his tactical pants.

Harper thought Ryder probably didn't understand the lust quality of an Australian accent for American women. No denying it. There was something about it that caught a girl's attention. And some guys' attention too. Carlos was all kinds of agog when he listened to Ryder talking.

Berlin turned her attention to Ridge. "Your turn!"

Ridge was slouched back, his eyes twinkling with

amusement. "I've got nothing that exotic. Everything I have is what you'd expect dogs, workouts, work, and domestic."

"Domestic? Like what?" Berlin asked. "You knit?"

"Actually, I do."

"Knit?" Harper asked.

"And I did ballet. So I guess I don't ascribe to all the he-man tropes."

"Just most of them," Berlin said. She leaned forward to see the pilot. "I want to go," she whined, then settled back into her chair and batted her hand at Ridge. "Go back to the knitting. There's a story there. Right now, you're losing out to Kiwi's kangaroo."

"Not much of a story. My nephew wanted to make a baby blanket for his baby sister. He insisted that he should knit it. We didn't know anyone who could knit, so I got some knitting needles and some practice yarn and figured it out on YouTube. Enough that I could teach him, anyway. Nothing fancy. He did an amazing job. He's an awesome kid—golden-hearted."

"Is it hard to do?" Harper asked.

"Once I figured it out, the repetitious movement and the counting, I found it meditative. I also like that it keeps my fingers nimble, especially if I'm using thin needles."

"My man knits," Carlos said with a laugh.

Berlin had lifted her coffee and was blowing on it when she said, "O.M.G. You're such a softy!"

"He's retired from Delta Force," Harper said flatly. "They don't have a reputation for being soft."

"Okay—I mean soft like that round French bread." She turned to Harper and snapped her fingers.

"Boule," Harper said, as Berlin set her cup in the holder.

Berlin pointed at her. "Exactly. Hard on the outside." She wrapped her hand around her bicep. Then formed her hands into a heart shape over her chest. "And squishy on the inside."

Ryder bent his head low, looking at his boots, trying to hide his snort behind a fake sneeze.

Ridge didn't have any reaction at all.

"What do you knit, though?" Carlos asked. "Scarves? No! Little toy animals?"

"I usually do scarves and hats."

"Do you have drawers full?" Berlin asked.

"No, ma'am. I donate them to a shelter that focuses on veterans with addiction problems. You know, I could buy a box full of hats and stuff and just hand them out, but it's nice, I think, to have something that a fellow veteran made for you. There's intention in what I do. My friend Lynx holds that the energy you put into something is embedded. I think good thoughts for them as I work. I like to believe Lynx is right about that."

"Lynx is the cat-woman with the pink dress?" Berlin asked. "She rubs me the wrong way."

Ridge didn't respond.

"This is the softer side of a hard man you're showing me." Berlin drew a finger across her chest from one shoulder to the other. "Not to say that I don't love my men hard. Kiwi makes me think of whips and leather, and with you… I could see myself baking some cookies and coming to the door in only an apron."

Ridge didn't respond. Not a sound, not a change of stoic face, he was giving her nothing. And *that* would make him a challenge. Berlin hated to lose. Snatch something away from her, and she became the junkyard dog, sinking in her teeth to hold on with tenacity.

"Is your nephew a cute kid? Photogenic? When we get back to D.C., we could do some photos—you and me and the kid knitting."

"You knit?" DeWayne asked.

"No, I don't knit." She scoffed. "Do I do half the things we put into photos? No. We're Hollywood. We create illusions. Listen, Ridge. We can get some attention to your charity that way. Folks eat it up, cute kids doing good."

"I'm going to nix that idea. Their mom keeps the kids' images off social media for safety reasons. And I don't want to exploit the situation the veterans are in for publicity."

Berlin shrugged. "Okay. It was a thought. I haven't forgotten that you said ballet, which intrigues me. Dancing the way your team does is cool. Ballet though? Kind of sissy, isn't it? Or was the ballet for your nephew again?"

"My nephew's more a hip-hop guy. I played high school football. Freshman year, they had a thing called 'Touchdown Tutus.' It was a charitable event to raise money for inner-city kids to have immersive arts programs. I was all for that. So what they did was have the university ballerinas teach us football players ballet on Sunday afternoons."

"Older girls, am I right?" Berlin asked with a sly smile. "And you got to lift them overhead with your hand on their crotch? It's a pubescent boy's wet dream."

"When we lifted, I supported them at their waist or thigh and only with their permission," he said evenly.

"Still—" Berlin sent him a 'come-on, we know the truth' smile "—college girls were an incentive for a fourteen-year-old boy."

"I'm sure it was there in the mix somewhere, but my mom brought me up to be respectful of women."

"And *my* sisters taught me to be terrified of women." Ryder laughed. "The women in my family were some nasty buggers."

"What?" Carlos asked. "Did they snitch on you?"

"See how my middle finger goes crooked like that? Yeah, that would be my sister Molly. She stomped on my hand and broke that finger when I wouldn't give her the last brownie."

"How old were you?"

"About eight or so. Scarred for life, I am."

"Oh, please." Berlin threw her legs over the arm of the chair. "You? Afraid? Then tell me this, how did you get the call sign, Ryder? Or should it be Ride Her?"

He pretended to zip his lips.

"Sad to say, Kiwi, boxing kangaroos wins in the interest category. Okay, two seconds while I put this story of us playing our game…kangaroo for the win… Yup. That should get a huge number of likes." She looked up. "You're ripped, handsome, and have that accent. Have you ever considered doing something with it?" She didn't explain what she expected him to do. "Tell me whom to Venmo my cash."

"Nah, it's all good," Ryder said. "Just remember to ask before you post a picture of any of us on your security team. Remaining anonymous is important to my safety and the safety of my future clients."

They all turned as the pilot came over the intercom. "Hello, everyone, I'm Captain Tony. Ready for your next adventure?"

Chapter 30

Harper

Harper stood, planting her hand on the galley counter. "Do you need anything, Berlin? If not, I'm going to go to one of the row seats."

"Harper hates to fly," Berlin announced.

Harper offered up a tight-lipped smile and a finger wave as she moved to the row behind Carlos and DeWayne.

Ridge followed her. "Can I sit with you?"

She nodded.

"Do you want a window or aisle?"

"Window, so if we go down, you can get out and drag me with you."

"I don't think it will come to that. But okay."

They clipped their safety belts in place. Harper tightened hers down to the point where she didn't have any circulation.

He leaned down and whispered in her ear, "Would it help if I held your hand?"

She reached over and slid her stiff fingers into the warmth of his hold. Yes. That felt better. Touching him felt better.

The good thing about Guam off the schedule was that Iniquus didn't give them two more Strike Force operators. They got to keep Ryder and Ridge. Harper was more comfortable with Cerberus than Strike Force because she knew them. Though Gator and Blaze seemed friendly, they were in work mode. Harper didn't know them in friend mode.

"You're okay," Ridge said as the engines started. "Which part is the hardest for you?"

"Takeoff. The flight—if there's turbulence."

He nodded.

"And landing."

His smile gave him wrinkles around his eyes. "Would it help to talk?"

"Let's talk about you."

"All right."

"I thought you were an only kid."

"Yup."

"The nephew is from one of Brandy's siblings?"

"I started dating Brandy in high school. We were off and on through college. Her family is my family."

"Big of you. I'm impressed. That takes a level of maturity that not many have."

"Brandy's brother Joe was a Marine. He was married to Rachel. I'm godfather to their kids. It's in Rachel's will that the kids will come to me if she's incapacitated. I made that promise to them on the day they showed me their first child's ultrasound."

Harper nodded.

"That day, I also took a solemn vow. Joe and I, we were having a beer in front of the fire. He asked me to swear that I'd step in for him if anything happened. He'd just gotten his deployment for Iraq."

"Oh."

"Yeah, he came home. Went back. Came home. Went back." Ridge rubbed Harper's hand with his thumb. "The last time he came back, it was to Dover in a flag-draped casket."

Harper's heart kicked up, and she felt a wave of sadness pass over her. She pressed her hand into her chest to still the pressure. "How many kids?"

"Three. At the time of Joe's death, there were the two boys. My sister-in-law was pregnant with my niece. I told her about my vow. That I'd step into his shoes. Provide what they needed financially, emotionally."

"Where is this in the timeline with your wife?"

"Ex-wife… We were still married at the time. It all kind of came to a head in the same space. Joe's death played a significant role in my decision to leave the military. My duty to my then-wife, to Rachel, and the children."

"What are the children's names?"

"Trinity is almost three, Jasper is five, and Maximillian— Max is eight now. His birthday was last week."

She nodded.

"My military pay wasn't enough for me to help Rachel and the kids financially. They get a monthly check from Uncle Sam. It doesn't go far. I needed to do more than a check and a video call when I could, anyway. They needed someone there to do things."

"Knit."

"If that's what it takes, yup."

"They live in D.C.?"

"Rachel? Her family is in Sterling, Virginia, about a half-hour from Iniquus Headquarters. I moved them up from Quantico when I took the job. Iniquus issues a pretty good signing bonus, and I was able to get her a little house for them."

"Iniquus gives you enough money to buy a house when you sign?"

"This is an expensive area to live in. The operators are joining straight out of the military, and you know an average SEAL earns around fifty thousand a year. My Delta brothers mostly lived in military housing at the fort. Iniquus makes sure their staff can move their families in close."

"And those without family?"

"Same thing. Signing bonus. Most of the guys who live at the barracks with me put the money aside. When they meet their person, then they can choose a home together. For me, it just made sense to set Rachel and the kids up in a place I can reach them."

"Where is your wife incarcerated?"

"Ex. She's remarried." He gave her a long look, making sure that got through. "Brandy is down in Colombia. I've told you about the obligations I feel to her. My connection with Rachel and the kids isn't an obligation. She's my sister. She's been in my life for fifteen years. I'm loyal to my family, whether it's my Delta brothers, Iniquus, or a heart family."

He seemed to be trying to convey something to her, and she wasn't clear on what. "Are there any other women that you want to tell me about?"

"That's it." He leaned in and whispered, "Unless you want to talk about us."

Us. There couldn't be an us.

She'd tell him over the phone when she got to California. Friends. Though sleeping with him was fun. Fun? Who was she kidding? Her toes were still curled from the orgasms. And there's nothing she'd like better than an "us," except, of course, staying alive.

These talks they'd been having lately had changed. Even someone with blinders on, like Harper, could tell the difference. These were housekeeping conversations, the kind that people who had lived for a while and accumulated responsibilities and baggage had. Logistical conversations. He had a family of sorts. He lived in a place she couldn't venture.

California, then New Zealand. Alone. And that was a conversation she wouldn't have with Ridge. She focused on her plan. Come January, she had a visa to live on the other side of the world, as far away from her nightmare as she could go. She had a gig teaching art in a private school there. She could stop looking over her shoulder. Stop hiding in the shadows. Breathe.

If only the teacher she was replacing would retire earlier, Harper would leave today.

Her nerves had been quietening, especially after the cocoon time at The Wild Mountain Lodge. They frayed again when the man stepped out of his car with a gun.

Ridge was distracting her from her task—staying alive.

Unless you want to talk about us.

The chemistry had been there when they were at the lodge. They'd become friends, touching base most days.

It wasn't always convenient, what with the time difference and their odd work schedules.

But yes, as she looked back, and somehow this was just hitting her, Ridge had been part of her every day, even if it was only a text back and forth. Every single day since they met. And Harper had categorized him as a friend.

Why? Because she was unavailable for a relationship. Period.

It was like being a priest, she would guess. The desire for intimacy, both physical and emotional, might be there, but she couldn't risk it. She couldn't become complacent. Or connected. Or even stationary. Dodge and weave.

January, and she'd have her work visa.

For now, she needed to make sure that Ridge was only a friend.

And, okay, yeah, a fantasy.

She felt her face flame. She cleared her throat. Time for a change of topic. "You live at Iniquus?"

Ridge gave her a long look. He probably realized that this was an inappropriate place for a conversation about "us."

"I pointed out the men's barracks. That's where our male operatives live. All men with a single female exception."

"How's that?"

"Striker Rheas, who heads up Strike Force, is engaged to Lynx. There have been times when Lynx had to be sequestered to the Iniquus campus for safety. She had some issues—she told you she'd been held in solitary in the Honduran prison."

Harper nodded.

"She had issues with her health, both physical and

mental, coming out of that situation. Command decided on the one exception, allowing her to live in Striker's apartment. There, she was under the highest security, and she had the emotional safety net of being with Striker."

"No female operators? They don't have housing?"

"For the most part, Iniquus culls its operators from special forces. Women in special force roles are fairly new. We do have female operators, ex-CIA and FBI. They have a cul-de-sac of houses down by the river."

Okay. Ridge still had that look in his eye; he wanted to have the "us" conversation.

"And you see Rachel and her family often?"

The look shifted. Ridge must realize that she wasn't going to have a relationship talk. And he'd figure it was because they were on the plane with ears all around them. She had to prepare herself for this to come up again the next time they were alone.

"I try to get out there a couple of times a week, dinner, and bedtime rituals. Reading bedtime stories, making sure they get their teeth brushed. We watch movies. That's the time when I knit. I think it's important for the kids to see a man cooking, cleaning, and knitting as well as fixing the car or the hot water tank. I want them to see broad horizons instead of boxes. It's best to set an example than just lip service."

"It was Max who asked to make the blanket for his sister."

"Yes."

"Tell me a story about Jasper."

"Ha! He's a character all right. Let me think of a— yeah, here's a story for you. So Rachel has a tradition each night as she puts them to bed, after their songs and stories. As she tucks them in, she says, 'Good night. Sleep tight. Don't let the bed bugs bite,' kisses them, then places a prayerful hand on their foreheads and says, 'Peace be always with you.'"

"That's lovely."

"I do the same when I put them to bed, for continuity." She smiled.

"One night, after I said good night to Max, I moved over to go through the ritual with Jasper. As I was getting up to leave, his little arm swung out from under the covers and splatted me right on my forehead. I like peace. Peace be with you, too, Uncle Caleb."

"Sweet." She pressed her hands to her heart and curved her shoulders.

"Mmmm. I thought so. And I thought this was a perfect moment for Uncle Caleb to have a poignant discussion with young Jasper. So I asked him, 'Hey, Jasper, tell me what you like about peace.' And he says in his wide-eyed innocent voice, 'Yup, they're pretty good. I like carrots, too, but not brush sprouts.'"

"What? He thought you were saying peas?"

Ridge laughed then shook his head. "Yup, the kid thought we wished him 'peas,' and I guess he thought we were imaginary rubbing them into his head each night."

"Little lovey."

"Yeah, he is." He sent her a smile that looked like paternal pride. "A beautiful soul." He pointed out the window. "We're here. You did great."

Berlin called back. "We're landing! Woohoo—shark tank, here we come!"

Harper released a heavy sigh.

Chapter 31

Ridge

Impressively, today was going off without a hitch. They stepped off the jet right on schedule. Three Lyft Lux cars lined up. Their drivers, in suits, stood by the passenger doors, ready.

The group rode in comfort to the end of a Camden peninsula. They were dropped off at The Pink Orchid Tea Garden.

"The Lily, The Pink Orchid, I'm seeing a pattern here," Ridge said.

Carlos and DeWayne, their equipment, and bags of wardrobe changes were in the first car.

Ryder, Ridge, and Harper had been in the last car. Having exited, they were now making their way over to the principals—the men's heads on a swivel.

CiCi and Berlin were being assisted from their car by

Strike Force. The operators were careful to stay out of the way of DeWayne and his fast-snapping picture taking.

The wind whipped at the women's hair and clothes.

"Stop, DeWayne." Berlin swatted at the photographer. "I need to get inside and have Carlos fix us. This wind is terrible." She sent a stink face to Harper as if managing the wind had somehow been overlooked on Harper's to-do list.

Harper had the patience of a saint; he'd give her that.

Inside, Harper bustled over to talk to the restaurant's hostess, then over to confer with DeWayne and Carlos. The two men slipped out of the room.

Ridge's phone buzzed. "Lynx," he said to Gator and stepped out of earshot.

"Ridge here."

"Lynx."

"What have you got?" He pushed through the front door and scanned the area. No one was near. Still, he moved out to the center of the parking lot and lowered his voice.

"I was doing a search to see if I could find out anything about Katherine Zelensky. There was a missing person article about her in the Washington Post. Beginning of January, a year and a half ago. Three weeks before Harper Katz, LLC. It has her picture. It's Harper, for sure."

Ridge spiked his hand to his hip and looked down at the toe of his boot. "You said there was no police record."

"There isn't. Isn't that curious?"

Ridge didn't answer.

"The article listed the police officer who responded. He's retired and moved out of state. It also listed the detective. I was also able to find the originating 9-1-1 call."

"Who made that call?"

"Gabby Goldman. The WaPo article said she was Kat's friend. Kat was staying with her. According to the article, Kat went out for a run. Didn't come home. Then she missed her big meeting with a D.C. gallery owner who wanted to do a show with her. At that point, Gabby called the police. Hide nor hair was found at the time the article came out. I did an AI search of police reports. There are none. Next, I had my neighbor Dave Murphy look into it. He's a detective with Washington PD. He knew the detective, but he died in a car accident—no way to follow up there. I showed Dave the WaPo article. He says he has no explanation for that not being an open case and not having a record."

"You followed up with Gabby?"

"To the extent I've been able to, I tracked her down. It turns out that she's a fellow artist slash best friend since they were in grad school together. When Kat disappeared, Gabby moved to Kat's house. After graduation, Kat had bought a small tract of land with a house out near Cape Charles on the water and had her studio out there. Gabby didn't want things to get messed up by no one being there, so she moved out to her house, waiting for them to find Kat or tell her what to do. Kat doesn't have any family."

"Gabby keeps in contact with the police?" Ridge lifted his gaze to do a sweep of the area.

"She said that she did until they moved her file to the FBI. Gabby said that the FBI wouldn't tell her whom to talk with over there."

"When was that?"

"Fairly quickly. Gabby said within the first month of Kat's disappearance."

"What did Dave say?"

"It's not normal for a case to disappear that way, even if there's FBI involvement. And then, I thought of Gage."

"All right." Gage, who killed two people to protect his DARPA scientist fiancée. Ridge didn't even need to know what Dr. Zoe Kealoha's expertise was to understand how deadly and clandestine that case had been. DARPA was the scientific arm of the military. They worked on the next genius way to protect the United States. Everything over there was highly classified. Who knew what foreign power would want Dr. Kealoha under their control—or stopped. "If Harper had accidentally seen something, learned something…"

But how could that be?

According to Gabby, Harper had been living on the Eastern Shore with the migratory birds and fish. Then the hummingbird flashed into his mind. How she ran with blinders to make her run seventeen percent easier.

Ridge pulled a hand over his face and quickly looked around to once again assure himself he was alone in the parking lot.

"Ridge?"

"Yeah, I'm listening."

"Gage and Zoe had a guy in the FBI helping them. His name is Damian Prescott. I know him pretty well. I reached out to him."

"He said the FBI doesn't have the case and has never heard of Katherine Harper Zelensky," Ridge guessed.

"Exactly. And, like Dave, he said that's not how things work. The police should still have a missing person case. Because Gage thinks he recognized Harper, Prescott's antennae are up. The case is classified—a big case with national security implications. The information is sealed for lots of reasons. I worked on the team when Gage was trying to save Zoe. This is what I can share; there were people of great power involved—senators, DARPA, the CIA, FBI, and Montrim Industries and, therefore, a connection with the Pentagon."

"Okay." Ridge put a hand on his head and worked to regulate his breathing as his heart hammered his ribs.

"Prescott and I looked at the time of Kat's disappearance to see what else was happening that day."

"Shit."

"Nothing in a direct line. Something to do with Zoe's case, though. Do you remember the attack on the D.A.'s home? A man dressed as an EXPress guy showed up and shot the D.A.'s housekeeper, who opened the door, her husband, and daughter in the living room?"

"Yeah."

"The D.A. was in the garage at the time. She was fine. The maid died. Her husband is paralyzed. Their daughter survived."

"The killer committed suicide. I remember this story."

"Yes. Now, what has this to do with Zoe? The D.A. was the one who was bringing the case forward about one of the executives from Montrim Industries. She was going to bring the case before a grand jury the next day. His name is Topher Bilik."

"Yeah. Was that near where Harper was running?"

"No."

"What happened with that case?"

"It was dropped."

"Dropped?"

"Yes."

"How does this tie to Kat disappearing and resurfacing as Harper?"

"The date. Vaguely from proximity. And Gage."

"Gage could have read the newspaper that day. That might be the point of contact and why he put the two together. You said Harper's picture was in the paper."

"Katherine Zelensky is a missing person. Harper Katz LLC is Katherine Zelensky. Prescott wants to run this down."

"Are our principals in danger from this?"

"Not that we can tell."

"Is Iniquus pursuing this?"

There was a long pause, then a sigh. "Not as part of our close protection contract with CiCi and Berlin. We're off the book as soon as you land back in D.C. However—"

"Shit."

"The FBI signed a contract for us to figure this out. Between now and then, I'll be working with my team to puzzle this through. When you get back to D.C., Prescott will be meeting the plane and would like to have a conversation with Harper. Now, as an Iniquus employee, you cannot forewarn Harper. You are forbidden from talking to her about any of this. No sign of danger. It might put her on the run."

"We have to support her."

"Of course we do. I insisted on that. Gage insisted on it, vehemently. And Command was in full agreement. Sy will remain Harper's assigned lawyer. I already talked to him. He's going to be there at the airport for the landing. And Zeus. He'll be there too."

"I hate this."

"You'd hate it a lot more if we let it go, and she was hurt or worse. You'd hate it a lot more if she had to spend her life on the run. A couple of hours of silence, then the whole dynamic changes."

"Thank you. And if this has nothing to do one with the other?"

"We say sorry for the inconvenience, and everything moves on." There was a pause. "What does your gut say, Ridge?"

"She needs help."

After disconnecting the call, Ridge slid the phone into his pocket and stalked across the parking lot to the front door. The CIA, DARPA, the Senate, the Pentagon, the FBI, Iniquus, the Washington P.D., Montrim's billion-dollar military complex, and Harper possibly thwarting them all.

Almost inconceivable.

He stepped through the massive carved wood door back into the cool, dim lobby of The Pink Orchid.

Harper, spotting him, paused mid-sentence, nodded, then turned back to Berlin and CiCi. "I've arranged for you to be in a private tearoom. DeWayne and Carlos are eating a quick bite now. In just a moment, they'll be doing your publicity shots while you enjoy your tea experience. You'll remove your shoes outside of the space and sit on a mat with a woman in traditional garb."

"Like a geisha?" Berlin asked.

"Traditionally dressed," Harper repeated. "You will have lunch—I've ordered it—all things you both like. Seafood, so you can post about that on your Instagram. Points you might bring up—why you want babies to grow up being able not only to enjoy the ocean but to preserve the nutritious proteins that we can get from the ocean. Promote seaweed. I've texted you a few facts that you could slip in to make yourself seem knowledgeable—the reason why Congress wanted to hear from you instead of, say, an oceanographer who has dedicated their lives to the study of the ocean's health."

"Oh, good, okay." Berlin nodded.

"Then you'll have a traditional tea ceremony—also great for pictures. DeWayne knows all this and is ready. After tea, our cars return and take everyone to the aquarium. They'll do the photoshoot for the most part—they have a photographer who dives. He knows you need this to look like you're out in nature. He says he can do that. First, stingrays."

The hostess swept her hands to get them moving down the short hallway.

"Isn't that how that guy died—the kangaroo guy from Australia?" She looked around at Ryder.

"Steve Irwin?" he asked.

"Yeah, him. The Crocodile Hunter."

"Yes, he did."

Harper turned bright red and sent an apology smile toward Ryder before turning back to Berlin. "These are safe stingrays. Kids pet them all day. You're fine. Next, you'll be in with the corals and tropical fish."

Berlin and CiCi turned to each other, gripping hands—squeeeee! It was high-pitched excitement, and Ridge had to work to keep his face blank.

Then CiCi put her nose in the air. "O.M.G.! Can you smell that? Wow!"

"It's incredible!" Berlin said. "What is it?"

Harper lifted her hand to point.

At the end of the hallway, they'd arrived in an atrium. Looking to the left, a curtain of blooming honeysuckle hung from the third-floor balcony to the floor.

"Tearooms, second floor," the hostess said, touching the elevator button.

Harper turned to the right, where the open doorways led to a meditation garden. Through the open veranda doors, hummingbirds darted in and flitted amongst the pink honeysuckle blooms.

It was a dazzling setup, and Ridge thought Harper would be mesmerized. He turned to her.

Harper dropped her bag and bent to put her hands on her knees. She was gasping for breath.

Her face and neck broke out in hives. Ridge grabbed at the medical backpack Blaze had slung over his shoulders. It held an EpiPen if Harper needed it.

"I didn't see her list a severe allergy," Gator said.

Harper held up a hand in a kind of keep-away gesture, then turned to dash back up the hall to the lobby and out the front door.

"I'll go." Ridge took off. "I'll radio in if I need support," he called over his shoulder.

As he moved through the front door, he whipped his head around.

Harper was gone.

Adrenaline shot through his system.

There. Movement off in the distance caught his attention. Harper wasn't going for fresh air. She was sprinting, not running, racing down the street as if hell was at her heels.

Chapter 32

Ridge

Ridge slung the supply pack onto his shoulders as he ran.

He had to get to Harper.

She wasn't looking where she was going. As she vaulted across a road, a car shrieked to a halt.

The driver was wide-eyed with the close call.

Harper didn't even turn her head.

She ran a steady eight miles per hour daily, getting ready for her next marathon. She was pouring it on now.

With her streaking out ahead of him, Ridge bent his head and pumped his arms, racing along the road. As he bolted forward, he was thankful that the streets had only light traffic.

If Zeus were here, that would have helped. Zeus would have caught up to Harper by now. He could tackle her on command. And comfort her with no prompting at all.

It was almost as if Ridge could feel Zeus there with him. It was the thing that Lynx had described. A *knowing*.

This *knowing* pressed him to run faster. Get to her, now.

Ridge was conditioned. But Harper was, too. And while he bit down and fought to make up the distance between them, she was a fire of adrenaline surge.

And Harper had on the blinders that helped her run seventeen percent easier than Ridge could as he tried to keep situational awareness for both of them.

Ridge pulled up a mental picture of the map he'd memorized at the airport this morning. If Harper kept going this way, she'd be safer. There was a park up ahead. It dead-ended in another peninsula.

He just had to keep her in view. Eventually, the adrenaline that was fueling her flight would ebb. He'd be able to catch her.

He was worried. And he was impressed.

He watched her take the next street without a glance left or right. She was in the park now. They were darting across the lawn, attracting attention. Harper was soft and feminine looking, even in her black pants and blouse. He was big and hard. If she had the same expression on her face that she had had when she dashed out of the restaurant, people would be on their phones calling the police. Or some hero was going to jump out of the bushes to trip him up or push him over.

Ridge kept his head on a swivel, wishing that the wind wasn't blowing off the water, and he could shout to her. He thought if she heard his voice, she might stop, slow, or at least turn her head.

Something made her think that she was in a life-threatening situation.

The hives and panting? Maybe her brain just snapped when she thought she might be suffocating from ana-phylaxis.

That made no sense.

If she was that allergic, she'd be on the ground, and he'd be administering the Epi.

She tripped. Ridge watched her arms shoot out to catch herself. His mind jumped to broken wrists, but no, she pulled one arm down across her body, tucking her shoulder and rolling. It was a martial arts fall that distributed the energy, so the person going down didn't absorb the shock into their systems.

That was a trained and practiced move—that sur-prised Ridge.

Of course, she could have been a gymnast or done ka-rate or something as a child, a body memory move. Or she could have asked someone along the way to teach her how to fall safely since she ran, and runners will on occasion trip.

Lots of explanations, he thought, for all of this. None of them made sense.

It was a new red flag that waved for him.

With a baseball slide, Ridge arrived at Harper's side. He grabbed at her before she had a chance to jump up and run again. "It's Ridge. It's Ridge."

She gulped at the air and nodded.

"Breathe."

She spun until she was on her hands and knees. Her breath came in gasps and hitches.

He put one hand on her back to give her emotional sup-port. The other, he hooked into her belt to hold her back if she was getting into position to vault again.

"Breathe."

"Hey! Is everything okay over there?"

Ridge raised his gaze to see the good citizen. Big guy. Dock-worker type. A piece of rebar in his hands. Ridge raised his hand to say yes. But he also wanted to show that he wasn't holding Harper down. She could leave if she wanted to.

God, Harper, whatever is happening, I'm here. I love you. We'll get through this, he thought.

He'd thought *love*.

He loved her.

And it was not a surprise.

Of course, he did.

She sat up wide-eyed, clutching her hand to her chest, then rolled over to lie on her back. "Oh my goodness. That was spectacularly crazy." She reached out and clutched at his arm. "I'm so sorry. I don't know what happened."

Ridge remembered her reaction on their run yesterday when she mentioned the memory of the hummingbird beacon. She'd said it fluttered into a garden to its nest hidden amongst some honeysuckle vines.

He was a hundred percent sure the hummingbird was the reason why Kat Zelensky transformed into Harper Katz.

An ongoing threat.

He was going to find it and destroy it.

Chapter 33

Ridge

Pressing his comms button, he said, "Ridge. I'm with Harper. She's stabilizing from a medical reaction to something in the teahouse. If you have everything covered, I'll stay outside with her." He released the radio button that he wore on a lanyard around his neck and taped to his chest. The team's magnetic earbuds helped them keep their communications covert.

"Ryder. We can handle the teahouse, mate. The principals are having a right big time. How about we meet you at the aquarium? Give Harper a bit of a breather."

"Ridge. Appreciated. Wilco. Over." He looked down at Harper, who was staring out at the water. "Better? Your hives are gone. That must feel more comfortable."

Harper tipped her head back to look at him. She pressed her lips together and gave a micro nod.

"Let's walk. After that sprint, you shouldn't stop cold like that." He reached for her hand and helped her stand. She was shaking, so he wrapped his arms around her, holding her against his body heat. If she didn't start to rally in the next few minutes, he'd take the next steps to counteract shock.

She stayed there until her breath was under better control, then moved away from him, walking in the wrong direction to get to either the teahouse or the aquarium.

"Aquarium is this way." He pointed. "Unless there's somewhere else you want to go."

She shook her head.

Ridge didn't like that. He wanted her talking so he could better assess. And, he reminded himself, he had to be very careful about his word choices. He searched around him for a neutral conversation starter. "Let's talk about colors. CiCi wore a green dress to the speech. You said that was helpful to deal with anxiety. Does walking across the grass help you?"

"It's a survival color." Her tone was cold and distant.

He reached for her hand. "Tell me about that," he encouraged.

"Did you know that the human eye can distinguish between more shades of green than any other color?"

"There must be a good reason."

"They speculate that it has to do with seeing snakes in the grass and fruit among the leaves."

"But you said that was pretty late in the color vocabulary, right? Black and white then red, yellow, then green."

She stopped and looked at him. "You were paying attention to me."

"Always." He jostled her hand and started walking again. "Tell me more."

"Fertility, life renewal, green increases creativity. That's one reason walking in nature helps us to problem-solve."

"Why?"

"No clue. It's being studied. It's why it's so important to get urban kids into green spaces. Brain performance increases after being in green spaces—though, if they really can't get out into nature, they could get similar effects to walking in the green space if they just see the color—so we know it's not something chemical in the air." They walked almost a block in silence before she added, "Yeah, but then…yeah, results can mix."

"What was that thought?" Ridge asked.

Her mouth tugged into a frown, looking out at the water. "The brain is strange. But survival is definitely built in. It's all about survival." She started trembling again.

Ridge wrapped his arm around her. "Your brain is one of the things I appreciate most about you."

"Yeah?" She turned to face him, tipping her head back. Her skin was too pale. Her pupils too dilated. Her facial muscles held rigid.

Seeing Harper like this after his conversation with Lynx revved Ridge's system. All he wanted to do was pounce on the threat and pummel it into submission. To take it out of Harper's life, release her from its hold.

He pushed the aggression down; she didn't need to be around feelings of violence. He wanted her to sense his compassion and his connection to her.

"Your lips." He kissed her very softly. "Your body." He paused at her frown. It was as if last night hadn't existed for her when it had meant *everything* to him. "They fit into that now, too." And then he allowed himself to say, "Harper, I care about you. Can you tell me what's going on?"

She scowled.

"Harper, I want us to be an us. I want to be there to support you as more than a friend."

She stepped aggressively back. "An us?"

"I know long-distance relationships are hard, but we've been doing pretty well, don't you think?"

"An us?" Her voice squeaked upward.

All right, this wasn't working. Ridge turned and took Harper's hand and started them walking again. Maybe the green would make him creative, and he could problem-solve this moment. "I thought after we were together last night, you might consider. California isn't so far away that I couldn't get there on my R&Rs. They're every three months."

She walked sideways, painting a hand down his arm, looking miserable. "I'm not going to be in California. Not for much longer. I'm going…"

She'd be back on the run? "Where?" He had to calm his racing heart.

"The other side of the world. I have an art gig in New Zealand."

Was this a lie? Did she latch onto New Zealand because Berlin kept mixing up Ryder's background? Harper, despite her false identity, wasn't a liar. "Why do you want to move to New Zealand? Seems pretty far away." It came out nonchalantly enough. It felt like he took a punch to the gut.

They'd come to a pier. Ridge turned and lifted Harper up to sit on the wall so they'd be eye to eye. She still hadn't responded. "I bet there's a psychological study behind it," he teased with a tap on the end of her nose.

"Psychological reasons?" She stared out at the water, avoiding eye contact. She shook her head. "See what life hands me. Perhaps another country and another opportunity. Something to feed my art and keep it fresh." She pulled out her phone and took a picture of the water, pointing the lens toward where the sun broke through a cloud, brightening the waters to turquoise blue.

"Remember I was telling you about the naked eye and the color captured by a camera—the aurora borealis and the bioluminescence? A camera sees differently than an eye."

Ridge gestured toward the water. "What do you see?"

"I'd break it down to about fifteen different shades on the blue to green spectrum. Did you know that if you have the word for a color like 'cerulean,' your brain can see it and pick it out amongst other colors? If you don't know that color, your brain will blend it into a known-name color."

Ridge shook his head. It all just looked…blue.

"This is how I frame that idea," Harper said. "If I see snow, I call it 'snow.' I might add an adjective if I knew enough about snow, wet snow, dry snow. It's pretty much just 'snow.' But in Scotland, there are over four hundred words and phrases for snow, including 'snaw,' snow; 'sneesl,' to begin to rain or snow; and 'skelf,' a large snowflake."

It was a strange conversation. But at least she was talking. Maybe she could shift to the processing part of her brain and away from the survival part.

He'd keep this going. Low-key.

"I thought it was Inuits who had all those snow words." Okay, things were evening out for Harper. Her eyes told him she was back to herself. They needed to get to the aquarium. Ridge lifted Harper down and pointed at the building out in the distance.

"That's a myth," Harper said. "I think they have like ten."

"I'm thinking of my niece and nephews. What would I do if I wanted to help them be able to see more colors?"

This time it was Harper who reached for Ridge's hand. Her fingers were stiff and cold. "You could start by getting a box of Crayolas and help them memorize the color names. Color with them and talk about the colors. But carefully. I mean, if they want to make a lavender-colored elephant, let them. Don't suppress their artistic expression. You know, encourage them by saying the word 'lavender' when you talk about art."

"Were you always this attuned to colors?"

She heaved a sigh, and they walked in silence.

As they approached the sidewalk, very quietly, she said, "My mom used to tell this story about me in kindergarten. Apparently, at circle time one morning, my teacher held up pictures of things and asked what color they were. My teacher said I'd always sit with my arms crossed, looking down and scowling. She thought it was because I didn't know my colors, and she was going to mark that on my report card. Then, on that day, the teacher, Mrs. Spencer, pointed at the grass in the photo. 'What color is the grass, children?' And everyone called out, 'Green.' I stood up, red-faced, fists balled, stomping my foot. 'It is *not* green. It is chartreuse. That grass is *chartreuse*!'" I was so mad that she had to send all the other kids back to their seats. She pulled out a crayon box, found the color that matched the picture and read the wrapper."

"Chartreuse."

A smile tickled the corners of Harper's mouth. "From then on, Mrs. Spencer would say, 'What color is the sky, class?' and they'd yell, 'Blue!' Then she'd turn to me. 'And what shade of blue, Ka—Harper?' And I'd yell, 'Azure!' or whatever I saw. Mom said I was much happier after that."

She'd almost slipped. Ridge had kept his face blank as she'd checked to see if he'd caught it. He pulled her closer and dropped a kiss into her hair. "I love that story about you."

And I love you. That was more than Harper could handle hearing right now.

But he made her a silent vow—I *will* keep you safe, Harper.

Chapter 34

Harper

The plane was descending at the small D.C. private airport.

Ridge had kept her talking the entire flight. He'd kept her thinking about lines and colors and the human experience. It had been the most comfortable flight she'd taken since that horrible trip home from Norway. He, though, had seemed...something. Concerned was the word she thought of, but it wasn't right.

Harper thought about their discussion about the box of Crayolas. The eye can't understand a color that it can't label. It was probably the same with emotions. In her art, she hadn't explored the emotions she saw in Ridge's hands and muscles. That flashed in his eyes. Harper had to assume that since she didn't have the vocabulary word, her brain wasn't settling on an understanding.

As they were landing, the emotion in his eyes intensified. Not true for the other Iniquus operators. Harper kept trying to grasp insight. Her mind offered up, "Mission ready." But why would that be right?

She finished answering Ridge's question about how enriching and creativity-expanding it was to date someone from outside of one's language and culture for a long period.

"Did you get to experience that?" he'd asked.

"No, not really. I mean, a guy from Canada for about six months. I learned a lot about hockey."

"Ridge," Berlin called. "Is Harper yammering on about one of her insightful topics again?"

"Do you consider it yammering?" Ryder asked.

Berlin pursed her lips. "She intellectualizes things to the point of boredom. Don't get me wrong, I use it all the time to my benefit. I just wish she'd cut to the chase sometimes."

Ryder stretched his leg out comfortably in front of him. "Sometimes, there isn't a chase to cut to, don't you think?" he asked.

Strike Force's Gator and Blaze didn't have the week at the Wild Mountain Lodge being on casual terms with Berlin. They kept themselves stoic and distant as one in close protection roles should. But Berlin and Ryder had a relationship. It was allowed for him to speak to her this way until Berlin decided to disallow it.

"I mean," he said. "Exploring a subject sparks useful thoughts. Sometimes people have to have the discussion to get there, right?"

"I guess."

"We do that when we're on the job," Ridge said. "You saw it happen when we were at the lodge, Berlin. Do you remember? We'd have scenarios set up on the table, and we'd talk them through. Our team members would add information. We learned from each other, tried out new ideas, found the holes, built new scenarios. It's the creative side of security."

"I don't have time for all that yammering, though."

Ryder pulled his leg in and leaned forward. "You like her ideas?"

Ridge reached over and took Harper's hand. That felt comforting.

Harper's ears were popping as they came in for a landing.

"Breathe," he reminded her.

"That's why I keep her on." Berlin sighed. "It's just looonnng to get from a 'look at that daisy.' To the perfect idea for an Instagram post. Looooonnnng." She focused over on Harper. "Just don't bore the security into a coma. I need them alert and ready if my life were on the line."

"Okay." Harper struggled to get the word out as bands of anxiety tightened over her lungs.

The wheels shrieked, lifted, shrieked, lifted.

Harper grabbed Ridge's arm and pulled it across her.

"I swear to god, Harper, you have been such a prima donna since we've come out here. Can you stop?"

Ryder pulled Berlin's attention away from Harper. "We're going to see you all back to The Lily Hotel. You'll be heading out again tomorrow morning. It's been a pleasure serving you."

As Berlin answered, Ridge leaned down to whisper in her ear, "Harper, can I stay with you tonight? We can take another run before you go."

Harper was looking out the window at the cars gathered near the hangar. Far too many cars were parked under the bright exterior lights. "I'd like that," she said automatically. Her focus was on the why of all those cars as the plane taxied to a stop. She put her finger on the pane. "Is that Lynx and Zeus standing out there? Who's that with her?"

Ridge leaned over her and looked out the window. "The guy on her right, that's Striker Rheas. He's Lynx's fiancé."

"Oh."

The engine powered down. The pilot rounded the cockpit to open the door and get the steps in place.

"We made it." She smiled at Ridge.

He averted his eyes.

Maybe now that they were landing, he was regretting asking to spend the night with her? His energy had definitely changed. Was something up? She scanned over the other men. No, nothing there. She'd find a way to let him off the hook. Develop a headache or something. She reached for her bag. No, she didn't want to lie to him. She'd just tell him he wasn't on a hook. She needed a private moment to do that.

Ridge leaned in and whispered in her ear, "Let's hang back for a second. Let the others off first."

See? She was right. Harper gave him a nod.

She saw the Iniquus men freeze mid-movement. Then each of them reached up and tapped their chests right where Harper knew their communications buttons were taped.

Ridge was the last to tap-tap.

Her system iced.

The tiny follicles lifted the hair on her arms.

What was happening?

Carlos and DeWayne got off first so they could get the photos.

Then Gator and Blaze.

Ryder.

CiCi.

Berlin turned to her. "Come on, Harper. No lollygagging. I'm exhausted."

Harper stood. She could feel Ridge wanting to stop her, but he said nothing.

Harper began to tremble. She had to force her feet forward. Had to make herself breathe.

Brains are amazing things, she told herself. They're primed to keep us safe. Mine has been on overdrive. What I'm seeing isn't what's happening any more than those hummingbirds or that honeysuckle portended death. She tried to talk herself off the ledge.

Down the steps. Out into the beautiful velvety Washington, D.C., night. She stopped and forced herself to look up at the stars, to take a deeper breath. Ridge was here. Ryder. Zeus. She was fine. This was fine.

She stepped away from the plane, heading over to give Zeus a scrub behind the ears.

Bang. The exterior lights went out.

Immediately the car lights went on. They were in darkness for only a moment.

Something landed near her feet. She twisted. And something hot brushed by her face.

"Shots fired. Shots fired. Shots fired."

"Kill the lights."

"Down. Everyone down. Down. Down."

She didn't down. She wouldn't down. "Zeus!"

"Shit. Harper, no. Get down."

She was running. It was what she did when she was scared. What had started as an experiment and a curiosity had become an obsession, to get faster so she could run away. She had no idea where the shots were coming from. But she knew she'd be safer in the tree line.

It was the direction Zeus had run. Animal instinct. Follow the animals…they know best.

And all those thoughts flew through her head in a nano-second as adrenaline dumped into her system.

It was like she was running through gelatin. Like one of DeWayne's videos, he slowed to a slug's pace to find just the right tip and tilt of Berlin's chin. Open eyelids. Sexy smile. She was like those frames. Slow. Slow. She could see Zeus's muscles in the full moon's light as they bunched and extended. He was single-minded. He ran with blinders on just like she did.

Wait! He was running toward danger. That's what Zeus did.

A great weight struck her, engulfed her, and held her immobile, her face in the dirt.

She closed her eyes.

This was it.

Now, she was going to die.

Chapter 35

Harper

Harper had stopped screaming when Zeus's rough tongue found her face.

She'd discovered it was Ridge who had tackled her and held her down.

She'd been bustled into an Iniquus car and driven at breakneck speed to their Headquarters.

Not Cerberus but the main Headquarters.

The sign on the door said Strike Force War Room.

War.

Now, she hunkered on the floor in the corner with a blanket wrapped around her. Zeus lay in her lap.

Sy strode through the door, searched her out, gave her a nod before talking to Striker, who was Gator and Blaze's boss.

Lynx moved over and joined the conversation.

And there was another man in a suit. He focused on Lynx as he spoke. There was a history between the two. They were both very serious about what was happening. But they trusted each other.

Harper trusted Zeus and Ridge. Zeus and Ridge trusted Lynx. Lynx trusted this man. He must be a good guy. Maybe. But Harper would have thought the Captain of the D.C. Police Department was a good guy, too.

Someone had been shooting.

Not at them—not the group. Her. Someone tried to kill her tonight.

Harper couldn't figure out how they'd found her.

And she really wanted to know.

If she knew, then she wouldn't make those mistakes again. She cleared her throat. "How did they find me?" she asked no one in particular.

Lynx looked at the man. They had a silent conversation, then he opened his hand as if ushering Lynx over.

Lynx picked up her tablet and came over to sit cross-legged on the floor next to Harper. She reached out and scratched behind Zeus's ears. "I know, buddy. I know."

Ridge had been standing with his back pressed against the wall, and he slid down until he was sitting with them.

"I'm going to answer your question. But I don't want you to say anything to me. When you speak, you need Sy beside you, do you understand?"

Harper nodded.

Lynx opened the tablet. "Bob said—and he's on his way—his house is about a half-hour away. He wants to be here, so you know you're supported."

Tears pressed behind Harper's eyes. She nodded.

"Bob said he showed you the video that Shawna's mother posted."

Nod.

"Our A.I. took it down. Another video of you was posted on CiCi's TikTok, Instagram, and Twitter accounts." Lynx pressed a button.

There was Harper and Ridge dancing. You could see Ridge's body, but not his face, thank goodness, Harper thought. It was the last few seconds of their hot as hell rumba. He spun her out. The crowd was clapping. The tag on it was: Ladies, no matter your size, *someone* will love you. And: Ladies, BIG is beautiful, go out and shake yo' fat a$$es!

The disparaging crap masquerading as body positivity.

Everyone read that about her.

It was a small thing in the grand scheme of her problems; she let it go.

"Now, CiCi and Berlin are friends," Lynx said, tapping the video off. "A lot of their followers are shared. This video migrated between their social media accounts. Our AI system didn't pick it up because those weren't the parameters we'd tasked our computer to look for."

Nod.

"We knew, before you left for New Jersey, that your real name is Katherine Zelensky."

Harper forced her head to freeze and not look around at Ridge. He knew. He said nothing.

She wasn't supposed to say anything, and yet her mouth was moving. "You knew my legal name, and so I'm assuming Iniquus did what it does and whirled the magical cogs in the supercomputer. You know when I got my first period, and where I popped my cherry."

"Not the kind of thing we usually research, Harper," Ridge said with a half-smile.

"Sorry. I'm thinking of things I'd rather keep private, and that's what came to me first."

"Understood."

Lynx put a finger to her lips to remind Harper to be quiet. "What we did know is that your friend Gabby Goldman had filed a missing person report January of last year."

Harper felt her bones melting.

Zeus turned and licked her face until she was able to scratch her fingers into his fur, telling him she was surviving this.

"We surmised that you were hiding from a dangerous situation. We don't know what that situation is, but now we have a good guess. I'm going to let my friends Gage and Prescott talk to you about that." She pointed toward the men.

Nod.

"I'm answering your question, 'How did they find me?' One of the things that social media enjoys is the hive mind. Imagine little worker bees all together, sharing their efforts. One person mentioned that person out with CiCi and Berlin looked like the person who had been in the video at the crime scene where Berlin's bodyguard had saved Shawna. That video had been downloaded to someone's computer, and it was reposted. Our A.I. found it and took it down. There was enough time lag for the followers to confirm that it was the same person. It was determined that you must be connected to Berlin. Who were you? And they were able to get various stills from the video. People said your name was Harper Katz, and then someone else mentioned that they had gone to college with you and your name was Kat Zelensky. And finally—"

Harper was shaking uncontrollably. She squeezed Zeus around the neck, so hard Harper was sure she was hurting him, but she couldn't make herself release.

"Someone said that this picture reminded her of a friend who went missing in Washington, D.C. She posted the Washington Post article. In that article was the map of where you'd told Gabby you'd be running before you disappeared, asking people along that route if they had seen or heard anything."

Harper exhaled.

"If someone had even done the very simplest thing," Lynx continued, "and put in a search app that they wanted to know if the name Kat Zelensky came up, they would know that you worked for Berlin Tracy. Berlin had posted over the last few days about Matteo's jet with the tail numbers visible. She posted that she was flying back to Washington tonight. A search of incoming flights would have given them the time and hangar. I don't know if you noticed, but someone flipped off the circuit breaker when you all were on the tarmac. Someone else was out in the parking lot, setting off the car alarms. One would imagine that the shooter and his accomplices wanted to distract the security they knew would be surrounding Berlin and CiCi. Not a lot, just enough to give them time to get their shots off. They were good shots. They came very close to hitting you."

"Why didn't I hear gunshots?" she asked.

"It was a sniper rifle, shot from across the highway. That's why Zeus didn't get to him. The barriers. Looking at the video, the high wind and your twisting kept you alive. Do you know why you were running for the shooter? What were you thinking?"

"I wanted to help Zeus." Which was moronic.

Lynx reached over and coaxed Harper's arms to loosen around Zeus's neck. "Zeus says, thank you. And that's his job, not yours. Your job is to look."

"Okay."

"Harper." Ridge's voice held none of the anger or disappointment that she would have expected. His voice was low and comforting. She didn't deserve that. She'd put them at risk. She'd put Zeus and him at risk. What if something had happened to them?

Harper started trembling again.

Ridge pulled the blanket tighter around her and petted a hand down Zeus's back.

Zeus was panting and yawned to release his stress. But he didn't budge from her lap. And so now she was crying. Again.

Ridge pulled a tissue from the box and pressed it into her hand. "Would it help to have the doctor give you something for your nerves?" Ridge asked.

She shook her head.

"So while we knew your name," Lynx said, "now the world knows who you are, too. Someone acted on that. They obviously think you know something that puts them in danger. We want to make sure you're safe, and the criminals are put in jail."

Harper nodded.

"Are you ready?"

Chapter 36

Harper

Harper was offered a chair at one of the long tables. She swiveled toward the door. Was it locked? They did that in movies, right? She'd go storming toward the door to leave and find that she was already a prisoner.

Sy was on one side of her. He bent in. "You're on the run, Harper. Would you like to stop?" he asked quietly, her lawyer asking her a private question.

Harper didn't know the answer. It had been a year and a half on the run now. It was her life. She was habituated to it. She thought of friendships that she'd set aside. Her house out at Cape Charles, the one where she'd spent her happiest childhood vacations, down by the water by herself, looking at nature and daydreaming. The wide-open space. Untethered by time. The canvases. The possibility of love and a future full of family. A husband's arms, children at her feet. Hope.

That's why she was going to New Zealand. To give herself this possibility.

And...

And she knew that even there, she could be in danger of high-dollar, high-placed men who felt threatened by what she knew and how she could prove she was right. A family would be leveraged against her.

Look at what happened to the D.A. Her child was shot. Her husband was paralyzed. Her housekeeper dead. That leverage had made the grand jury go away for that Montrim man, Christopher Bilik. The murderer, Jim, had died that day by suicide, though she was unconvinced that it had been a suicide. She was the witness. She was the only one who knew—the single threat.

She wasn't willing to sacrifice her life at the chance to make Bilik pay for something that had nothing to do with her. "I want to live."

Sy patted her hand in his fatherly way.

They'd made Bob and Ridge sit off to the side. The men did as Special Agent in Charge Prescott told them to, so they could stay in the room.

Harper wished she could talk to Ridge, and he could tell her what to do. She opened her mouth and wiped at the corners.

Everyone's eyes were on her.

At least they'd let her have Zeus. He planted himself between her knees as she sat in the high-backed chair, and he hadn't budged.

"We can protect you," Sy said. "You're safe now."

Harper wasn't sure she could believe him. He had no idea, after all, what he was talking about. This wasn't about a man with a gun, jumping out of his car like on Wednesday.

She glanced around at Ridge. He couldn't hear what Sy said. He leaned into the wall. His arms crossed over his chest, looking formidable.

She couldn't be with him. Ever. Luckily, no one had outed Ridge. CiCi's video didn't capture his face, just hers.

If there was a relationship between her and Ridge, the bad guys could go after the kids—Trinity, Max, and Jasper would be at risk.

Were these men high-powered enough that they might be able to track Ridge down? Cold washed over her. He was Berlin's bodyguard. Harper's phone was in Berlin's name, the I.P. address was wherever Berlin was. Berlin had no filter. If someone called and acted interested, she'd spill everything.

Harper could disappear.

Ridge couldn't.

He had to work a job with a good salary to support his family obligations.

Rachel shouldn't have to run with her kids.

She, Katherine Harper Zelensky, was putting innocent people in danger with her cravenness.

"I'm done running." She said it before she weighed the ramifications of that sentence.

"Let's start there," Ridge said, pushing off the wall. "Can you paint the picture for us? Tell us like an artist would. One day in January last year, you went for a run in Washington, D.C."

He wasn't supposed to talk. All the heads spun his way.

Ridge moved toward the table, pulled a chair, and sat down across from her, breaking the rules. "You run with blinders on to save yourself seventeen percent of the effort. It was a year and a half ago, so you would have been running about six miles an hour at that point. You set a beacon on a hummingbird. Normally, you'd run until you passed it and set a new goal. But the hummingbird caught your interest. You slowed, didn't you? You watched as it flew to its nest amidst honeysuckle vines. Not the white ones we usually see by the side of the road. These were special. They were pink. When you run, you think about images you want to work with. Tell me about the art." He laced his fingers, his elbows resting on the table. Ridge looked at Harper with warmth.

She nodded. Okay, that much she could do. "I was supposed to talk to a gallery owner later that day. The show I was putting together was a study I'd embarked on. In this study, I wanted to convey scent through my paintings." She tapped her nose. "I wanted to see if I couldn't trick the viewers' brains into thinking that they could fill their olfactory senses."

"Why scent? Is there a psychological study?"

"Lots." Okay, this was safer ground. The fog lifted from her gray matter. "The gist is that scent is the sense that triggers memories. My goal was to capture a common experience in such a way that someone would inhale the air." She stopped to breathe in deeply, filling her lungs. "I wanted them to try to smell the subject of my painting. I had decided not to do something easily evocative—a lemon, chocolate chip cookies coming out of the oven. But something that would have been explored and would have innocent connotations." She licked her lips and looked at the FBI guy, then focused back on Ridge. "Not criminal innocence. Childhood innocence. I was looking for that experience as I moved through my normal day. A vague awareness that I was looking for inspiration. When I was following the hummingbird on my run, it turned into an open gate. I caught a glimpse into the garden. It was exactly what I was looking for. The back garden had a brick patio off, I guess, the kitchen door. I was going to paint it that way. Maybe put hands placing a berry pie on the windowsill to cool. Shadows framed the patio then faded to black. On the left, fuchsia, magenta, and chartreuse from a bed of caladiums sprinkled their colors like gemstones in a fairy tale book."

Ridge sent her a nod of understanding.

"On the right, there was a tree with a craggy trunk, lots of wonderful texture there. Beyond it, the sun illuminated a wall of pink honeysuckle. And there was the hummingbird suspended in bejeweled flight. I stepped around the trunk of the tree, slowly, quietly. I pulled my phone from my pocket, and I started videoing, trying to capture the moment so I could remember the details. It was such a sensory-rich environment, and I was mesmerized."

"She's describing Faulkner's backyard," the FBI guy, Prescott, said.

She sighed out heavily. "The sweetness perfumed the air in such a heady way that I was transported. I was standing there thinking, how can I capture this moment so that from the art viewers' personal memory, they will experience being enwrapped in this perfume? How could I get them to physically breathe in, trying to fill their nostrils with childhood nostalgia? Then the gate to the garden banged shut. I realized I was trespassing. Foolishly, or not, I stepped back into the shadow of the tree." She stopped and kneaded her hands around Zeus's ears.

Zeus tipped his head back, and his tongue made little licks of pleasure.

One good thing about tonight was that no one had been hurt.

Zeus had gone after the man trying to kill her. *Kill*

her. With a bullet. Dead. She leaned over him and kissed him between the eyes.

It wasn't fair to put Zeus or anyone in danger for her.

She was going to do this. She was going to push the story out, no matter how unwilling her lips were.

She dropped a second kiss onto Zeus's head.

"I didn't tell the man I was there. Instead, I pressed myself back toward the trunk, thinking he'd go in, and I'd slip out. But I was awash in fear, and it was inexplicable to me." She swallowed. "I thought, I'm dressed in black. I'll just wait until the coast is clear, and I'll leave. I pulled my hoodie up to cover my head and shadow my face. If I was very still, I told myself, I'd be fine."

"Was your video still running?" Prescott asked.

"Yes. I have it all on video."

"Tell me what 'all' means," he said.

She made a horrendous noise, something in her throat. She wasn't even sure how she made that noise. It was a startling sensation that sent radiant waves up through her head, down through her body. She seemed to swell and contract. She thought she might faint. And then the room came back into focus, her stomach burbling.

"A man came out of the back door. He spun around, arms out, showing off his EXPress delivery uniform. The man—"

"Do you know the name of the man?" Prescott asked.

"The one in the uniform was called Jim. The one in the suit was called Mr. Bilik. And they talked about the man who died in prison before his trial. Uhm. Colonel Guthrie…yes, they talked about his being dead under suspicious circumstances and…and…and they laughed."

"Go on," Prescott said.

She breathed in and let the air flow out in one big gust. "Okay. So Mr. Bilik put a paper bag down on the patio.

A grocery bag. He pointed at it and said something like, 'There's the gun you're to use. Do you have gloves?' Jim pulled some doctor gloves from his pocket and slid them back away. He said, 'There's the money and the phone'—no, he called it a 'burner.' Mr. Bilik was talking to the man, Jim, who was wearing the delivery uniform," she repeated. "He had stolen it. The uniform. Taken it from the driver. He took the keys and the truck. And Jim wanted to get on the road quickly because he wasn't sure if the drivers called in periodically, and he'd be missed." Harper put her fist to her mouth and burped. She was swallowing too much air with her odd little mouth moves. "Mr. Bilik said, 'I want zero blowback, or you know the consequences.' Jim reached into the bag and took out the gun. He put it in his belt." She rubbed her back. "Here."

"What else did they say?" Prescott asked.

"Uhm. Mr. Bilik asked, 'Where is your change of clothes?' Jim told him they were in his car at the parking deck. He said he'd be able to pull up right behind the half-wall, crawl over the back, change his clothes, put the uniform in a plastic bag to burn, and drive on down the road. Everyone thought he was on vacation at his beach house. Then Mr. Bilik asked if the man was dead. He was talking about the driver."

Harper looked up at Ridge. He nodded at her.

She looked over at Prescott. He nodded at her.

Lots of nodding.

"Jim said that he left him naked in the mud with zip ties." She held up her fingers to make air quotes. "'I thought he'd be easier to move alive. Deadweight can be a problem.'" Harper's body juddered. "Mr. Bilik told him that was good thinking. Then he said, 'It's never good when you get taken to a secondary location.'"

Harper stopped and looked around the room.

Lynx stood up and brought her a wastebasket.

Sy stood up and brought her a ginger ale.

Harper waited for her stomach to calm enough to say, "His men would take care of it. He asked if he—the naked man—could scream."

Prescott leaned forward.

"Jim said no. He'd ball-gagged him and stuck in a...a...a plug with a horse tail. Put some fetish ears on him, so if anyone came near him, it would look like they'd accidentally come upon sex play, and people would shun him and probably not call the police."

"'Yeah, but they were new, right? None of your DNA could be found?' Mr. Bilik asked," Harper continued. "'Are you kidding me?' Jim had said. 'I don't share my sex toys. They were new from the package. And the package is in the trash right beside the guy. No prints. No receipts. No way to trace them back to me. I stole them from a hooker.' And they laughed."

Prescott used his fingers to tap a drum beat onto the table. A big grin spread across his face. "That's a detail that we held away from the public. Good. Keep going."

"Jim gave Mr. Bilik the address where he'd left the driver, and said something like, 'Good enough, I'll send over a crew to dispose of him, now.' There was more. I have it on the video. Jim patted his pocket and said, 'Okay, I'm grabbing my keys, and I'm heading out. I have a fine bottle of scotch out at my beach house. I've been saving it for something special. I'll toast you in absentia. This is a win-win.'"

Harper scratched her head. This was the part where she broke the law.

So... Here goes nothing.

"Jim went into the house. Mr. Bilik turned to leave. I peeked out the gate and saw his driver pull away from the curb, and the house was, you know, a corner house. They turned. I grabbed up the grocery bag, stuffed it under my sweatshirt in the waistband of my running tights, and left. I'm…a curvy girl, so no one could tell that it was a bag and not my stomach."

"Why did you take it?" Prescott asked.

"Because I'm prone to knee-jerk reactions, apparently. I can't really tell you. Without the money and the burner phone, maybe Jim wouldn't do whatever it was he was going to do. At any rate, there's no point in even more self-recrimination. I saved the driver. I didn't save the family. The driver saw my face. I knew I was on the run. I could have walked away, but I didn't. I think Ridge, you call that a system one failure. My brain did what my brain wanted to do. Not a failure. I saved a man."

"That's right," Ridge said. "Tell us about that."

"Let's see." She stared down at the table. "I ran across the street and hid behind a car, so I could play the video and get the address where the real driver was tied up. On Google maps, it wasn't far. Far to drive because of the way the streets were laid out, one-ways, turns. Short to walk. So I ran there as fast as I could. I cut the zip ties on the guy. I told him to run for his life. They were coming to kill him, and then I just started walking."

"With the grocery bag under your hoodie."

"No, in my arms like a grocery bag. I gave my hoodie to the driver. He was naked, and…he was naked."

Prescott nodded. "That fits."

"You had a phone. Why didn't you call the police?"

"Yeah. That. There was more to the conversation. I knew if I called the police that I'd be killed. It's in the video."

"Harper," Lynx said. "Can you tell us where the video is?"

"In a tree."

Everyone sat still.

"So I was walking and in shock. I just kept walking and walking until I found myself outside of a library. I used the computer to look up how to hide. Me and the stuff. I didn't want the stuff on me. I had taken the batteries out of both phones. I knew to do that much. The Internet search brought up websites for geocaching. I got on a Metro, and I went out to the geocache place. On the way, I bought some kitchen plastic storage bowls and some black, uhm, garbage bags. This is a jumble. There was a lot that was happening. Uhm. I went out to find the geocache. If you find that spot and walk 22 steps directly west, there's a tree that has four branches that come together." She held up her hands. "Just over my head. I put the phones in the plastic bowl, the bowl in a garbage bag, and the bag in that tree. Then I took the rest of the stuff in the brown bag, the money, and I walked, I think it was forty-seven steps to a bunch of rocks. I crammed the bag under there in case there was a radio following something or other in the bills. I saw that on a show. An FBI sting." She frowned at Ridge. "Yeah. They should be separate but together."

"Where, Harper?" Ridge asked.

She pulled out her phone, pulled up the geocache website, found the particular game, and slid the phone to Ridge.

Striker picked it up and said, "I'll take Strike Force. We'll be back."

Chapter 37

Ridge

Striker came through the war room door and set a box on the table in front of Prescott. Black plastic garbage bags rounded out of the top of the box.

"Can you bring the cameras down? I want to get all of this," Prescott said.

"Affirmative," Deep, their computer guy, said. "Go."

The money was piled on the table. The burner phone was whisked off by the forensics lab tech.

A battery was put into Harper's phone. A cable attached; the video of the patio chat came up on the screen.

It was chilling.

No wonder Harper ran.

That she took the bag to try to spook them into not proceeding, that she got to the man in time to save him, that she developed a plan of escape on a library computer with some printed instructions, all of it was remarkable.

They watched the video in silence. Now, they were watching it again. It was just as Harper described the exchange. The vicious tones of voice. The coldness of how they described the murder. The lists of people who would keep the men safe. The things they had on them. Harper made it sound like it was a quick exchange, but this went on, both men—friendly enough that they were at ease with each other—sharing the dirt they had, pressure points, smoking guns. In his parting comment, Jim Faulkner said, "Thanks for letting me be the one who does this. I've wanted retribution since she put my brother away. This is going to feel good." He'd laughed.

And then Bilik said, "Just remember Colonel Guthrie, if things go sideways, we won't give you the chance to turn. And it won't be a fun ride from here to Hell."

It was so cold and so truthful.

Two hours later, Faulkner was dead. Suicide. Though, that now was questionable.

"You didn't call the police immediately?" Prescott asked.

"No… I… I… I had thoughts about calling the police. It's in the video. You heard him. Mr. Bilik was reassuring Jim that the police captain, the A.G., the FBI guy, at the top, Mr. Bilik said. They were deep in his pocket. It wasn't a problem. He just needed to get this D.A. gone. Mmm, and the other one, the Acting United States Attorney. The one who brings federal charges. How could I make that call?"

"I'll remind you of a couple of things here," Lynx said. "The missing person report that was filed on Kat Zelensky doesn't exist in the police files. Kat Zelensky's photograph was in the paper with her route drawn out, soliciting community input. Tom Cassidy had a rendering done of the woman who had saved him. They were looking for her to serve as a witness. The Washington P.D., according to the newspaper, had a copy of the picture but was holding it away from the public. I had a friend check on the rendering. Tom Cassidy's file was gone. No one is trying to solve the crime."

Prescott nodded. "The FBI will be following up." He turned to Harper. "So, you went and got the delivery guy free."

"I told him to run. I told him what was going to happen to the D.A. and her family. That the guy Jim, wearing the EXPress uniform, would deliver a package, and he planned to kill everyone and drive away. I told the guy he should call the police, so they were warned. I mean, Jim already knew who the delivery guy was. The delivery guy wasn't increasing his danger. They'd know I was there, but they didn't know who I was. I was random. Right?"

"Yes, that's right," Prescott said. He pointed at the table. "Is this all the cash?"

"No. It's all but thirty thousand dollars of the cash." She shot a look toward Ridge. *Wasn't this part of why Brandy went to prison?* "I took enough to help me stay safe. I was afraid of it because money can be traced, according to the website. I did the things on the papers that I copied at the library. I just went down the line doing each one."

"You laundered the cash?" Prescott asked.

She looked at Sy.

Sy nodded.

"I went to a place where you can get cashier's checks. I went from one to another and did five thousand in each.

The Internet said more than that, and they had to report it. I had taken three mustard straps. Bundles. A mustard wrap meant one hundred, hundred-dollar bills. Uhm. Ten thousand dollars." She pointed at the pile of money.

Several hundreds of thousands of dollars were piled on the Iniquus table.

"Then I went to another check cashing place and cashed the cashier's checks. So none of the money was the same money. I felt I could spend it without being followed."

Prescott tipped his head. "Where'd you go?"

"Back to New Jersey, where I did my undergrad. I knew the area. It was easier for me to lay low while I did the things on the list. Setting up my LLCs and waiting for the paperwork to come in. I bought a van for cash and traded with this mechanic. I did murals in his shop, and he built out my van so I could live in it. Hit the road. I lived like a vagabond. Did art."

"You met Berlin in Canada, right?" Prescott asked. "You felt comfortable going over the border to Canada?"

"I had a friend who borrowed my van, who went up there. I told her I was on the run from an abusive husband. Many van-lifers are. I crossed over at Niagara Falls on tour. My friend picked me up. She met up with her wife, who was driving their van. I thought the bad guys might discover that I'd gone over the border, but my van life kept me safe. So I could go up legally. I did have my passport. It was the one thing I allowed myself to take from my house. I was up there and planned to stay up there, then Berlin hit me. Buying a new van up there with registration and insurance put my identity in danger. I needed to get back to the United States and start again."

"How did you get back to the U.S.?" Prescott asked.

She rubbed her hands together. Then rubbed her arms. Striker picked up her blanket and brought it to her. She looked up at him and said thank you. But instead of wrapping it around herself, she hugged it. "With my van totaled, Berlin had offered me the job. After the contracts were signed, I convinced Berlin it would be fun to take a boat along the coast. We went out from Canada and came back down in California."

"You've had quite the adventure," Prescott said.

"That's one way to describe this." Her face was rigid; she was blinking mechanically. "I have the money to pay back the thirty thousand dollars. It's in an offshore account."

"That's what you had on your list from the library?" Prescott asked.

"Yes. I can PayPal it to whomever. It wasn't my intention to be a thief. I was trying to survive. They'll kill me. They already tried. I'll need to start over with a new alias."

Gage, who was sitting off to the side with Lynx, suddenly leaned forward. Lurched forward. It was such an aggressive move that Harper startled.

Ridge understood that this guy Bilik had come after Gage's fiancée. And now Ridge knew what that would feel like to have someone you loved in such terrible danger.

Lynx put her hand on Gage's arm, and Gage forced himself to sit back.

"We need you here, Harper," Prescott said emphatically. "We need your testimony."

She shook her head. Ridge didn't think Harper would be willing to stick around.

The emotions that engulfed him made Ridge feel like

he was drowning. He couldn't imagine being in Harper's shoes. All alone. All this time.

He needed to keep her safe. If she disappeared, he wouldn't be able to do that.

"We have a plan to offer you," Lynx said. "It's running up the chain of command now. Give us a minute to get our ducks in a row."

"I saw on the news that the delivery guy was fine." Her voice squeaked with panic. "*He* could testify."

"He only saw Jim Faulkner. Faulkner's dead. The delivery man can only testify to what happened to him." Prescott looked over to the desk in the back corner. "Deep," he said to the guy sitting at the computer. "Can you bring up the sketch?"

The lights dimmed. "As Lynx said. The file was missing at the police department. But we had this in our system. This was done by a forensic artist interviewing the driver."

A pencil drawing showed on the screen. Ridge stared at it. It was very similar to Harper. The nose was wrong. The cheeks too full. Her eyes were too close together. But she was recognizable.

Prescott tapped a finger onto the table in front of Harper. "We've been looking for you."

Sy popped the top on the ginger ale he'd offered her earlier and handed it to her. "How are you feeling, Harper?"

"Numb. Fine. Stressed, I guess." She tipped back to take a long drink. "I'm bracing for the next shoe to drop." She laughed without mirth. Setting the can down, she said, "They'll arrest me this time, won't they? I keep taking things that aren't mine."

"It's a habit you'll want to break," Sy said. "In this

case, the benefit you provided is significant, just like it was with the car on Wednesday."

Deep called out, "Lynx, the housing is a go."

"Let's make a plan," Sy said. "This case is important to Iniquus because it ties to us directly. We want this man, Christopher Bilik, in jail for the rest of his life. Normally, we put our clients in safe houses. Because of the capabilities that Bilik has, the people under his thumb—as you pointed out. We're hesitant to move you out of our control. We'd prefer that until the judge has stipulated that Bilik is jailed without bail. And possibly longer, until he's tried, that you aren't out in public."

Harper frowned at Ridge.

"Here on the Iniquus campus, we have a women's residential area."

"That's only for operators. Iniquus doesn't allow people to be here without an escort," Harper said.

"Right, the female operators have a cul-de-sac of what looks like houses, very much like Cerberus Headquarters. Inside there are apartments. We have an apartment open."

"Didit lived there," Ridge said. "She was married just before Wild Mountain Lodge. She lives off-campus with her husband now."

Harper nodded.

"It's very nice," Sy continued. "It has a Florida room that might be someplace you could paint. Lots of light. A view of the river. This is a high-security campus. Harper, we'd like you to stay here. Now, mind you, here means *here*. You cannot go into this Headquarters unescorted. But the cafeteria is at your disposal with an escort. You cannot go in the men's barracks at all. And it may be months. If it's longer, and you want to do something else, a foreign country under an alias, we can try to arrange that. Being here means we can get you to the courts safely. We *need* your testimony."

"But my living at Iniquus would put you all in danger."

"No one will know you're here. And they won't know when you leave or how you get to the courthouse."

She trusted what Sy was telling her. "And I can go see the dogs?" She reached down to lay her hand on Zeus.

"Yes."

"And." She kept her gaze focused downward. "My friends are on Cerberus. I was told no women are allowed in the men's barracks. Can I have visitors to the women's barracks?"

"That's allowed since each unit has its own outside exit. Males aren't allowed to go in through the front door to the common space."

"There are running trails," Ridge added.

She nodded. "Okay. Yes. Thank you. I can do that. It will be a little bit like being out at my house on the estuary, I'd imagine."

"We're wrapping up here," Lynx said, walking over to them. "Ridge, can you take Harper down, please?" She smiled encouragingly at Harper. "We have your bags from The Lily already in the apartment. The apartment is fully furnished. Tomorrow, when you've got your feet under you, we can talk about the details and figure out what you'd like brought in for you."

Prescott extended his hand for a shake. "Harper, I'm glad this came to light. You've done a remarkable job laying low. I understand why you did it. We're going to bring this to a close."

"Yes, sir," Harper said, shaking his hand then looking up to Ridge.

She'd hit her wall.

* * *

Ridge held Harper's hand as they walked toward the river to see her apartment. While they were done for tonight, the FBI would have more questions tomorrow.

It could be challenging, stuck in one place. But if Harper needed to cloister for safety, this was the place to do it. It was a beautiful campus. Lots of nature. Friends. Dogs. *Him.*

"I want you to feel safe, Harper. I promise you, I'll keep you safe. Zeus and I."

She tucked herself under his arm.

Here it goes, he said to himself. "We've been friends, Harper, but in my heart, I know that you're my person. My last call. My touchstone." They walked a few paces in silence. "Since we met, I think about you throughout my day. I tuck away the stories I want to share with you at night. I'll be eating a meal and think, I bet Harper would like this. Or I'd see something, and it would go on my list of things I'd like to show you one day."

"Yes," she said. "That's how it's been for me."

"At Rachel's house with the kids, I think about how I'd projected all that out in front of me. A wife. Children. The messy, loud glory of banality. I didn't have that in my marriage with Brandy. She didn't want kids, and that's fine. That was fine. As we got deeper into the marriage, I was glad we didn't have kids. A father who was gone all the time. A mother on heroin. I'm nervous," he said with a laugh. He walked them off the path to a rock. He wanted to see her face while he said this.

"I get a little wedge of that life from Rachel and the kids. I get to be the involved uncle. It makes me yearn for that for me. Selfishly mine. My dirty laundry and my kids' lunches to pack. Me climbing in between the sheets at night with my wife snoring beside me. I was ready to look for a match, but I couldn't find her. Lots of dates. Lots of amazing, talented, intelligent women. None of them fit. And then there was our time at the lodge, and you were perfection. It was so easy to be with you."

Harper didn't say anything.

Ridge swallowed.

"I thought you thought of me as just a friend, and I'd take what I could get. I'm a thirty-six-year-old man with a ton of baggage and a difficult job to fit into any kind of pattern. I wanted something better for you. But when I imagine you in another man's arms...it makes me physically ill."

Zeus lay down at their feet, making whining noises in the back of his throat.

Ridge didn't know how to interpret that except that he was picking up on Ridge's stress. What if she said that friendship was all she was willing to allow?

"When we made love—" he reached for her hands "—I thought that was the corner we needed to turn. I thought my feelings weren't mine alone. It didn't feel like sex to burn off some energy. It was meaningful. To me, it was, anyway."

She frowned at him, sadness in her eyes.

"If we can take the threat away, would it free you up to consider other choices? Me. Would you consider a relationship with me?"

She exhaled one long breath.

She closed her eyes and breathed in so deeply that it tipped her head back.

When her head came level, eyes still closed tight, she whispered, "I love you." Then she popped her eyes open as if to see if that had shocked him.

He brushed the hair from her face and just smiled at how beautiful she was, inside and out. "You're safe. You're home. I love you, too."

Chapter 38

Harper

September

"How are you feeling?" Rachel asked before Harper could get a "Hi" out of her mouth. This was the first time Rachel was allowed to come down to the women's residential area.

"I think 'existential dread' might be the right term," Harper said with an attempted smile. She stepped back, allowing Rachel to move into the living room.

It was normally against the rules for non-Iniquus people without business at Headquarters to be allowed on campus. It was definitely against the rules for them to be back in the residential area. She was a special case. A first, Harper had found out. Iniquus didn't house their protectees here. Ever.

Harper had only met Rachel over video chat, and they had become good friends. As good of friends as one can be, speaking mostly in the future tense.

Ridge had brought Harper copies of the kids' favorite books, and he'd go visit them for their bed-time rituals, turning the pages for his niece and nephews as Harper read the stories.

Ridge had told Rachel about the situation as he dropped her at the guardhouse this morning. One of the guards had driven Rachel down to Harper's apartment, as Ridge left with the Cerberus team to get in place at the courthouse.

It was all very cloak and dagger.

Harper hated all of it. She didn't have an ounce of Berlin's thirst for drama.

In another hour, Harper would be heading to court to stand against the big bad wolf. If all went well, this would soon be over.

Harper extended an open palm toward her other guest. "Do you know Zoe?"

Dr. Zoe Kealoha stood in Harper's Iniquus apartment. Her long black hair in a low bun and her big black geek-girl glasses made her look like she should be headed to her lab at DARPA rather than making them lunch.

As if Harper could eat.

Harper had met Zoe when Harper had given her secret testimony at the grand jury hearing. And they had hit it off in that neither one of them needed conversation. They were comfortable quietly being in their own heads while together.

The team thought having Zoe and Rachel here might have a calming effect on her.

There really wasn't anything that would do that. Girls' lunch as a distraction, yeah…that wasn't going to work.

Lynx stood at the open door. "Knock. Knock. We're here."

"Hey," Harper said, watching Didit from Cerberus and a woman named Margot from Panther Force move into the room.

"I see we're doing the heart attack scenario," Harper said after seeing the women dressed as first responders.

The teams—three of them, Cerberus, Strike Force, and Panther Force—were all involved in getting Harper from Iniquus to the courthouse to testify. They had developed four scenarios for getting her in there safely. This one was the most complex.

Ridge had told her that it was a system two event until she made it a system one. He said that's what they did in Delta Force as well as at Iniquus. They planned it on the table. Then they practiced, practiced, practiced, and when they thought they had it, they practiced again until their bodies knew how to move without thought.

It was like learning a dance. The people who do it well don't have to count the beats in the music; they can feel it in their bones. They don't have to remember the steps; their bodies are already there. "Think of it like a dance, Harper," Ridge had said.

So Harper had learned how to be a first responder, pulling up to a scene, getting the equipment ready, heading in to save the guy.

She did it dozens of times, to the point where the stress was gone, and it was just part of her every day.

Someone would be collapsing in the courthouse. A 9-1-1 call would go out. An ambulance would head out. Only, it would be the Iniquus ambulance that responded.

This was Harper's least favorite scenario because Ridge and Zeus wouldn't be directly with her. They'd be positioned in the courthouse.

The K9s had already gone over the area and the courthouse, looking for explosives. They would be patrolling inside and out. Zeus and Ridge would be allowed in to support her as she testified. The judge had okayed Zeus after she'd been advised of Harper's panic attacks.

"I'm putting on a video," Margot said. "I want you to see what's happening, so you're not surprised. There's a lot of noise and a lot of bodies." She tapped her tablet.

They had known in advance that it was likely that protesters would show up. Folks who wanted the powerful to pay for their abusing the system and those who tried to stop the war machines would be on one side. The counter-protesters, who thought this trial might embolden big government to step on their rights, would clash against them.

There were police officers in riot gear.

And Harper broke out in a sweat. She had to get from the ambulance, through all the chanting and sign-waving, the fists in the air, and the anger, into the courthouse.

"Breathe, Harper," Lynx said, petting a hand down her arm. "You've got this. Look at the video. See?" She pointed. "That's Gator. There's Blaze. Deep. That guy there is Honey. He doesn't blend as well as the others."

At almost seven feet tall, it was hard for Panther Force's Honey to blend.

One of the scenarios the teams had anticipated included protesters. It was the operators' job to mix in, and when the ambulance showed up, block the crowds.

Cerberus Alpha and Bravo teams were in their uniforms with their K9s inside.

They weren't allowed hand weapons in the courthouse, but fur weapons were a different story.

Harper just needed to get from here to in there, then she'd be fine.

With the video Harper made in Jim Faulkner's garden, this was a slam dunk case. Bilik was going to prison for life.

Having listened to Bilik in that garden, Harper couldn't imagine a scenario where Bilik would allow that to happen to him.

So far, Bilik had claimed he was innocent.

So far, he'd kept his mouth shut about those high-powered men he had in his pocket.

But today, the jury would hear her video.

The video laid bare the corruption of ambitious men.

Harper couldn't imagine that those men would allow Sy Covington to play that video or for her to testify.

But everything she wanted—freedom to walk out of the shadows, freedom to be in love with Ridge, and for them to move into a future together—all of it depended on her stepping into that witness box.

Chapter 39

Harper

Lynx changed Harper's appearance. A wig. Makeup. Glued-on eyebrows. A bullet-resistant vest. And her first responder's uniform.

Didit, Lynx, and Margot all wore the vests too.

Harper sat in the back of the ambulance with Didit, waiting for the call.

Margot was the driver. Lynx sat beside her up front.

An all-woman crew was supposed to hide Harper better. Once she got into the building, there was another woman who was built like Harper, dressed like Harper, waiting in the bathroom.

Simple, they'd said. Harper would walk in. They'd wait a moment, flush a toilet, run the water, and the other woman would walk out, returning to the ambulance with Didit, Margot, Lynx, and some guy on the gurney.

Ridge and Zeus were waiting for her in that bathroom. She'd wipe off her makeup, remove the wig and fake eyebrows, put on her dress.

Ridge and Zeus would walk her down to the courtroom. They'd be covered by Cerberus.

She'd go in. She'd put her hand on the bible. She'd be done.

It sounded so easy the way they painted the picture for her.

The siren sounded.

This was it.

A very short drive down the road, they slowed to a crawl. "Protesters," Lynx said.

Harper knew the men were out in front, trying to both look like they were part of the bedlam and, at the same time, move folks back.

The ambulance came to a complete stop. "This is it," Didit said. She squeezed Harper's hands. "System one. Just like we practiced. Our job is to get in there and save the guy having a heart attack, right?"

"Right." Harper nodded.

The back door swung open. Lynx reached for a first-aid supply bag.

Margot reached for the gurney, tugging it toward her.

Harper and Didit jumped down.

They started in.

As soon as the door shut, an officer over the loudspeaker announced, "This area is declared a riot zone. This is a riot zone. Disperse. Disperse. Disperse."

"They know this is a ruse. They're coming," Margot said. "Move it."

With her hands still on the gurney, the women swung around the end of the ambulance, still in character.

Then the area filled with smoke. The air grew painful with pepper gas.

"Disperse. Disperse. Disperse."

Lynx grabbed hold of Harper, dragging her to the ground. "Roll," she shouted into Harper's ear.

It was Harper's instinct to run. But running wouldn't get her into the courthouse.

Harper fought her instincts.

They hadn't practiced this with her.

Under the ambulance, Lynx opened her bag, pulling out black cloth. "These should fit over your clothes, pull them on. Do it now."

The way Lynx made the command, it broke through the bright cacophony exploding in Harper's brain. With trembling hands, Harper complied. Not the easiest thing to do wedged between the asphalt and the undercarriage.

Lynx was changing too. They tied bandanas over their noses, pulled protective goggles into place, hoodies up.

"Wait for it," Lynx yelled past the explosions.

"Disperse. Disperse. Disperse. This area is declared a riot zone."

A hand shot under the undercarriage of the ambulance flashing a hand signal.

"Roll out, lay facedown," Lynx yelled.

"Okay." Roll out, facedown was easier for someone Lynx's size. Would she be trampled? What was happening out there?

Lynx yelled, "Roll, Harper."

As directed, Harper was facedown on the pavement. A knee went into her back. Her hands were dragged around, and she felt handcuffs close around her wrists. Everything in Harper's body told her to fight for her life.

Who had her?

It was one of the bad guys, she decided. And now, she was cuffed.

At their disposal.

She was just like the delivery guy, crouching naked in the mud. Only, Harper was being moved to a secondary location.

Nothing good ever happened at a secondary location.

"Disperse. Disperse. Disperse."

The man in heavy black boots and black pants had his hands on her, lifting her to her feet.

Harper swung around and saw that the same thing was happening to Lynx.

How had Harper let this happen?

Not only was she going to be killed, but they'd kill Lynx, too.

Harper could barely breathe for the smoke and her panic.

"Disperse. Disperse. Disperse."

She was moved, stumbling and terrified, down the street, around the corner, down some stairs.

Pushed into the building, she could see the men who had her. Huge men. Dressed head to toe in black protective clothing—riot shields in their hands.

One reached out and dragged back her hoodie, pulled down the bandana, and slid her goggles from her head along with her wig.

And there stood Ridge with Zeus.

"We've got you, Harper," he said.

The SWAT-looking guy at Harper's back was uncuffing her.

Lynx wriggled her shoulders, shaking off her own discomfort from the handcuffs. She tugged off her own disguise.

Harper stood there, trembling. "That was planned?"

"We plan for every contingency." Ryder pulled off his helmet. "Riot was far down our list. But it was on the list."

"Let's get you into the courtroom," Lynx said.

And that's how Harper arrived. Bullet-proof vest under an ambulance uniform under protester-black clothing. Hair disheveled. Makeup smeared. Zeus at her feet.

Sy was at the lawyer's table next to the government lawyer.

Ridge sat in her direct line of sight. His eyes intensely on her. Harper could feel the love pictures he was sending to her. The "it's almost over" pictures.

Harper put on her blinders, just like when she was on a run, hoping it would make this at least seventeen percent easier. She focused on Ridge as her beacon.

This next step had to be taken for a lot of reasons. But Ridge was definitely high on that list.

Harper stood, raising her right hand. When she asked if she solemnly swore to tell the truth, the whole truth, and nothing but the truth, Harper said, "I do."

Epilogue

Ridge swept Harper into his arms to carry her across the threshold of their new house on the same block as Rachel and the kids.

"We're home, at last, Mrs. Hansen." He set her on her feet, next to Zeus, leaving the door standing open to the beautiful October day.

On the entry table, a vase of bright flowers was placed along with three pictures colored by her new niece and nephews, welcoming their Aunt Harper.

She blinked up at Ridge. "I have a family."

"You do. And they love you. Just not as much as I do."

She wiggled her fingers into Zeus's fur as she looked around the rooms he and Harper had decorated together before their wedding. Some boxes were still stacked in the various rooms, waiting to be unpacked, but the main part of the house was complete.

Even still, the décor felt like them.

"We're going to be happy here." Ridge held her tight and kissed her softly. It felt like he'd traveled a long road to get here, but there was satisfaction that they'd arrived.

"I think we will." She pulled away and took a step back. "There's one thing I think we need to change, though." She looked up the staircase. "I'd like to paint the room across from ours."

"We just did that before the wedding." Ridge tipped his head, confused that the wall color was the thing on Harper's mind right now. "You want something different?"

"Yeah, well." She reached in her purse and pulled out a piece of plastic with a little yellow ribbon tied around it.

When she turned it toward him, Ridge saw a pregnancy test with a plus sign showing in the window.

"Perhaps something more soothing for our little one. Don't you think?"

Ridge's grin lit the room. "Yeah, I think." He swept her into his arms and twirled them around. With Zeus barking and dancing around their feet, Ridge threw back his head and laughed with the pure joy of it all.

* * * * *

Thank you for reading Ridge and Harper's story.

The Iniquus World of books continues to grow with more great stories from the ex–special forces security team members who live, work, and love in the tightly knit Iniquus family.

Look for—
Defender's Instinct
Ryder, Sabrine, and Voodoo's story

**IF YOU ENJOYED THIS BOOK
WE THINK YOU WILL ALSO LOVE**

HARLEQUIN
ROMANTIC
SUSPENSE

Danger. Passion. Drama.

These heart-racing page-turners will keep you guessing
to the very end. Experience the thrill of unexpected
plot twists and irresistible chemistry.

4 NEW BOOKS AVAILABLE EVERY MONTH!

Get 4 FREE REWARDS!

We'll send you 2 FREE Books plus 2 FREE Mystery Gifts.

FREE
Value Over
$20

Both the **Harlequin® Special Edition** and **Harlequin® Heartwarming™** series feature compelling novels filled with stories of love and strength where the bonds of friendship, family and community unite.

YES! Please send me 2 FREE novels from the Harlequin Special Edition or Harlequin Heartwarming series and my 2 FREE gifts (gifts are worth about $10 retail). After receiving them, if I don't wish to receive any more books, I can return the shipping statement marked "cancel." If I don't cancel, I will receive 6 brand-new Harlequin Special Edition books every month and be billed just $5.24 each in the U.S. or $5.99 each in Canada, a savings of at least 13% off the cover price or 4 brand-new Harlequin Heartwarming Larger-Print books every month and be billed just $5.99 each in the U.S. or $6.49 each in Canada, a savings of at least 20% off the cover price. It's quite a bargain! Shipping and handling is just 50¢ per book in the U.S. and $1.25 per book in Canada.* I understand that accepting the 2 free books and gifts places me under no obligation to buy anything. I can always return a shipment and cancel at any time by calling the number below. The free books and gifts are mine to keep no matter what I decide.

Choose one: ☐ **Harlequin Special Edition**
(235/335 HDN GRCQ)
☐ **Harlequin Heartwarming**
Larger-Print
(161/361 HDN GRC3)

Name (please print)

Address   Apt. #

City   State/Province   Zip/Postal Code

Email: Please check this box ☐ if you would like to receive newsletters and promotional emails from Harlequin Enterprises ULC and its affiliates. You can unsubscribe anytime.

Mail to the Harlequin Reader Service:
IN U.S.A.: P.O. Box 1341, Buffalo, NY 14240-8531
IN CANADA: P.O. Box 603, Fort Erie, Ontario L2A 5X3

Want to try 2 free books from another series! Call 1-800-873-8635 or visit www.ReaderService.com.

*Terms and prices subject to change without notice. Prices do not include sales taxes, which will be charged (if applicable) based on your state or country of residence. Canadian residents will be charged applicable taxes. Offer not valid in Quebec. This offer is limited to one order per household. Books received may not be as shown. Not valid for current subscribers to the Harlequin Special Edition or Harlequin Heartwarming series. All orders subject to approval. Credit or debit balances in a customer's account(s) may be offset by any other outstanding balance owed by or to the customer. Please allow 4 to 6 weeks for delivery. Offer available while quantities last.

Your Privacy—Your information is being collected by Harlequin Enterprises ULC, operating as Harlequin Reader Service. For a complete summary of the information we collect, how we use this information and to whom it is disclosed, please visit our privacy notice located at corporate.harlequin.com/privacy-notice. From time to time we may also exchange your personal information with reputable third parties. If you wish to opt out of this sharing of your personal information, please visit readerservice.com/consumerschoice or call 1-800-873-8635. **Notice to California Residents**—Under California law, you have specific rights to control and access your data. For more information on these rights and how to exercise them, visit corporate.harlequin.com/california-privacy.

HSEHW22R2

HARLEQUIN
PLUS

Announcing a **BRAND-NEW** multimedia subscription service for romance fans like you!

Read, Watch and Play.

Experience the easiest way to get the romance content you crave.

Start your **FREE 7 DAY TRIAL** at
<u>www.harlequinplus.com/freetrial</u>.

Was she really considering allowing herself to be captured by the man who'd killed Amber? Even though he'd insisted he hadn't murdered Jeremy, how did she know for sure? She could be putting herself into the hands of a ruthless monster.

The sound of the back door opening cut into her thoughts.

"Hey there," Trace said, dropping into the chair next to her, one lock of his dark hair falling over his forehead. He looked so damn handsome her chest ached. "Are you okay? You look upset."

If he only knew.

"Maybe a little," she admitted, well aware he'd see straight through her if she tried to claim she wasn't. In the short time they'd been together, she couldn't help but notice how attuned he'd become to her emotions. And she to his. Suddenly, she understood that if she really was going to go through with this risky plan, she wanted to make love to Trace one last time.

Moving quickly, before she allowed herself to doubt or rationalize, she turned to him. "I need you," she murmured, getting up and moving over to sit on his lap. His gaze darkened as she wrapped her arms around him. When she leaned in close and grazed her mouth across his, he met her kiss with the kind of blazing heat that made her lose all sense of rhyme or reason.

Don't miss
Protected by the Texas Rancher *by Karen Whiddon,*
available October 2022 wherever
Harlequin Romantic Suspense books and
ebooks are sold.

Harlequin.com

HRSEXP0822